W9-BVW-347

DEATH
ON A VINEYARD
BEACH

A Martha's Vineyard Mystery

PHILIP R. CRAIG

SCRIBNER

SCRIBNER
1230 Avenue of the Americas
New York, NY 10020

SCRIBNER and design are registered trademarks of Simon & Schuster Inc.

Manufactured in the United States of America

Text set in Baskerville

1   3   5   7   9   10   8   6   4   2

Library of Congress Cataloging-in-Publication Data
Craig, Philip R., 1933–
Death on a vineyard beach: a Martha's Vineyard mystery/Philip R. Craig.
p. cm.
1. Jackson, Jeff (Fictitious character)—Fiction. 2. Private investigators—
Massachusetts—Martha's Vineyard—Fiction. 3. Martha's
Vineyard (Mass.)—Fiction. I. Title.
PS3553.R23D43   1996
813'.54—dc20
95–45861
CIP

ISBN 0-684-19717-0

For two of the Other Women in my life:
my agent, Jane Otte, and my editor, Susanne Kirk,
who forgive my literary trespasses
but don't let me get away with them.

". . . On the trees no leaf is seen
Nor are the meadows growing green,
Birds build no nest, no song is sung,
And hapless beasts shall bear no young,
So is it while the sinful king
Shall evil on his people bring.
For Jesus Christ does punish well
The land wherein the wicked dwell."

SONE DE NANSAI, 11. 4848–56

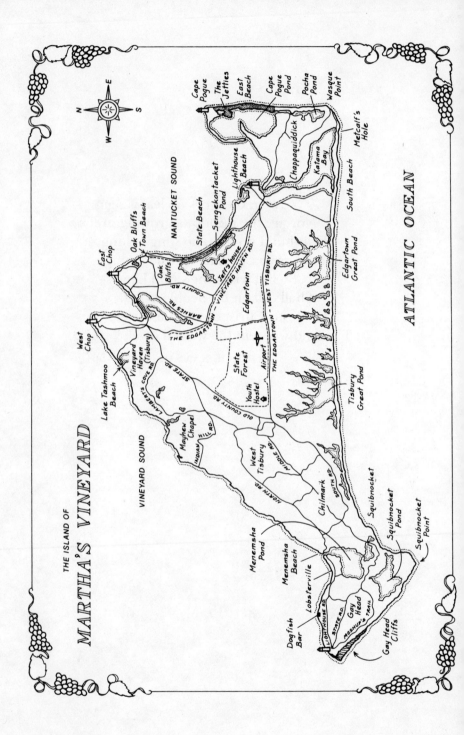

DEATH ON A VINEYARD BEACH

— 1 —

Zee and I got married at noon on July 13, a date artfully chosen by me in the hope that since it was my birthday, one of the four dates I usually remembered—the others being New Year's Day, Christmas, and the Fourth of July— I had a fighting chance of recollecting my anniversary in the future.

It was a beautiful Martha's Vineyard day, with a warm sun in a cloudless sky, and a gentle north wind to keep things comfortable for all of us who had abandoned our summer shorts and had dressed up for the occasion. There were people with regular cameras and video cameras moving around shooting pictures. Apparently we were going to get the whole thing on record.

We were in our friend John Skye's yard, between the farmhouse and the barn, and there were more people there than I had thought we knew. My sister and her husband were there, in from Santa Fe; the Muleto family—Zee's parents and brothers and the brothers' wives—had all come over from Fall River and New Bedford. And there were island people, friends of Zee's and friends of mine, including the chief of the Edgartown police and some other cops. It was quite a crowd.

The justice of the peace performed the ceremony, and a young liberal Catholic priest, ignoring the fact that Zee wasn't Catholic anymore and I never had been, blessed the whole affair. I had met the justice of the peace, but

I'd never seen the priest before. He was the work of Maria, Zee's very religious mother, who, when unable to convince her daughter to have a church wedding, arranged a compromise and brought in the priest to make things as legit as possible in her God's eyes. Zee and I had each already had one church wedding, and that seemed enough to Zee, since neither marriage had worked out in spite of the blessings of religion. This time she thought we'd try it without benefit of clergy.

The food and drink were laid out in abundance, and as soon as they could manage it, people filed by with handshakes and kisses and headed for the bar. I could hardly wait to join them.

I was in a rented summer tux, and was beginning to feel sweat trickle down my neck. Zee, in something swirling and pale blue, looked as though she'd stepped out of a magazine about brides. On her left ring finger she now wore my grandmother's engagement ring and a narrow band of matching gold. Once again I wondered why the wedding ring was on the inside of the engagement ring instead of the other way around, which made more sense to me since we'd gotten engaged before we'd gotten married. I decided I'd not ask that question today.

A young woman came by. "Hi," she said to me. "I'm Maggie Vanderbeck. Congratulations!" She kissed Zee and went on her way.

Zee said: "Maggie volunteers at the hospital when she's home from college and isn't working in her sister's shop."

"One of the Gay Head Vanderbecks?"

"One of the very same."

"Congratulations," said the chief, who was the last one

through the reception line. He kissed Zee and shook my hand.

"An honest woman, at last," grinned Zee. "Is it true that you're going deer hunting in Maine this fall? Word has it that you just got yourself a brand-new 30.06."

"Yeah," said the chief. "I have it zeroed in at a hundred and fifty yards. I plan on venison for Christmas dinner." He looked down at my wedding ring and then back up into my face. "The smartest thing you've done since I've known you, J.W. It's good for a man to be married. It's the way things are supposed to be."

The chief had been married over thirty years, and like most such long-married men couldn't imagine a better life. Neither could I.

From the tables came the sound of corks popping. I glanced over and saw John Skye and Manny Fonseca pouring champagne.

"Come on, you two," I said, taking Zee's hand. "I'll buy you both a drink."

The chief glanced at his watch. "One glass, then I got to get to work back downtown." He allowed himself a smile. "Crime never sleeps, you know. Not even in Edgartown."

"Well, maybe it'll doze until you get back on the beat," I said.

We went up to the tables and got glasses. Somebody dragged Zee off to join other people. Around us, the sound of voices filled the air. People seemed happy. I was happy, too.

"Got the boat ready to go?" asked my sister's husband, Mike.

"Ready to roll. You and Margarite will have our house and the cats to yourselves while we're gone, and you'll have both trucks, so you can get down the beach and back."

"How romantic," said Margarite. "A sailing honeymoon to Nantucket in your own catboat."

"It'll be romantic as long as the weather holds. If it breezes up or starts to rain while we're out on the sound, an eighteen-foot catboat won't be an amorous conveyance."

"I'm sure everything will be wonderful," said my sister, whose own romance was with Mike and the mountains and deserts of northern New Mexico. She squeezed my arm. "Your Zeolinda is about the most beautiful woman I've ever seen. You're a lucky guy!"

"I consider it skill," I said, knowing she was right. "It took time and work, but now I've got her in my clutches."

"And I've got you," said Zee, coming out of the crowd. "It's a high price to pay to finally get to go to Nantucket, but I've always wanted to see the place and this is the only way I could swing it."

The chief had his glass in his hand and was looking around at people in that way that some cops do, even when they're off duty. I noticed his eyes stop moving and focus toward the driveway, which was lined with cars. I turned and followed his gaze.

A man was walking casually away. I couldn't see his face, and wondered who he was. Someone else from the hospital where Zee worked, maybe. Maybe a friend of Zee's, or the husband or boyfriend of a friend. Was there something familiar about the way he walked? The chief was still looking at him when I turned away.

On the porch, the band was tuning up. A glass and a half later, they started off with a country-and-western tune, and people began to dance on the lawn. Ties were stripped off and coats were piled up on the porch. Women kicked off their shoes and tossed their hair.

"Come on, Jefferson," said Zee, and led me away from the bar. We danced, which is to say she danced and I walked around and kicked up a heel now and then, hoping that I was stepping to the music. I do my best dancing standing still since somehow rhythm doesn't reach my feet very well. Still, we danced fast, then slow, then alone to the "Tennessee Waltz" while everybody else watched.

"You and Fred Astaire," said Zee, nimbly escaping one of my shoes. "You're a matched pair."

"Fred and I are twins," I said. "People can't tell us apart."

After a while, someone in the crowd said, "Enough of this. A round of applause for the bride and groom, then let's get dancing ourselves!" The applause came and the lawn filled again with dancers, all of whom were better at the sport than I was.

John Skye took Zee out of my arms and whirled away with her. I went to a table and ate some pumpernickel with mustard and sliced salmon on it, washed down with champagne.

Iowa, Walter, and Dick Dirgins, three of the island's dedicated fishermen, were ahead of me, enjoying the fare.

"Not a bad party," said Dick. "You should get married more often."

"I'm going to try to make this one last," I said.

I looked down the driveway. At the end, under a big oak tree, I could see a man standing. He was leaning lightly against the tree, looking back at the crowd. He had a hand on his chin and was wearing dark glasses, so I couldn't make out his features. He was wearing a light blue summer suit and a dark tie. He was thick through the shoulders and chest, and long-waisted, but didn't have much in the way of hips. His hair was black and straight and a bit longer than was fashionable that year. Maybe he saw me looking at him, for something seemed to pass between us. Then he straightened, turned, and walked out of sight beyond the corner of the farmhouse.

"Jeez, J.W., I never been to such a good party before. I think it's really good, don't you?"

I turned and found Bonzo beaming at me, champagne glass in hand, gentle eyes smiling emptily up at me.

"It's my wedding," I said. "It's supposed to be really good."

"Yeah," said Bonzo. "You and Zee are gonna be married. That's good, J.W. You and Zee are good friends." He nodded approvingly.

Bonzo had once been a promising lad, they tell me, but some time in the past he'd gotten some bad acid that had touched his brain. Now he worked with a broom and bar rag in the Fireside Bar in Oak Bluffs, and lived with his widowed schoolteacher mother, who adored him and treated him like the little child that he would always be.

"Are you having a good time, Bonzo?"

"I sure am. Look, I got champagne. I don't get that much. Usually all I get is a beer. This champagne is good." He smiled his sweet smile.

"I'm glad you and your mom could come and help us celebrate. I wouldn't have wanted to get married without having you as our guests. And Zee feels the same way."

"Say," said Bonzo, sidling nearer and beginning to blush. "Do you think it might, maybe, be okay if I have a dance with Zee? Would that be okay, do you think? I mean, I never hardly dance, but today is special. What do you think? Do you think she'd let me have a dance?"

"Wait right here," I said, and walked out and found Zee and John. I told them what Bonzo had said.

"Allow me," said John. He took Zee's arm and led her to Bonzo.

Zee smiled her dazzling smile at Bonzo, and Bonzo stared at her with awe.

"I'd love to dance with you, Bonzo," she said. "Let's go."

John and I stood and watched them.

"Well, I'll be damned," said John a moment later. "Will you look at that."

I looked and felt myself grinning, for Bonzo—kind, mindless Bonzo—was a beautiful dancer. He and Zee seemed to be floating over the lawn, swirling and striding, riding the air. Zee's long, blue-black hair glinted in the sun, and her skirt swirled as they stepped and spun to the music.

I glanced down and saw Bonzo's mother beside me. She was looking with wonder and joy at her son.

"He's terrific," I said. "I had no idea he could dance like that."

"Yes. He's beautiful," she nodded. "Very beautiful. Look at them!"

Others were looking, too, and soon everyone else stopped dancing and watched Bonzo and Zee weave and spin over the lawn. When the song ended, Bonzo listened to the applause and grinned and ducked his head, and led Zee back to me.

"You were a lovely pair," smiled Bonzo's mother. "Just lovely."

Bonzo shook Zee's hand, and smiled shyly. "Thanks, Zee. That was fun for me. I hope it was fun for you, too."

"It was a lot of fun, Bonzo."

"Maybe someday we'll all go to another wedding, and there'll be music again, and you and me can dance another time. What do you think? Would that be okay?"

"That will certainly be okay, Bonzo. Thank you for dancing with me. You're a fine dancer."

He nodded solemnly. "Dancing is good, you know. It makes you feel good when you do it, not quite like you feel good doing other things like, maybe, fishing or listening to the birds, but real good." He nodded his head. "Yeah, it's good, all right."

The justice of the peace came up to Bonzo. "Hey," she said. "You can really trip the light fantastic! How about dancing with me?"

She and Bonzo went off together as the next tune began. And when that dance was done, another woman asked to dance with Bonzo. And after that, another. He danced with Maggie Vanderbeck. Bonzo danced and danced.

We all had more champagne. The band took a break and joined the guests at the bar and food tables. Then we danced some more, and partied until mid-afternoon. Then people began to fade away. By four o'clock, my sister and Mike and Zee's family were helping John and Mattie Skye and their twin daughters clean up the wreckage.

"We'll help," said Zee.

"No, you won't," said Mattie slapping at her hands. "Time for you two to be off."

And off we went, trailing good-byes as we drove out of the yard. We went to my house—our house now—and got out of our wedding duds and into our summer clothes: shorts, tee-shirts, and Tevas. We fed Oliver Underfoot and Velcro the last cat food meals they'd get from us for a while, then I called a taxi and had it take us down to Collins Beach where I keep my dinghy chained to the bulwarks so the summer yachtsmen won't steal it.

We rowed out around the Reading Room dock and fetched the *Shirley J.*, which was swinging on her stake halfway between the Reading Room and the yacht club.

I had provisioned the boat the day before, but also found an iced half-case of champagne, along with some caviar, in a Styrofoam container in the cockpit. A welcome gift from some anonymous donor.

The wind was still gentle from the north, so we raised the big sail and reached out against the incoming tide, through the narrows where the On Time ferry links Chappaquiddick and Edgartown. Clear of the lighthouse, the wind seemed fresher.

Boats were coming in for the night, and among them I saw the *Lucky Lil*, the nice conch boat that had once been the pride, joy, and livelihood of Jimmy Souza, but now belonged mostly to Albert Enos, but also partly to me, since Albert had needed a couple thou more to swing the deal, and I, at that moment, had a couple of thou to loan.

For being sharp, Albert had shortly afterward gotten a black eye from Jimmy's angry son, Fred, who, already mad about his father's decline, figured that sodden Jimmy had been suckered once more.

But the sale had stood, and where once Jimmy had been captain, and his testy son had worked as his sometime crew, now Albert was captain and red-nosed Jimmy was his crew.

There were different stories about why Jimmy had gone belly-up. He and his boy claimed it was because the draggers and trawlers had destroyed too many of his pots and other gear; others claimed it was because Jimmy had succumbed to the fisherman's traditional companion and enemy, the booze. Whatever the case, I hoped that

Albert would have better luck, and was once again grateful that I was only part-owner of the boat, and not a real fisherman or farmer, the two chanciest professions that I knew of. On the other hand, I didn't have a profession of any kind. Was that better? I decided to follow Scarlett's advice and think about that tomorrow.

"There's my retirement plan," I now said to Zee. "The *Lucky Lil*. If I go first, my share will all be yours."

"A big spender from the East," said Zee. "A shipping tycoon. My favorite kind of husband."

We passed through the boats and headed for the Cape Pogue Gut.

The tide and wind carried us smoothly into Cape Pogue Pond, around John Oliver Point, and down to the south end of the pond, where I dropped the hook.

There, ignoring Edgartown's regulation forbidding overnight anchoring in the pond, Zee and I spent the first night of our married life on the cockpit floor, since the bunks in the cabin were singles, too narrow for two.

Sometime during the night I drifted half awake, and found myself wondering who the man in the driveway had been. But then Zee sighed in her sleep and curled a long, sleek leg over mine, and the man went out of my mind. Until morning, when the explosions came down into my dreams, and I woke with Zee shaking me and saying, "Wake up! Wake up! What is it?"

— 2 —

I don't often have the dream, and when I do it's more surrealistic than real, but it's real enough. There's blood and noise and splintering trees and breaking earth, and I'm filled first with paralyzing fear, then the cold certainty that I'm going to die. I start dragging myself through the explosions and bodies toward the radio, but I never get there. I wake up making the kind of sound that frightened Zee that first morning of our married life.

She had me in her arms, and her voice was gentle. "It's okay, it's okay. It was just a dream. It's gone now."

My brow was cold and wet. I lay there until my breathing was normal again. Then I said, "Sorry. Just a nightmare. I have it sometimes."

"Are you all right?"

"I'm fine." I put a smile on my face and looked up at her. "Don't worry."

She tightened her arms around me. "What's the dream?"

"It's nothing. The day I got hurt in the war. I almost never have it anymore."

"You've never told me about that."

"There isn't much to tell, but I was pretty scared at the time."

She rocked me in her arms. "Poor baby. I'm sorry."

"Don't be," I said.

The boat was wet with morning dew. We put the sleeping bags in the cabin, had breakfast, and motored out of the gut into the sound as the sun climbed out of the sea and the morning wind rose.

I raised the sail and cut the engine, and we headed east around the tip of Cape Pogue.

"One interesting thing," I said. "Remember me asking you about that guy I saw at our wedding? I think seeing him triggered the dream. I didn't recognize him then, but I do now. He was my sergeant. A guy named Joe Begay. They called him Lucky Joe, although he wasn't so lucky that day."

"Let's not think about those days anymore," said Zee. "Let's think about now."

"Good idea." But I wondered what Joe Begay was doing on Martha's Vineyard. I hadn't seen him in over twenty years.

Although the islands are within sight of each other, a lot of Nantucket people have never been to Martha's Vineyard, and a lot of Vineyarders have never been to Nantucket. Zee and I were two of the latter, although we'd often seen the low outline of Muskeget on the horizon while we were fishing at Wasque Point. Muskeget is a tiny island at the west end of Nantucket, where, I'm told, seals gather in February to give birth to their young. Wasque, where I spend a lot of time, is the southeastern corner of Chappaquiddick, and is probably the best place on the east coast to surf cast for bluefish. I'd seen a few seals there as well.

Once we'd cleared Cape Pogue light, we'd stripped and were now naked and sopping up the rays of the sun as we sailed slowly eastward. I was at the tiller, and Zee was stretched out on a sleeping pad on the cockpit deck. She looked like a bronze goddess, and her long black hair was spread like a dark halo around her head.

"Well, how do you like being married?" I asked.

"It's better than having a sharp stick up your nose."

"How sweet. And they say that the language of lovers is a thing of the past."

"What would happen if you let go of the tiller and slacked the sheet, and came down here for a minute or two?"

I looked around the horizon. There were some tall sails to the north of us, and some fishing boats to the south, down toward Wasque or maybe even farther. Two trawlers, their outriggers spread wide so that they looked like great birds or insects sitting on the sea, were moving across the channel. There were no signs of a shoal close by.

"Let's check it out," I said, and loosed the sheet and tiller. The *Shirley J.* turned slowly and drifted broadside down wind and stream. I eased down beside Zee.

Afterward we lay together while the boat wallowed gently on the small waves.

"Is your mast all in splinters, are your shrouds all unstrung?" asked Zee, flashing her dazzling smile.

"Only momentarily." I ran my hands over her smooth tanned body. "Skin," I said. "There's nothing like it."

"Look up there," she said, staring at the sky.

I looked at the clouds moving across the blue.

"A cloud-eating sky." She pointed.

Sure enough, amid the light, fluffy clouds there was a patch of cloud-eating blue sky. As the windblown clouds moved into it, they grew rapidly smaller and then disappeared. Clouds that didn't enter that bit of blue sky kept right on blowing down wind, intact and undiminished. More proof that nature is weird.

We lay and watched the clouds being eaten up.

"Are we going to have babies soon?" asked Zee.

"If you want babies, you get babies."

"Or should we just have the two of us for a while?"

"If you want just two of us, you get just two of us."

"But what do you want? I don't want you just to want what I want. I want you to have some wants of your own."

"But I do want what you want. I know you want to have babies, so if you want them now, that's okay with me. Or if you want to have them later, that's okay, too."

"But you do want to have them."

"Actually, I do," I said. "I just don't want you to feel that you should have them right away just because I'd like to have some."

"How many do you want?"

"I think two. Or three at the most. My parents had two. One of each kind. That seemed to be a good number and a nice variety of genders."

"My parents had three. Two boys and me. That seemed like a nice selection, too. Do you want a boy or a girl first?"

"A girl, because they're made of sugar and spice and everything nice. And I want her to look just like you. Later we can have a boy. Or if we don't, that'll be okay, too."

"What if we get boys instead of girls?"

"I think boys would be okay. You can teach them how to fish and I'll teach them how to cook. We'll do the same with the girls. We'll both teach them how to garden, and Manny Fonseca can teach them all how to shoot."

"I don't know if I want them to know how to shoot."

"In that case, I'll have to sneak them off to the Rod and Gun Club range by myself while you're at work, because I want them to know how to handle weapons."

"Are we having our first argument about the children?"

"Nope. But since there are guns in our house, I want you to learn how to use them, too, and how to be safe with them. But I may have gotten to you too late. You may already be molded."

"Mold, shmold. I just don't like guns. We never had any in our house."

In a locked gun cabinet, I kept the shotguns and the rifle that had been my father's, and the .38 pistol that I'd had when I'd been a Boston cop. I didn't do much hunting anymore, but I kept the guns anyway. Now and then I used one.

I got up and took the tiller and hauled in the sheet, and the *Shirley J.* turned and headed east once more.

Zee, the sea goddess, lolled on the deck and looked ahead. "Say, I do believe that's Nantucket there."

"I do believe it is."

"What's that ship doing there? It looks like it's aground."

"What keen eyes you have, my dear. It is, indeed, a ship gone aground. It's been there several years, I believe."

"How romantic. A wrecked ship on the fabled island."

"How about the two of us on the fabled island. That's even more romantic."

She came and sat beside me and put her head against my shoulder. "I like being married," she said.

The sun was swinging low when we entered the channel leading into Nantucket harbor and became one of a steady stream of boats headed in. An hour before, as we had closed with the island and the sea around us had grown less empty, we had exchanged nudity for shorts and shirts, and were now models of well-dressed summer sailors.

We sailed in past the lighthouse and the ferry dock, found a spot where we'd have room to swing, nosed up into the wind, and dropped anchor. I lowered the big mainsail and lashed it to the boom, and we were there.

Zee came up from the cabin with champagne, glasses, caviar, and crackers. We sat and watched the busy harbor while we downed the wine and hors d'oeuvres. When the bottle was empty, I looked at Zee.

"Go get into some going-ashore duds, my love, and pack whatever you'll want when we explore this unknown island tomorrow. You and I have reservations for supper at eight at Vincent's, and then two nights at the Jared Coffin House."

She looked at her watch and leaped to her feet. "Eight o'clock? Good grief, why didn't you warn me?" She ducked down into the cabin. Then she hurried back out and gave me a large kiss. "You are so sweet! I thought we were going to be living on the boat!" She disappeared again.

For two days we played tourist, enjoying our inn, taking the tour bus out to the east end of the island, walking the cobbled streets of the town, and finally finding a Jeep and going out over the sands to Great Point, where the rip reminded us of Chappaquiddick's lonely beaches, and we'd felt much at home and had missed our surf-casting rods.

Then we sailed for Chatham in front of a south wind.

"Well, what do you think of Nantucket?" I asked, looking across the shoaly waters toward the sands of Monomoy and Cape Cod.

"Not a bad island for a honeymoon," said Zee, balancing a Sam Adams on her flat belly as she lay in the sun. "Not many trees, of course."

"They make up for the trees by having lots of fog."

"The Gray Lady," agreed Zee. "I'm glad we went. Maybe we should just keep sailing from place to place forever. Maybe we should sail up to Boston to see the opera."

One of our presents was a set of tickets to see *Carmen* the coming weekend. After that, the honeymoon would officially be over. I wasn't sure I wanted it to be.

We sailed into Chatham Harbor and anchored and walked that lovely town for two days. We spent a good deal of time on the cliffs overlooking the opening in the eastern barrier beach, noting how the recent wicked storms had savaged the waterways and beachfront properties.

"Remind me not to build my next house too close to the ocean," said Zee.

"Okay. Don't build your next house too close to the ocean."

"Thank you, thank you, thank you."

The wind was still from the south when we left Chatham and sailed west along the south shore of the cape. Zee wrote thank-you notes as we went. One long reach took us to Hyannis, where we went ashore long enough to mail the notes and get ice for our last two bottles of champagne. The next morning we had an east wind that blew us to Hadley's, where we found a far corner of the harbor, popped those bottles, and ate the last of our caviar.

"How did you arrange for such a fine trip?" asked Zee.

"A gentleman never sails into the wind," I said. "I made a deal with Neptune before we left. Nep and I are just like that." I held up a hand with fore and middle fingers side by side.

The next day we caught the tide and sailed back to

Edgartown, where I managed to fetch our stake so perfectly that I knew that nobody was watching, since people are only watching when you mess things up.

I rowed us ashore, found a taxi to take us home, and carried my bride across the threshold. My sister and her husband were gone, but the cats were waiting, looking well fed and lazy.

"The honeymoon isn't officially over yet," I said. I kicked the door shut behind us and walked straight into the bedroom. Zee laughed.

The next day, having arranged for the Skye twins to tend to Oliver Underfoot and Velcro in our absence, we shoved suitcases into the back of Zee's little Jeep, and headed for Boston, where we planned not only to see *Carmen*, but to catch a Sox game.

As things turned out, there was moderate conflict at Fenway, but two violent confrontations at the Wang Center. One involved Don José and Carmen, and the other included me.

3

It's arguable that anyone who deliberately leaves Martha's Vineyard in July and drives to Boston for a weekend deserves whatever wretchedness he encounters, the principle being that stupidity is its own reward.

It's not that Zee and I never go to Boston at all. We usually drive up there once a year, in the fall, just before the Bluefish Derby starts, to catch a Red Sox game. By that time, all hope for Sox success is usually gone, and we can relax and watch without any actual expectations of winning the World Series as the local guys last did in 1918. Going to the city during the summer is something else entirely. Who would do such a thing unless they were fools or had been given opera tickets, or both?

We went north over the Bourne Bridge up to 495, took a right onto 24, another onto 128, and a left onto the Southeast Expressway, and so on into the city. From my Boston cop days I had a little local knowledge, so we managed to find a fairly cheap hotel not too far from the Wang Center that provided a decent room for us and a parking place for our car, which I had no intention of using while we were in town. It was Saturday morning, so the traffic hadn't been bad, but not even I was such an idiot as to drive in downtown Boston when I didn't have to. Better by far to take the T, or grab a cab. Or, better yet, to walk, since Boston is a very walkable city. Like London, someone once told me, although I wouldn't know, never having been to London.

Boston was hot and full of exhaust fumes, but Fenway Park would be better. Under a pale blue sky, we walked across the Common and through the Garden, stopping briefly on the bridge to watch the swan boats in the pond, then strolled up Newbury Street, window-shopping. Zee picked out several extremely expensive items that she said she would accept from me as tokens of my esteem, and I promised her we'd get them all on our way back to the hotel. She held my arm and smiled at passersby.

The far end of Newbury is shabbier than the Garden end, but it leads toward baseball, so we didn't care. We crossed the Muddy River, and then, without getting killed by Sox fans looking for parking places, made it to the old ballpark, America's finest and quirkiest.

You never know quite what a ball will do when it's hit down either line or off the left field wall in Fenway Park. It can take crazy bounces that will drive outfielders mad, and turn a routine play into something quite bizarre. Oh, for the days when Yaz and Dewey were still out there in left and right, playing the angles with grace and winging the ball back in. The golden days of yesteryear.

But this was this year, and Yaz and Dewey and Jim Rice and the rest of the old Sox sluggers were only distant memories.

But they still had Roger, if not a lot else, and they were playing almost 500 ball, in spite of their usual shaky infield, limp bull pen, and sore-kneed, bingle-hitting outfielders.

We managed two pretty good tickets behind third, where we could see everything but the left field corner, and bought beer, hot dogs and popcorn, the necessities.

"Home at last," said Zee, sitting down and looking at her program. "Warm beer and cold hot dogs, instead of the other way around. It must be Fenway."

"Pennant fever," I said, looking at the noisy, mid-summer lazy, shirtsleeved crowd.

The wind barely moved the flags, and it was warm. The teams and the crowd stood for the national anthem, and the Sox took the field.

"Our team," said Zee, clapping.

Our team, indeed. For better or for worse. Like marriage.

"Go get 'em!" yelled Zee, as the pitcher put one down the middle and the first batter popped up.

More beer, more hot dogs, more popcorn. Not too much scoring, but just enough for the local guys to win. We were carried out of the park by a happy crowd.

"How long is our winning streak?" asked Zee.

"One game. This one."

"The pennant for sure. Nobody can stop us now!"

Across the street from Fenway is the Boston Beer Works, where they make and serve their own beer. We shouldered our way in and actually found seats in the back.

Their Amber Ale is good. Maybe not quite up to Commonwealth Brewery standards, but good. One of the really positive signs of good health in America is the increasing numbers of micro-breweries across the country. Boston alone has a half dozen or so, and there are others everywhere, all making good, local, English-style beers.

I said all this to Zee and smiled a masculine smile. "It makes a man proud to be an Amurican."

"I think that's American, with an *e*."

"I'm pronouncing it with the Ollie North accent, which is the truly Amurican one."

"As in 'Amurica the Beautiful.' "

"That's it. Spoken like a truly Amurican woman."

"The kind that made our nation great."

"The very kind."

Later, as darkness fell, we walked back downtown, and were not mugged, held up, or otherwise assaulted on the mean streets.

"Dinner at Jake Wirth's?"

"Nothing could be finer."

Jake's dark beer, wurst, and sauerkraut were delish, as always. We wandered home through the dark streets, sated and happy.

"Not a bad first day in the big city," said Zee later, sleepily wrapping her arms around me.

"Not bad at all."

We breakfasted at McDonald's, a treat to folk such as us, who live on a McDonaldless island, thanks to a successful effort by our Vineyard neighbors to repulse a Big Mac attack intended to establish a place in Vineyard Haven. The successful defenders of the blessed isle hold that it is too classy a place to want or need an off-island fast-food joint. Personally, I think that Mac's or its equivalent is exactly what the island needs—a place to get cheap, dependable, high-cholesterol, all-American food. But nobody has yet asked me my opinion on the issue. At any rate, now being in America, Zee and I feasted on Egg McMuffins and coffee, and called them good.

"Mac's in Paris, you know," said Zee, munching. "A guy told me a while back that the trash containers in Luxembourg Gardens are stuffed with empty McDonald food containers. So if it's good enough for a Parisian, it's good enough for me."

"Fried food without guilt."

We walked up to the MFA and had a look at things, then walked back downtown just in time to have a beer and sandwich before hitting the Wang for the matinee.

The Wang Center is just a few seats smaller than Fenway Park, but our tickets were front and center, so we had a good view of everything. Zee was pleased to note that our fellow opera lovers were not dressed too much differently than we were, in slacks and shirts, sans formal garb. There were exceptions, of course, including an elderly man and his younger companion who were seated a row in front of us. They, unlike most of the men in the audience, wore neckties and suits. No doubt there were others of their ilk scattered here and there, lending an aura of civilization to an otherwise casual-looking crowd.

I listen to a good deal of opera, but I had never attended a performance. I thought it was terrific, the perfect first opera for anyone who'd not seen one before. Carmen was slinky and beautiful, Don José was perhaps a tad overweight, but in good voice, and Escamillo both looked and sang well. There was passion and dancing, a lot of good music, and just enough violence. We gave everyone several good rounds of applause, and I was happy.

" 'The Toreador Song' was good enough to make one consider becoming a baritone instead of a tenor," I said to Zee as we jostled our way out of the auditorium.

"Surely you're not giving up the idea of singing 'Nessun dorma' some day?"

"Well, no. But I don't see why I can't do both."

"Along with learning how to play 'Amazing Grace' on the bagpipes. You're a musically ambitious man, Jefferson."

"It's true that I aspire to great things."

"As for me, I think I can see myself doing the habanera."

"Perfect casting. Dark-eyed Portuguese beauty that you are, doing the flamenco bit."

"Gee," said Zee, "with our musical drive, it's really too bad that neither one of us can actually sing very well."

"Maybe we could become musical scholars. For instance, did you know that the habanera came from Cuba and isn't really Spanish at all?"

"Neither was Bizet, for that matter."

"It's so swell to be smart. I really love it."

We came out into the afternoon sunlight, and the crowd, chatting and cheerful, moved away in both directions along Tremont Street, seeking food or transportation home.

There was an old, well-maintained black Cadillac at the curb. It had those dark windows that prevent you from seeing who's inside, but the driver's side window was rolled down and there was a young guy sitting there, looking at the people coming out of the theater. He saw who he was looking for, got out, and opened the rear door. I noted that his party consisted of the older man and younger companion who had been seated in front of us, decked out in ties and suits. The two of them moved toward the car, with Zee and me only a step or two behind.

Then a car that had been double-parked down the street to the right moved up and stopped beside the Caddy. A shapeless figure wearing a long, unzipped, hooded sweatshirt, baggy pants, and high-top sneakers stepped out and came around behind the Cadillac. This popular inner-city attire caught my eye, since it was a warm day for a sweatshirt, however fashionable such garb might be.

As the older man reached the car, the hooded figure spoke one word: "Marcus."

The older man paused and looked at him, and the hooded figure brought out a sawed-off shotgun from beneath his sweatshirt.

As the shotgun came level with the older man's chest, his younger companion, half a step behind, lurched forward, too late, to protect him.

Closer, and ignored by the shootist, I took one step and knocked the muzzle of the gun into the air as it went off.

I was aware of the sound of breaking glass as the shot hit some window or streetlight, then I had both hands on the gun and had spun my body between it and its owner. For a moment we struggled for possession, then I slid a hand down, found the little finger of the shootist's trigger hand, yanked it back and broke it. There was a cry of pain from behind me, and a sudden release of the shotgun. I turned in time to see the hooded figure race around behind the Caddy. I grabbed, but caught only the sweatshirt, which its owner slipped out of like an eel. He cast one look at me, then dived through the window of the car beyond the Cadillac. The car's engine roared, its spinning tires squealed, and it tore away up Tremont.

Turning back, I found myself looking into the wild eyes of the older man's companion. There was a large pistol in his hand, and it was pointed at me. I was aware of the shotgun in my own hands. For an instant he seemed poised on the brink of decision: Was I friend or another foe? Should he shoot or not?

"Get out of here," I said. "That guy might not have been alone."

Perhaps a second passed. Then he nodded. "Yeah." He pushed the older man into the car. "Get us out of here, Vinnie," he said to the driver, whose face was white and tense. He and Vinnie got into the Cadillac and drove away.

All around us, shocked theatergoers were staring or cowering away. Who could blame them? I thumbed on the safety, then held the shotgun close to my thigh, where it was less conspicuous.

"Come on," I said to Zee, taking her arm. "We'll go inside and call the cops."

She was pale as snow. "Are you all right?"

"I'm fine," I said, but I felt pretty pale myself.

We went back into the theater and made our phone call. It took Boston's finest about five minutes to get there. They weren't used to shootings at opera matinees.

4

The uniforms who showed up first felt better when they'd separated me from the shotgun. They didn't trust the safety any more than I did, and they didn't trust me, either. We were all glad when the lab boys took the gun away.

Meanwhile, some detectives had arrived and taken turns asking us questions. They did the same of some other people who had hung around long enough to be nailed as witnesses. As might be expected, not all stories corresponded in detail. A couple of people even testified that I was the shootist, which didn't surprise me or the cops, but which made Zee angry.

"What kind of klutzes are those people? Don't they even understand what they see with their own eyes? My God!"

"Now, take it easy, Mrs. Jackson," said detective Gordon R. Sullivan, who was going over things with us one last time. I wondered what the *R* stood for and how many Sullivans were on the Boston PD these days. Detective Sullivan had a soothing voice. "Eyewitnesses are notorious for getting things messed up. We'll get this all sorted out. So you don't know the guy who seems to have been the intended victim?"

"I never saw him before."

"And you, Mr. Jackson?"

"Never saw any of them before."

"What made you involve yourself like that? That was a very dangerous thing to do."

I'd been wondering about that. "I haven't the slightest idea," I said. "If I'd had time to think, I probably never would have done it. It just happened."

He looked at me. "Just happened."

"Yeah."

"And you don't know any of the parties?"

"No."

"Or, like where we might catch up with any of them?"

"The older guy and his friends drove off in an old black Cadillac with those tinted windows. The car had a Mass plate, but I didn't get the number. The perps were in a light-colored sedan. A Chevy, maybe, but I'm not sure. I can't tell the difference between one make and another these days. They took off up Tremont. I didn't get that plate, either. And I don't know how many of them there were. A driver and the shooter, at least."

"Describe the shooter."

"We already did that," said Zee. "Young guy. White. Short. Light build, about a hundred forty pounds or so. Dark hair. Dark eyes."

Sullivan gave her an expressionless look. "You remember a good deal, considering you only saw him for a second."

"I'm a nurse," said Zee. "I see a lot of people in the emergency room. I'm used to quick ID's."

"I guess so." He looked at me. "Anything to add? Maybe you remember something you forgot before."

"Don't forget the broken pinkie."

"I won't." The detective looked at his notes. "Wiry type. Wearing gloves."

I nodded. "Maybe those surgical ones. Pretty strong kid, for somebody that size. Gave me a real tussle for the gun."

"You say the shooter said a name. Marcus."

"Yeah. And the older guy looked at him. So maybe the older guy is Marcus."

"Why would he call his name?"

"I don't know. Maybe he wanted him to know he was about to get shot."

"Or maybe he wanted to make sure he was shooting the right guy."

"Yeah. He didn't show the gun until Marcus looked at him."

"Reacted to hearing his name, you mean?"

"That's how it looked to me, but it all happened pretty fast."

"And after the shooter took off, you turned around and the younger guy with Marcus had a gun pointing at you."

"I'd hardly call him a young guy," said Zee. "I'd say he was more fortyish. But, yes, he did point a gun. I was only a yard or so away, and I saw it all. He jumped in front of the older man and jerked the pistol out from under his coat. I thought he was going to shoot Jeff!"

The detective looked at me. "And that's when you told him to take off."

"Yeah."

"This fortyish guy was a bodyguard, you think?"

"That's what I think."

The detective grunted, and got out a cigar. Then he looked at Zee and put the cigar away. "Lessee. An older guy named Marcus complete with bodyguard and a driver and a black Cadillac with Mass plates. Shouldn't be too hard to track down. The perps are another story. You both sure you never got a look at the driver's face?"

"Not even a glimpse."

Sullivan stood up. "You gonna be in town long?"

"About thirty seconds after you let us go," said Zee. "I'm on my honeymoon, and I don't want to spend the rest of it in the Wang Center."

"Honeymoon, eh?" Sullivan arched a brow. "Congratulations, Mr. Jackson. Best wishes, Mrs. Jackson."

A policeman came up to us, and gestured toward the door with his thumb. "Gordy, there's some reporters out there. You want I should let them come in now?"

"No reporters," I said, getting up. "I don't need any reporters sharing my honeymoon. There's got to be another way out of here."

"Come with me," said Sullivan. "We'll sneak out the back way and go down to headquarters so you two can look at some mug shots and sign your statements and be on your way."

So we went and looked at mug shots, but didn't see the kid with the shotgun.

Sullivan was disappointed, but not surprised. "The thing is, we get shotguns, but they aren't the weapon of choice around here. Nines are what the bad boys like these days. But since spring, we have had two shotgun killings. Not the usual thing, so maybe this shooter is the same guy. You're the first people who've seen his face, so I thought maybe we'd get lucky."

"Who got shot?" I asked.

"The sort of people you'd expect to get shot sooner or later. Two would-be bad guys from in town."

For the most part, people who die violently live that way first. It's pretty rare for a peaceful person living in a peaceful place to get shotgunned.

Of course, it does happen.

Sullivan thanked us and told us that he might be in

touch. "Not unless we nail the perps, though, or unless
something comes up." He shook hands. "I'll have somebody run you back to your hotel. If you think of anything else, give me a call." He gave me his card. "Now
get back on that honeymoon."

A young cop drove us back to the hotel. There, I
looked at Zee. "What do you say, wife, shall we stay
another night or head for the blessed isle?"

"I've had about as much city as I want for now. To the
Vineyard, James."

We checked out and headed south. It was now early
evening, and we had the road pretty much to ourselves
since we were driving toward Cape Cod and the cape
weekenders were all coming home, filling the north-
bound side of the highway.

Zee was pretty silent, I thought. Finally, she spoke.

"You scared me, Jeff. You could have gotten yourself
killed."

I was uncomfortable about the whole incident myself.
Years before, after having been shot, I'd left the Boston
PD for Martha's Vineyard in part because I hadn't
wanted any more to do with defending the city from its
bad guys. When I'd learned that I would have to live the
rest of my life with a bullet lodged against my spine, and
when I'd had my first wife leave me for a man in a safer
profession, I had decided to let some other people save
the world. "It all happened pretty fast," I said now. "I
didn't really think about it, I just did it."

"I know. That's one of the scary parts. I just got married. I don't want to be a widow."

"It was just a fluky thing. It'll never happen again. We
should just put it behind us and not think about it anymore. I plan to live a long time, and tell my grandchildren

lies about the good old days when all the bluefish weighed at least twelve pounds and the bass weighed fifty."

"Good. We'll grow old and gray together." She put a hand on my shoulder and squeezed. But when I glanced at her, she still had a thoughtful, solemn look on her face. Feeling my eyes on her, she looked at me.

"Now, don't think about it anymore," I said.

She put a smile on her face. "Okay, I won't think about it anymore."

"The past doesn't exist."

"At least we should only remember the good and useful parts."

"You've got it, kid."

We arrived at the Sagamore Bridge traffic circle and took a right. Driving along the road paralleling the canal, we saw several boats making the transit from Buzzards Bay to Cape Cod Bay, all motoring briskly along.

"Someday we'll do that in the *Shirley J.*," I said. "We'll make a giant sail up Buzzards Bay, through the canal and out across to Provincetown. Then we'll go down the outside of the cape and home again."

"In the *Shirley J.*, that will take some time," said Zee.

"We'll have the time. We're going to be married for at least an epoch."

"How long's an epoch?"

"Long enough to circumnavigate Cape Cod in the *Shirley J.*, and then some."

"And to produce grandchildren."

"That, too."

We looped onto the Bourne Bridge and drove to Woods Hole where, by happy chance, it being a Sunday evening, we managed only a short wait in the standby line before catching a freight boat to Vineyard Haven.

At our house, the summer stars were out, and Boston seemed far away. There was a soft wind from the southwest, and it stirred the leaves of the trees. An owl hooted somewhere off to the north. Zee put her arms up and around my neck and I drew her to me. We stood in the warm darkness, then went inside.

Oliver Underfoot and Velcro, sleeping together in their favorite chair, yawned at us.

We went into the bedroom.

"Home," said Zee, smiling.

Two days later, Zee went back to work at the hospital. In her absence, I cleaned the house, checked on the *Shirley J.*, and then went clamming down at the Eel Pond. By the time Zee got home, I had supper ready to go in the oven, and chilled Lukusowa martinis and smoked bluefish pâté waiting for her.

"Not bad," said Zee, kicking off her shoes, and lighting up the room with her smile.

We took the hors d'oeuvres and the drinks up to the balcony and watched the evening settle over Vineyard Sound, out there on the far side of the barrier beach that carries the road between Edgartown and Oak Bluffs.

A few last sailboats were leaning across the darkening waters, heading for harbors, and motorboats were leaving white wakes behind them. The beach beside the highway was emptying of its last families, and there were only a couple of bright surf-sails moving back and forth along the shore. The evening darkened into night, and I went down and got supper heated.

We ate a lazy meal.

"This is nice," said Zee, reaching across the table and touching my hand. "I'm glad we're here."

"Yes."

The next morning, as I was putting my rod and my quahogging rake on the Land Cruiser's roof rack, I heard the phone ringing. When I was single I sometimes didn't answer the phone on general principles, but now I was a married man with responsibilities, so I made the dash and swept up the receiver.

"Mr. Jefferson W. Jackson?" It was a voice I did not know.

"Yes."

"Mr. Jackson, my name is Thomas Decker. I work for Luciano Marcus. He'd like to invite you to dinner."

5

I looked at the receiver, then put it back to my ear.

"Marcus as in Wang Center and *Carmen*?"

"That's right, Mr. Jackson. Mr. and Mrs. Marcus would like to invite you and your bride to dinner, so they can thank you in person for what you did to prevent a serious incident. Would Saturday night be convenient?"

"How did you get our telephone number?"

"Mr. Marcus has spoken to the police in Boston."

"And they told him who we were."

"Mr. and Mrs. Marcus are greatly in your debt, and would very much like to make at least a gesture of repayment."

I wasn't interested in a gesture of repayment, although I was curious about who Marcus might be.

"I'm sure the Marcuses would like to put the whole thing behind them," I said. "So would my wife and I. Tell them that they owe me no debt, since I only did what anyone else in my position at that time would have done. Tell them my wife and I just got home and we don't want to leave the island again right now. But thank them for the invitation."

"Ah," said Decker. "But you don't have to leave the island. Mr. and Mrs. Marcus live in Gay Head. They will be pleased to send a car for you and Mrs. Jackson, at your convenience. On their behalf, I implore you to accept their dinner invitation. They will be deeply disappointed if you do not."

Implore. It was a perfectly good word, but one that

few people used. I tried to remember the last time I'd heard it, but could not. I wondered, too, how long it had been since someone had been deeply disappointed because I couldn't show up for dinner. It had been some time. Probably forever. Finally, I wondered if Zee was as curious about Marcus as I was. I decided she might be.

"All right," I said. "Saturday night."

"Excellent. It will be a very informal evening, so please wear casual dress. Our driver will pick you up at seven."

"You know where we live?"

"It's a small island, Mr. Jackson. Until Saturday, then. And thank you for accepting the invitation. Mr. and Mrs. Marcus look forward to seeing you."

The phone clicked and hummed in my ear. The Vineyard was, indeed, a small island, but not so small that most people in Gay Head knew where we lived, down island in the woods of Edgartown. Not that our location was a secret. The mailbox on the Edgartown–Vineyard Haven Road identified our driveway for anyone who cared to find us. And Luciano Marcus, or at least Thomas Decker, apparently cared enough to have done that.

I went back out to the Land Cruiser, completed loading my fishing and quahogging gear, and drove south, inching through the not yet too bad traffic jam in front of the A & P, passing Cannon Ball Park and the cemetery, taking a right on Pease Point Way, and driving on to Katama. There, early-morning arrivals on South Beach were already spreading their blankets, setting up their umbrellas, and getting their kites into the air, their cars filling the tiny parking lot and lining Atlantic Drive.

In earlier years, there were parking lots all along the beach, inland from the sand dunes, but these were, for reasons which eluded me, no longer available, being fenced off from the road. Some ecological theory rooted in the notion of the fragility of island beaches was no doubt behind the decision to block off the parking lots. Probably it included the argument that parked cars hastened the eroding of the beach, a popular notion that ignored the fact that the beach had steadily been eaten away since records had been kept, long before there were cars on the island. As early maps attest, South Beach was once a barrier beach at least a half mile farther out to sea than it is now, and the great ponds on the south coast of the island were connected by water passages that would allow you to row a boat from Edgartown to Chilmark inside that barrier beach.

But that was then and this is now, and the authorities, like God, work in mysterious ways their wonders to perform. So things go.

Not that it really made much difference to me, since I never went to the part of the beach populated by the drivers of two-wheel-drive cars. Like other four-by-four owners, I now left the pavement and headed for the less populated sands of Norton's Point Beach, which separates the Atlantic Ocean on the south from Katama Bay on the north and leads finally to Chappaquiddick.

I was bound for the shell-fishing grounds along the southern edge of Katama Bay in search of the wily littleneck.

A recent hurricane, another of nature's tools to keep man mindful of his real status on the earth, had broken over the beach and deposited much sand in Katama Bay, once again changing its shape and depth, as so often had happened in the past and would happen again. One result of this latest storm was that some of my favorite grounds for raking littlenecks had become barren deserts, and I was still hunting for a dependable spot to capture, cajole, or otherwise entrap those most tender of quahogs.

But I didn't mind the search, since the joys of quahogging do not consist entirely of finding and harvesting them, but also include the lonely pleasure of exploration and occasional discovery, accompanied by a simultaneous and wonderful freeing of the mind to play with subjects other than catching hard-shell clams.

So while I raked, and raked some more, first finding nothing but seed quahogs, too small to keep, then, finally, finding a promising spot on a flat out beyond the channel that parallels the beach, I waded in thigh-deep water, basked in the warm July sun, and thought about Luciano Marcus.

Who was he? Why did he need a bodyguard? No, I knew why he needed a bodyguard: Somebody wanted to kill him. But why? Was he a criminal? Mafia, maybe, or whatever those guys are called these days? An organized crime lord? Or was he a good guy that the bad guys wanted dead? Or was he none of the above?

In any case, he lived in Gay Head. Did gang lords live in Gay Head? My chief knowledge of that westernmost of island townships, famed for the colorful cliffs that gave it its name, was that it was the home of one group of the Wampanoags—"a federally recognized tribe," as more than one sign attested—that it was surrounded by some of the best bass and bluefishing waters on the east coast, and that its government seemed intent on making things difficult for fishermen and other visitors by banning parking almost everywhere, overcharging in the town's one central parking lot, and, worst of all, charging money to use the town toilets. Obviously a money-grubbing bunch of bloodsuckers. Would a rich gang lord live in such a town?

Could be. Jackie Onassis had owned a place there, not far from Squibnocket Pond, and there were surely other much moneyed people in the town. So why not a gangster? Maybe he got a cut from the town's ill-gotten gains. No wonder he was rich.

If, indeed, Luciano Marcus was a gangster. Maybe he was just a regular guy with an armed bodyguard and a chauffeur. Maybe he wasn't even rich. Maybe the chauffeur and bodyguard belonged to somebody else, and he had just borrowed them for the trip to Boston. When you went to Boston, after all, you could do worse than to let somebody else drive and to take along a bodyguard.

I found a mother lode of quahogs and my basket began to fill. A mixed colony of littlenecks, cherrystones, and stuffers. This was more like it. I took sightings on the beach to the south, on Chappaquiddick, off to the east, and on the western shore, triangulating my location. In the future, I wanted to be able to find this spot again.

The sun rose higher and grew hotter. I was wearing my Tevas, my baseball cap with "H-S 9" on the front, and my daring bikini bathing suit (fashionable, I'm told, on the Riviera, but not quite kosher on the Vineyard, which allows its sweet young things to wear tiny bathing suits, but prefers its men to wear boxer trunks). So now I luxuriated in the contrasting warmth of the July sun on my body and the cool waters around my legs. Life could be worse.

I thought about Marcus some more, and recalled Balzac's saying. Behind every great fortune is a great crime. Was the opposite true? Was there great virtue behind poverty? If so, maybe I had a halo. I looked up but saw none. Oh well.

My basket was full, and I waded ashore, passing off the flat, down into the chin-deep water of the channel, and back up onto the sandy beach. I put the basket and rake in the Land Cruiser and looked at my watch. Not yet noon, but somewhere or other the sun was over the yardarm. I got a Sam Adams out of the cooler and popped it open. Ahhh. Still America's best bottled beer, although there are more and more contenders every day.

It was not a good time of day for bluefishing, but you don't know if you don't go, so I went to Wasque Point, where the bluefish love to eat anything moving. There, although others were before me and not a rod was bent, I parked and got my eleven-foot graphite rod off the roof. I put a redheaded Ballistic Missile on the leader, walked down to the rip, and made my cast.

The many fishermen leaning on their trucks with coffee cups in their hands watched me with lazy, mildly ironic looks, and the few still making desultory casts into a sea that apparently had been fishless for a long time continued their sleepy work, with no hope of actually catching anything, but simply because making casts was better than not making casts.

Then came a rare joy. I'd reeled about halfway in when I got a hit. What could be better than to arrive just before noon, make one cast, and nail the only bluefish caught all morning? It's one of life's finest moments, and you have a duty to make the most of it when it happens. While the coffee-drinking fishermen abandoned their cups, grabbed their rods, and rushed down to the surf, I reeled in a nice eight-pound blue, cut its throat, put it into the fish box, waved to a couple of fellow fishing friends, and drove away.

At home, I filleted the fish on the table out in back of my shed, and tossed the bones into the woods for the bugs, birds, and other denizens of the wild to enjoy—the smell, until the bones were clean, would only come back to me if the wind came around to the northeast, an occurrence that was not foretold by my radio weatherman. I put one fillet in the freezer, and the other in the fridge. Then I rinsed and sorted the quahogs. I put two dozen littlenecks in the fridge for the evening's hors d'oeuvres, and the rest, bagged, into the freezer. I also bagged and froze the cherrystones for future clams casino. Then I steamed the stuffers.

When the shells opened, I cooled and ground the meat, mixed in minced onion, chopped celery, chopped green pepper, bread crumbs, and a few doses of Dos Gringos hot sauce to pep things up, and put the mixture back into the shells. I put a bit of bacon on top of each shell, and put the shells into the fridge. Stuffed quahogs would follow the evening's littlenecks on the half shell and precede the baked bluefish with dill sauce.

I had a ham and cheese sandwich, washed down with a couple of bottles of Sam Adams, then, abandoning my bathing suit so as to ensure the quality of my all-over tan, and clad only in Tevas and dark glasses, I mowed the lawn, filled the bird feeders, and washed a couple of loads of clothes, hanging them afterward on the line of the solar dryer.

By the time Zee got home from work, I was dressed again, and had the littlenecks open and the Lukusowa waiting. She got out of her uniform and into shirt and shorts, and we went up on the balcony, where we sipped and nibbled and I told her about the telephone call.

"I said we'd go, but I can change my mind if you don't want to."

"I've been thinking about that whole business," said Zee. "I can't decide whether this Marcus guy is some sort

of crook, or what. I mean, why would he need a bodyguard? Who needs a bodyguard?"

"I don't mind guarding your body," I said, leering.

"How sweet." She fluttered her long, dark lashes and
patted my thigh. "Anyway, I think I do want to go. Just
to see what kind of a man he is. How about you?"

"Me, too. For the same reasons."

"Then let's do it."

Like many casual decisions, this one had unantici-
pated consequences.

6

Shortly before seven that Saturday, a dark-windowed Cherokee came down our driveway and turned around in the yard. The driver's door opened and Vinnie got out. I recognized him as the driver of the Cadillac I'd seen at the Wang Center. We left the screened porch and went out to the car.

"Good evening," said Zee.

Vinnie thought about that. It didn't look easy for him. "Good evening," he said, as he opened a rear door for us.

Vinnie drove efficiently. He took a right at the end of our driveway, a left at the blinker onto the Airport Road, another right onto the West Tisbury Road, and drove on through West Tisbury and Chilmark to Gay Head. There, he turned off into one of those unobtrusive dirt driveways that lead away from the island's paved roads. There was a mailbox beside the driveway with the name Gubatose written on it.

Tangled trees and undergrowth were on both sides of the driveway. About fifty yards from the pavement we came to a gate. There was a weathered sign on it saying PRIVATE PROPERTY, and forbidding hunting, fishing, and trespassing. On this side of the gate was a space where cars could turn around and go back. On the other side of the gate, about halfway up a tree, the evening light glinted momentarily on a partially hidden object that appeared to me to be a camera of some sort, aimed at the gate.

Vinnie touched a button on his dashboard, and the gate swung open. We passed through, and it swung shut again. We drove another fifty yards, and the narrow, dirt driveway widened and became paved. It wound up through increasingly manicured grounds until it emerged onto a rolling lawn that rose to the top of a hill. The road curved up toward a white slash just below the ridge, and as we approached the white slash, I saw that it was the front of an astonishing house.

Vinnie stopped in front of the house, and we got out. The front door opened, and the older man we'd seen in Boston came out, accompanied by a woman who was a few years younger. The man appeared to be in his late seventies, and although he was tanned and apparently fit, there was something fragile about him. The woman, by contrast, struck me as strong and healthy. They were wearing casual summer clothes. The man spread his arms, smiled, and came to meet us.

"So good of you to have come." He shook our hands. "Your driver is my grandson, Vincent. This is my wife, Angela. Angela, these are the young people I've been telling you about."

Angela Marcus shook hands with Zee. "Welcome. Luciano didn't tell me how beautiful you are." Then she took my hand and held it. "And you, Mr. Jackson. How can I thank you for what you did?"

"I was just in the right place at the right time. No thanks are necessary."

"Well, you have them just the same. Come in, come in."

"An amazing house," said Zee.

Marcus beamed. "First a drink, and then a tour, if you'd like. We're quite fond of our house, and we love to show it off."

We went up a circular stairway and out onto an immense veranda that surrounded a swimming pool. There, a young woman stood near an umbrella-topped table that was encircled by comfortable lounge chairs.

"Priscilla, please bring us some drinks." Marcus turned to us. "What would you like? My wife and I will have gin and tonics. I have both Italian and Greek wines, in honor of the countries of my ancestors. All of my other liquors are American, since I am an American and believe in buying American goods. It is an idiosyncrasy of mine. I hope, therefore, that you don't like scotch." He gave a small laugh.

"Vodka," said Zee. "On ice."

"Two," I said.

"With anything? A twist? An olive?"

"With two ripe olives, if I have a choice," said Zee.

"With a twist," I said.

Marcus glanced at Priscilla, who nodded and went into the house.

I looked to the south. The lawns fell away down the hillside, where I could now see walking paths lined with flowers. Beyond the lawn were trees, and beyond the trees, at the foot of a long slope of land, was what looked like a cranberry bog. On the far side of the bog was Squibnocket Pond, and beyond the pond was Squibnocket Beach, where there is wonderful bass fishing. Then there was the sea and the little island of Noman's Land, which somehow manages to be both a bird refuge and a navy bombing range.

Luciano Marcus came and stood beside me. "Terrific view. I never get tired of it. But it's not the only one. Come over here."

We walked to the east side of the veranda. From there

we could see Menemsha Pond, with Menemsha village on its far side. Beyond it, the north coast of Martha's Vineyard faded to the east into the haze that hid Cape Cod. It was as fine a view of the island as I had seen.

"I keep my boats in the pond," said Marcus. "I like to go out for fish, or sometimes Angie and I will take the boat over to Buzzards Bay just for the ride, or maybe to New Bedford, for lunch. I used to sail, but now I don't do that so much, so probably I should sell the sailboat. But you know how it is. I say I'm going to do it, but I never get around to it. So the sailboat just sits there at the dock. A hole in the water into which you pour money, just like they say."

Priscilla reappeared with a tray of drinks. We took them, and she went away. Marcus looked at Zee, and smiled. "Two ripe olives in vodka. I never saw that before. Come on, let us show you our place. I think you'll like it."

The house was on the side of the hill, its huge windows looking out over Squibnocket Pond. It was built into the ground rather than upon it, and depended on the natural elevation of the hill to provide it with the sweeping vistas it offered its inhabitants. It was a candidly modern house, making no pretense of being traditional in any way. It was built on many levels and was fronted on the topmost of these by the huge veranda where Priscilla had served us our drinks.

A walkway led from the veranda along the crown of the hill, then dipped down to a tennis court that was cleverly tucked into the earth and hidden on three sides by surrounding oak trees so that Zee and I were surprised when we first saw it. A four-car garage was built under the court, as were storage rooms and the small apartments where, we learned, Thomas Decker, Vinnie, and some of the groundskeepers lived. Stairs led from the garage to the tennis court, and an underground passageway led to a lower level of the house. I noticed dog kennels on the far side of the apartments.

Marcus pointed here and pointed there, happy with his home. "The president of the outfit that designed the place studied under Frank Lloyd Wright. You know about Wright? Quite a guy. I read a book about him, and when I decided to build here, I found this pupil of his and gave him the job. He did all right."

The architectural firm that had designed and built the house had indeed done its work well. It had taken great care to use the configurations of the land to maximum advantage when planning the house, toward the ends of not only grand and comfortable living, but security and complete privacy. For all its size and modern grandeur, the house, like the tennis court, was difficult to see from the public road that links Gay Head to Chilmark, or by most other houses in the area. Only from the direction of Squibnocket Pond could it clearly be seen: a white slash across the top of the green hillside. It presented no roofline, being built into the rock and soil of the hill, and only the winter smoke from its vast fireplace chimneys gave any sign, said Marcus, to people on the public roads or in neighboring homes that a house was there at all. There was, in fact, a lawn over part of the main house and over the attached guest house farther down the hill, and Marcus confessed to taking pleasure from the fact that even from that grassy roof, the buildings were next to invisible.

The outer walls of the house were white, and the wood of the terrace and decks was natural in color. There were huge earthen pots of flowers on those decks.

In spite of its modern design, there was something Aegean or Mediterranean, and a sense of antiquity or timelessness, about the place. Marcus, who believed that he could trace his lineage back to medieval Greece and Rome, savored this ambiance.

His cellar was, as he had said, stocked with the wines of Greece and Italy, and his house had been decorated by New York's second most expensive firm.

"The most expensive did not have good taste," confided Angela Marcus, with a smile. "I'm no interior decorator, but I know bad taste when I see it."

Throughout the house could be found classical pieces of sculpture. We paused before three particularly intricate panels.

"These are Roman," said Marcus. "They call 'em fourth style panels. They came into my hands in a business deal. Later on I learned that they came from a Roman villa excavated in Sardinia. I don't think whoever took them did it quite on the up and up, if you know what I mean. But I like them, so I keep them." He flashed me a veiled look.

In the master bedroom, one wall was decorated with a floor mosaic of the second century, portraying scenes from the *Iliad*.

"This came from a Roman villa outside of Toulouse, and was supposed to go to a museum in Paris. Instead, it got over here to a guy who found out that I liked things like that, and got in touch with me. Nobody ever came looking for it, so now it's mine. You like it? Those old Romans were really something."

These classical works were not the only decorative arts in the house. Interspersed with them were maps, globes, and bookshelves filled with leather-bound volumes that reflected Marcus's interest in geography and political history.

"I always liked maps," said Marcus, touching an atlas. "Even when I was a little kid. And I like to read about why things happen. History. It's interesting to me. Now that I got the time, I read. It's good. Everybody should read. I wish I could get Vinnie to do it." He shrugged.

Paintings of nineteenth- and twentieth-century masters hung on the walls, and a Calder mobile floated in a corner of the living room that looked out upon the veranda and pool. The furniture of the house was modern, clean-lined, and comfortable. The rooms were large and uncluttered, yet never cold or impersonal since wherever my eyes roamed they found some object of interest or beauty to occupy them.

The kitchen was huge, filled with work counters, ovens, freezers, and cabinets that held every sort of pot, pan, and appliance. It was capable of producing food for large parties at short notice, and was, at the moment, rich with the fragrances of cooking foods. The cook, however, was not in sight.

"Jonas, that's Priscilla's husband, is our cook," said Angela Marcus. "He must be up in the gardens, looking for some herb he needs. He runs this kitchen with an iron hand. When we were young, before we had much money, I used to do all the cooking, but Jonas is better than I ever was. He caters to Luciano and me and no one else. Mediterranean and American food, like we like.

"When he can't find what he wants in our gardens, he shops at island markets. He's very picky. Only the freshest vegetables and meat and fish will do. If something he wants isn't available on the island, he has it flown in from New York or Boston. He keeps a big account book where he lists all of his expenditures, and he gives Luciano a report every month. I don't think Luciano even looks at it. He just pays the bills." She laughed.

In the garage were four cars: the black Cadillac sedan I'd seen in Boston and three identical green, four-door Jeep Grand Cherokees, like the one that had picked us up that evening. All four vehicles had darkened windows.

"Like I told you," said Marcus. "I believe in buying American whenever I can, except for Greek and Italian wines."

"And Greek and Italian olive oils," amended his wife.

He put his arm around her. "Yeah, except for that, sweetheart."

Zee, who approved of signs of affection between married folks, smiled up at me.

"Privacy is hard to get," explained Marcus. "We like ours, and I'm lucky that I have the money to buy it. Other people have to put up with a lot of long noses."

We walked out along a flower-lined pathway. Luciano Marcus had his wife's hand in one of his. With his other hand, he gestured while he spoke.

"We got about three hundred acres here, and men to take care of it. Angie and I like to walk, so we have these paths winding around. You almost can't see them, but they're there. It's nice to walk on an evening like this."

Around us were rolling meadows and carefully tended trees and shrubs. The flowers lining the path smelled sweet. We paused at a small overlook, and Marcus pointed down the long hill below us.

"We have blueberries down there. A lot of them. See the bushes? And beyond the bushes, bending out of sight beyond that rise in the ground, is my cranberry bog." A hard note was suddenly in his voice. "That bog has produced cranberries for as long as anybody remembers. It's a damned fine bog, and I plan to keep it."

I glanced at him, and saw Angela pat his arm and gently steer him on along the path.

In various places on the property, there were native oaks, beetlebung trees, swamp maples, wild cherries, and ancient-looking apple trees. Although the grounds gave the impression of being in an informal, almost natural state, they were in fact so carefully designed and maintained that a crew of well-paid men would be needed to tend them. Those same men, I thought, would preserve not only the beauty but the security of the estate. Luciano Marcus, for all his apparent openness, was a man who made no bones about liking his privacy.

We crossed the driveway and paused again. Marcus looked at me. "You notice the mailbox when you came in?"

"I did."

"I thought you might have. You see the name?"

"Gubatose."

"That's right. Gubatose, not Marcus. That's so people will think somebody named Gubatose lives here, not somebody named Marcus. It works, too. Not many people have come up my driveway. When they do, they come to that gate. When they get there, they mostly turn around and go back. Sometimes somebody climbs over the gate and walks on up the driveway. You know who they meet?"

"An armed guard?"

Marcus laughed. "No. They meet a pleasant guy who tells them he's renting the Gubatose house for the summer, and then tells them that his Gubatose and their Gubatose are, too bad, different people, and who, gently but firmly, like they say, takes them back to their cars and watches them drive away. You know how we know to go down there and meet them?"

"The video camera in the tree?"

"You saw that, too. Good. Not many people notice it. I have others here and there around the place, so people won't come wandering through without me knowing about them. And at night we got dogs. My glass has been empty too long. Let's go back to the house for a refill."

"We have gardens, too," said Angela. "But we can look at them another day."

"Angie has the green thumb you hear so much about," said her husband, proudly. "My thumb is black. Whatever plant I touch wilts and dies, so I stay out of Angie's gardens, and let the men tend to the grounds." He laughed.

As we came up onto the great veranda, we found two men were standing on its west side, looking down the rolling meadow toward Squibnocket Pond. Vinnie the driver held powerful field glasses, and the other man was bent over a telescope. Both the binoculars and the telescope were directed at the pond. Beside them, mounted on a tripod, was a camera with a long telephoto lens.

"Birders," said Vinnie, as we walked out behind them.

The man with the telescope grunted. "Probably." Hearing us, he turned. He was the bodyguard I'd seen in Boston.

"Thomas," said Marcus. "Meet Mr. Jackson. Mr. Jackson, this is Thomas Decker. You met briefly in Boston, and Thomas spoke to you on the phone the other day."

Thomas, not Tom, Decker was a medium-sized man with red hair and freckles. I remembered his gun as well as his face. His face was hard and he had a firm grip. "How do you do? Let me add my thanks to you for what you did in Boston."

"There's no need for thanks."

"You have them anyway." He showed a thin smile. "If it hadn't been for you, I'd be out of a job."

Marcus laughed, then gestured toward the veranda railing. "What are you looking at?"

Decker hesitated, looking at Zee and me.

"It's all right," said Marcus. "As you know, Mr. Jackson saved my life. You can speak freely."

Decker nodded reluctantly. "There's a man and a woman down at the pond, the other side of the blueberry bushes and cranberry bog. The guy's got a floppy summer hat that makes his face hard to see, even with the binoculars. They have backpacks, and we've seen them take out books, water bottles, and sandwiches. They have field glasses and a camera with a telephoto lens like this one, mounted on a tripod. They act like they're looking at the birds in the pond and along its shore. They jot notes on clipboards and look at the books they get out of their packs."

"Birders," said Angela.

"You know, Grandma," said Vinnie, "I've been thinking of getting myself one of them bird books. There are a lot of birds around here, and I don't know one from another."

"You should do that, Vincent," said Angela. "It would give you a great deal of pleasure."

"I don't know that they're birders," said Decker. "They look up this way now and then, instead of at the birds on the pond. What are they doing now, Vinnie?"

Vinnie lifted his binoculars again and looked down the slope. "The woman just wrote something on the paper on her clipboard, and now she's looking through her field glasses at something I can't see.

"And now she's sort of turning, and now she's turned her glasses right up here toward the house. Jees, it looks like she's studying me just like I'm studying her. Weird."

"Excuse me for a minute," said Decker, turning away and lifting his telescope. "You better get a shot of her face," he said to Vinnie. "You get a good look at the guy yet?"

"Not yet. That hat flops down and he's wearing shades. Hey! Look. He just took his hat off, and he's wiping his brow. I'll get him now." He put down the binoculars and went to the camera.

"Well, well," said Decker, looking through his telescope while Vinnie snapped shots with the camera.

"I don't know how much detail we'll get at this distance," said Vinnie.

"No matter," said Decker, "I know who the guy is."

"Who?" asked Marcus.

"Joe Begay," said Decker. "That Navajo guy that's been nosing around. I should have known it would be him."

"Those damned Indians!" Marcus paled under his tan, and drew a small box from his pocket. He took out a pill and put it under his tongue. Angie gave him a worried look.

I was pretty shocked myself. "Can I take a look?" I asked, and without waiting for a reply I picked up Vinnie's binoculars and looked down the long slope. It was Joe Begay, sure enough, but now a middle-aged Joe Begay instead of the young man I had known. The woman beside him was younger, and as bronzed as he was. While I watched, the couple packed away their gear and moved toward the beach parking lot.

Some small movement about halfway down the hillside caught my eye. I looked that way and saw birds fly out of a bush and soar away. I looked some more, but saw nothing else. When I looked at the pond again, Joe Begay and the woman had walked out of sight.

I lowered the glasses. My past had become my present. More than twenty years had passed since Joe Begay and I had been blown up together in Vietnam. Now, after I'd almost forgotten him, he was back in my life. First at my wedding, and now here. I looked at Luciano Marcus and saw hatred in his face.

7

I turned and found Zee giving me an odd stare. I put the binoculars down, and walked back to her.

Luciano Marcus seemed to be recovering his emotional balance. He gestured at the camera. "Vincent, take this stuff away, but don't go too far. You'll be taking our guests home later in the evening."

"Yes, boss." Vinnie scowled, picked up the camera, telescope, and binoculars, and went away.

"Thomas, you stay and eat with us." Marcus turned to Zee and me. "Thomas is part of the family. Another son to me."

Angela's mouth tightened as he spoke.

"It would be my pleasure," said Decker in his oddly formal fashion.

"Our own children come for visits, but they don't live here," said Angela, moving away. "I just happen to have some pictures of the younger grandchildren, in the living room. Excuse me while I get them."

"We just happen to have about several albums of pictures of the younger grandchildren," said Luciano. "Our youngest and his family were here last week. When the kids come, Angie and me get to spoil the little ones while their parents escape to the beaches by themselves. Of course, when the babies act up, we shove them right back at their parents and escape ourselves. It's the great advantage of being grandparents."

"Oh, we do not," said Angela, reappearing. "Don't listen to him. He's a total softy when it comes to the babies. He lets them get away with anything. Now let me show you these pictures. I just got them back from the developers. Did you ever see anything cuter?"

We looked at the pictures and agreed that we'd never seen anything cuter, then we all went and sat beside the pool. In the gathering night we sat and sipped a second round of drinks provided by Priscilla.

"Tell me about Joe Begay," said Zee in an innocent voice.

Decker glanced at Marcus, who took a sip of his gin and tonic before replying.

"Mrs. Jackson, have you heard the saying that if you save someone's life you must care for him afterward?"

"I think that's some sort of oriental wisdom," smiled Zee.

He smiled back at her. When Zee smiles at men, they almost always smile back. "Well, if it's true, then you and your husband are now responsible for my life."

Zee laughed. "We're pretty busy just taking care of ourselves."

"Of course you are. Still, my life is yours in the sense that I now exist because of you. That being the case, I should have no secrets from you." A smaller, slightly ironic smile played across his face. "I'm not going to say that I will confide everything to you, but certainly I can tell you about Joe Begay. In fact, I want to do that."

I glanced at Angela Marcus, and saw again the worried look that I'd seen earlier.

Marcus took another sip of his drink, seemingly to gather his thoughts. Then he spoke. "They say that Joe Begay is a Navajo Indian from out West some place. Anyway, now he's married to a Wampanoag woman who lives here in Gay Head. His wife is the daughter of a woman named Linda Vanderbeck. Linda Vanderbeck is one of those Indians who thinks that my cranberry bog belongs to the Wampanoags and not to me. Something about some illegal land sale a long time ago. Or maybe it was a treaty of some kind. My lawyers can tell you more about it than I can.

"Anyway, this Linda Vanderbeck goes around making trouble for me any way she can, trying to get that cranberry bog, which, I can tell you right now, she's never going to get. And now that this Joe Begay is in town, she's got him helping her out." He looked at Decker, then back at Zee and me. "We see him down there at the pond, don't we, Thomas? And all around the edges of my property here. And they say that he's down at the Historical Society in Edgartown, looking at records, or up here looking at records, or maybe even in Boston or Washington looking at records. All he does is snoop!"

"He hasn't broken any laws, yet," said Decker. "But a couple of times he's tried to get up here to the house. Both times, we stopped him at the gate."

"You mean, he tried to sneak up here?" asked Zee.

"Yes!" exclaimed Marcus.

"Now, Luciano," said Angela in a soothing voice. "You know that's not quite true. He phoned first both times."

"And I told him no both times, but then he came to the gate anyway, and climbed over and came on up the driveway, just like we'd invited him!"

Angela nodded. "But when Thomas met him and told him to leave, he did."

"Only after an argument!"

"Not much of one," said Decker. "I asked him to leave, and he left."

"But he came back!"

"And left again."

Marcus's face was red. He took a deep breath. "I know I get excited, but it makes me mad. All this stuff about my land. Who do these Wampanoags think they are, trying to take a man's land away from him?"

"Linda Vanderbeck says somebody took theirs away from them," said Angela.

"Well, it wasn't me," said her husband. He looked at me. "You know, when I think of what happened up in Boston, I wonder if it had anything to do with this cranberry business."

Thomas Decker didn't look surprised at this notion, but Angela did. She opened her mouth, then shut it again.

I put my glass on the table. "That wasn't Joe Begay up in Boston. I just saw Joe Begay through Vinnie's glasses. Begay is a big guy, and a grown-up. The kid up in Boston was only about five six or so."

Decker raised a brow. "The kid could have been a hired gun."

I thought about that. Were Wampanoag passions running so high that one of them would hire a killer to remove an obstacle standing between the tribe and the contested cranberry bog? I had no idea. On the other hand, since history began, and no doubt before that, people have regularly been killed over trifles—a casual word, a pair of shoes, a few pennies, an imagined slight. Or sometimes just for fun. 'Twas ever thus.

"I don't know much about hired guns," I said. "The shooter up in Boston looked like one of those kids I read about in the *Globe*: hooded sweatshirt, baggy pants, floppy sneakers. The only difference was that he used a sawed-off Remington 12-gauge instead of a Nine, which seems to be the weapon of choice among teenage hood-lums these days."

"What's a Nine?" asked Zee, looking at me. "I meant to ask you about that up in Boston."

"You haven't been keeping up on the latest street slang," I said. "A Nine is a nine-millimeter pistol. If you read your *Globe* carefully every morning, you'd know these things."

"Some of us have to go to work in the morning, sweets. We don't have time to read the *Globe* from end to end. We only have time to do the crossword puzzles and read the sports page."

Priscilla appeared and informed us that dinner was served, and we went inside.

The dining room had a cathedral ceiling and a table that could be extended to seat at least a dozen people. Tonight, however, the table was sized for five, and adorned with an impressive amount of silverware, dishes, and wineglasses. We used all of them as we downed a many-coursed Mediterranean meal with a separate wine per course. Our host and hostess made small talk, and Zee and I, who normally concentrate on eating when face-to-face with fine food, did our best to reply in kind. When the coffee and dessert, a flan in the Spanish mode, were behind us, Marcus pushed back his chair.

"I allow myself one or two cigars a year. I smoked Cuban before Castro, but now I have them made in Florida. Tonight I'll have one, and I invite you to join me. Gentlemen, and you ladies, too, if the smell of cigars doesn't offend you, let us retire to the library."

"I think I will pass on that offer," said Angela. "Mrs. Jackson, please feel free to join the gentlemen."

"My name is Zeolinda," said Zee. "Most people call me Zee. While the men have their cigars, perhaps you and I can have more coffee on the veranda."

"Excellent. You're Zee and I'm Angela. Gentlemen, please join us later."

Decker and I followed Marcus.

I had given up pipe and cigarettes long ago, and had never been a cigar smoker, but that night I accepted one as I settled into a leather chair and looked at the room. There was an oriental carpet on the floor, a desk, and there were other comfortable leather-covered chairs such as mine, and good reading lights. The walls were lined with shelves of leather-bound books, and, unlike other libraries I have seen, this one looked as if it really was used.

From a cupboard Marcus produced a bottle of Italian brandy and poured. Priscilla brought in more coffee. Smoke rose and drifted toward the ceiling. My cigar was mild and sweet, and I felt sated and quite civilized. This was the way life should be. Or one of the ways, at least. Another, of course, was the way I usually lived.

Marcus looked appreciatively at his cigar. "Forbidden fruit, Mr. Jackson. My doctor would not approve."

"I'm not up on the latest church rules," I said, "But I doubt if an annual cigar is a mortal sin."

Beyond Marcus, Thomas Decker blew a set of perfect smoke rings. The desire to blow smoke rings was what had started me smoking when I was a kid. I tried one myself. Not as good as Decker's, but not bad. Like riding a bicycle; you never forget how.

"Mr. Jackson," said Marcus, "I have a business proposition for you."

On Martha's Vineyard, if you live the way I do, with

no steady job, you're always willing to consider new ways to make money. I supplement disability incomes from the federal government and the Boston PD by harvesting and selling fish and shellfish, by taking care of some houses over the winter, closing them up in the fall, and opening them in the spring, and by looking after some boats in the off season. That had been fine in times past, but now I was a married man, and suspected that perhaps I should become more fiscally responsible.

"What do you have in mind?"

"The incident in Boston was a deliberate attack. The gunman called my name before attempting to shoot me. If it hadn't been for your prompt action, I would be a dead man now. I need to know who that gunman was and why he tried to kill me. I want to hire you as an investigator."

I let that sink in, then shook my head. "No, you don't. The Boston Police are your best bet. They're professionals, and it happened in their town."

"Overextended professionals, as you know. I have cooperated fully with them, and will continue to do so, but I am not content with that. I want a private investigation as well."

But I had come to Martha's Vineyard to get away from the business of saving the world.

"I'm not a private investigator. There are some good firms in the city. I recommend Thornberry Security. It's a big outfit, and Thornberry is good at running it."

"You will be amused to know that I've already employed Thornberry Security. In fact, Mr. Jason Thornberry mentioned you, when I told him where I live and what I wanted. I've also employed a private investigator on Cape Cod. Perhaps you know him, too. A man named Aristotle Socarides."

"No."

"I have business interests in Provincetown that might be linked to the incident in Boston. Mr. Socarides is looking into that possibility, just as Thornberry Security is investigating my business interests in Boston. Some other people are making inquiries in New York City, where we have our winter home."

"You seem to have things pretty well covered."

He tapped the arm of his chair. "Not here. Not on Martha's Vineyard. You saw Joe Begay, and I've told you of the Wampanoag interest in my land. I need someone to work for me here."

"Why me? You don't even know me."

He lifted his glass. "Actually, I know a good deal about you. Thomas has been making inquiries. Thomas?"

Decker took a notebook out of his pocket and flipped through it until he came to the page he wanted. "You grew up in Somerville, where your father was a fireman. Your mother died when you were quite young. You have a sister living in Santa Fe, New Mexico. You lied about your age and joined the army when you were seventeen. You were in Vietnam at the very end of hostilities, were wounded, and received various citations. After you returned to America, you joined the Boston Police, where you served five years. During that time your father died when a wall collapsed during a warehouse fire; you married, and you graduated from Northeastern University. A month after your graduation you were shot during a robbery attempt and subsequently took a disability retirement. Your marriage ended in divorce, and you came to Martha's Vineyard.

"You live in a house that you inherited from your father. Earlier this month, you married Zeolinda Madieras, who is a nurse at the Martha's Vineyard Hospital. You were on your honeymoon when you saved Luciano's life in Boston. You drive a, shall we say, rather elderly Toyota Land Cruiser, and you supplement your disability income by fishing and doing a variety of other jobs. You know the island very well, having vacationed here since you were a child and having lived here since leaving Somerville." He looked up at me. "There's more."

I pointed a finger at Decker. "There's the man you should have doing your investigating."

"Not at all," said Decker. "It's all on public record. I just made a few phone calls."

"The important thing," said Marcus, "is that you not only have experience as a police officer, but you know this island and its people. Thomas does not. He can make the sorts of inquiries he made about you, but he has no—what do you call it?—local knowledge. He doesn't know the islanders. You do. I want to buy your experience and your knowledge. Moreover, you have already saved my life, and I am, therefore, certain that I can trust you. I am a wealthy man, Mr. Jackson. I can pay for my desires, and I desire your help." He mentioned a sum, and I'm sure my eyebrows went up.

The money he mentioned was considerable by my standards, and the bluefish were beginning to head north, away from Vineyard waters, as they always did at the end of July, which meant that I wouldn't be spending as much time on the beach as I did when the fish were in. Still, I hedged. "I'd need to know as much as I can about your life and your business. You might not want me to know things I might want to know."

"I'll tell you whatever you need to know."

"Who decides what that is? You, or me?"

His voice was like iron covered with silk. "I suggest that we cross that bridge if we come to it."

I realized that I was tempted, but threw in one more caveat.

"Some people are willing to work with people who tell them lies. I've done that myself, but I never liked doing it. If you don't want to tell me something, just say so, and I'll live with that or quit the job. But no lies."

"Fair enough." He lifted his glass. "It's a bargain, then. You please me, Mr. Jackson."

I think it was the idea of Joe Begay being on the island that decided me. Then there was the money, of course. And there was Luciano's family. Like the Oblonskys, the Marcus household seemed unhappy in its own way, and that was interesting.

"Call me J.W.," I said. "All my friends do."

— 8 —

"I like Angela," said Zee, when we got home. "She invited me back to look at her gardens. She's a very down-to-earth person."

"I have to go back myself," I said. "Luciano gave me a job. He wants me to find out who tried to kill him, and why. He has several other people working on it, all on the mainland. I'm the island rep."

She was quiet for a while. Then she said, "I thought we had policemen to do that sort of thing."

"I have a reason for taking the job." I pulled the reason out of my shirt pocket and handed it to her.

"He must want you pretty badly," said Zee, looking at the numbers written on the check.

"Try to keep that astonished expression off your face. You're not supposed to be so surprised that somebody would think I was worth that much."

"Oh dear, I've done it again, haven't I? I've just got to train myself to keep a straight face." She gave me a quick kiss. "Luciano must not be worrying about where his next meal is coming from."

"I guess not. I've got another reason, too. Luciano Marcus didn't have any trouble finding out that we were the ones who helped him out up in Boston. I figure that if Luciano could do that, so can the guys who did the shooting. If they think that we can identify them, it'll be better for me to find them before they have a chance to find us."

She shook her head. "Don't you really think it's pretty unlikely that some kid in Boston is going to come down here to Martha's Vineyard to try to kill two people who maybe can't even identify him?"

"You're probably right," I said. "But I think we should keep the possibility in mind."

"I'll tell you what," said Zee. "If I see somebody in a hooded sweatshirt hanging around the island in August, I'll keep a careful eye on him. How's that?"

"Good. But maybe the kid doesn't have another sweatshirt. Maybe I got his only one. Anyway, while you're keeping an eye out for him, I'll keep an eye on you."

"Oh no you won't! I don't need any husband of mine hanging around being my bodyguard. I can guard my own body!" Her eyes got fierce, the way they do when she's irked.

"All right, you can keep an eye on me, instead."

The fire died. "That's better. I can do that with one hand tied behind me." She gave me a prim smile. "Now tell me about Joe Begay."

I'd known that she'd ask me sooner or later.

"It was in Vietnam," I said. "At the very end of things there, though I didn't realize it at the time. I was just a kid, and Joe Begay was my sergeant. On his third tour, I think. He was a sort of famous guy. The called him Lucky Joe Begay, the way they used to call Leif Eriksson Leif the Lucky, because he was very tough, very good, and he took very good care of his men. When the guys in camp heard I was going on patrol, they said I was lucky to be going with Joe Begay, and I was. We got nailed by Viet Cong mortar men, or maybe artillerymen, I never knew which, and he carried me back to where the choppers could pick us up and get us out of there. He saved my life."

She put her hand on my thigh. "And that was what the nightmare was about."

"Yeah. Anyway, we were in the same hospital for a while, but then they sent us different directions. I never saw or heard of him again until the wedding, and I didn't recognize him then until I had that dream on the boat."

"So now Joe Begay is on Martha's Vineyard, and came to our wedding. Why?"

"I don't know. My new boss, Luciano Marcus, says he's married to a Wampanoag woman up in Gay Head." I told her about Luciano's land dispute, and his anger with Linda Vanderbeck and her son-in-law, Joe Begay. "I want to talk with Luciano some more, anyway, so I plan to drive up to his place tomorrow. While I'm up at that end of the island, I think I might try to see Joe Begay, too."

"Linda Vanderbeck," said Zee. "You remember Maggie Vanderbeck. You met her at the wedding. She volunteers at the hospital sometimes when she's home from college. I think her mother's named Linda. And she's got an older sister named Toni, who has a shop up at the cliffs. Maybe that's Joe Begay's wife."

I got the Vineyard telephone book. There was no listing for any Joe Begay, but there was one for Toni Vanderbeck. There were a lot of other Vanderbecks in Gay Head, too, including Linda.

"Maybe they haven't been married long enough for their phone to be in his name," said Zee. "Of maybe she kept her own name when they got married."

"I'll ask him that when I see him."

"And I'll go with you," said Zee. "I want to meet the man who saved your life."

The telephone rang. It was the chief, from Edgartown. "Just a rumor," he said, "but I thought you should know about it. Fred Souza apparently just found out that you own a piece of the *Lucky Lil*. He gave Albert Enos a shiner, you'll recall, and there's talk he may want to give you one, too."

As they say, if it ain't one damn thing, it's another. I thanked the chief, and gave Zee the message.

"I don't think it would be very smart of Fred Souza to try to give you a black eye," said Zee. "He only comes up to about your shoulder."

"You don't have to punch somebody's lights out to hurt him," I said. "There are other ways."

"For instance?"

"For instance, he might try to punch your lights out. You're more his size."

"He'd better not try it." She made a small fist.

True. A thought appeared in my mind of what I might do if I ever heard that Fred Souza had taken a swing at Zee. The thought had a reddish glow to it. I pushed it away, but the glow lingered. I pushed again and it went out of sight. Barely.

"He's just a kid," I said. "He probably blew his stack when he heard about my share of the boat, but calmed down later."

"Yes," said Zee, who was not a good hater, and rightly figured most other people weren't, either. I hoped she was right about Fred.

The next day was Sunday, and we had breakfast and the *Boston Globe* spread out all over the living room when we got another phone call. Zee, who was closest, put down the crossword puzzle and picked up the receiver.

"Yes. Speaking." She listened for a minute, then said, "Just a moment, please." She put her hand over the mouthpiece of the phone and frowned at me. "It's a reporter from the *Boston Herald*. He wants to talk to you about the shooting up in Boston. It seems that he's dug up your name, and he wants to get your side of the story. I think he has in mind a heroic-citizen-prevents-murder piece. Do you want to talk to him?"

Drat. "No. And ask him not to include our names in his story."

She did that, listened, then looked at me and shook her head. "He says he's not the only one who's got our names. He wants to talk to you."

"Tell him I just went fishing."

She spoke into the phone. "I'm sorry, but he just went fishing." She paused and listened, then said, "I'm afraid not. No, no comment at all. Sorry. Good-bye," and hung up.

"Rats," she said.

"There's nothing we can do about it now," I said. "It was only a matter of time once some reporter got interested in the story."

"Maybe he'll decide not to print our names."

"Maybe." But I didn't think I'd bet on it.

After lunch, I called the Marcuses to let them know we were coming, and we drove west to Gay Head under white clouds and blue sky. Another Vineyard beach day, with about a fifteen-knot wind from the southwest in case you decided to go sailing instead.

We found the right driveway, and came to the locked gate.

"Now what?" asked Zee.

"Observe." I punched the button on the gadget I'd gotten from Thomas Decker the night before, and the gate swung open. We drove through and another button punch swung the gate shut behind us.

"Magic," said Zee. "What is that? Some sort of a garage door opener?"

"I'm a trusted employee. This is like the key to the executive washroom."

We drove up to the house, passing a couple of frowning groundskeepers who were clearly unused to seeing as old and rusty a vehicle as my Land Cruiser on the estate. As we passed, one of them took a transmitter from his belt and spoke into it. Two other men were walking toward us when we stopped in front of the door.

As we got out, Thomas Decker came from the house. He gestured at the two men, and they turned and went away.

"Security," he said. "Next time, they'll know you. Come in." He nodded to Zee. "It's nice to see you again, Mrs. Jackson."

Zee was always nice to see. We followed him into the house and there was Angela Marcus. She was wearing old clothes and had a floppy straw hat on her head.

"Welcome back," she said, shaking our hands and smiling. "I'm just on my way out to my garden, Zee, and you're welcome to join me if you'd like. It bores me to listen to men talk about business."

Zee didn't hesitate. "I'd love to see your garden."

I followed Decker down a hall to a closed door. He knocked, and we went in. Luciano Marcus sat behind a large desk. We exchanged handshakes and greetings and he waved us into chairs.

"What can I do for you?"

I got right to it. "I need to know as much as I can about you and your business. You don't have to tell me about how much money you make or how you make it if you don't want to, but it will help me to know about anyone who might think that you're ripping him off. I also want to know if there's anybody in your past or present who might have it in for you personally. People usually don't try to shoot other people without a reason. If I can find the reason, I might be able to find the people who are mad at you."

Marcus looked at me without expression. "That is perfectly sensible thinking, and I will tell you what I can. My business concerns are fairly extensive and complex, and Thomas will brief you on them. Meanwhile, as to people who might, as you say, have it in for me, I will tell you that no businessman is without enemies, and I have made my share. However, I am, for all practical purposes, nearly retired, and cannot imagine any business enemy deciding now to take revenge upon me for past actions." He paused. "As for personal animosity toward me, when I was younger I made my share of enemies, but for many years now I have lived a very private life." He smiled a crooked smile. "I can think of no one who knows me well enough personally to hate me." He frowned. "Except for some Wampanoags, that is."

A lot of haters don't know their victims at all. And vice versa. I thought, but did not speak, of John Lennon and other casualties of fame. I said: "Most violence involves booze, dope, hormones, or stupidity, or some combination of the same. Can you think of any way any of that could make somebody try to kill you?"

Marcus looked at me steadily. "Personally, I like a drink and I have my annual cigar. When I was younger, my hormones were more active than they are now. I suspect that there are a good many people my age and younger who have tried, at least experimentally, illegal drugs and chemicals, but I've never dealt with them per-

sonally or professionally. I try not to be stupid or to
employ or associate with stupid people. Does that answer
your question?"

"Two other reasons to kill people are revenge and
defense. People want to get you for what you did, or to
prevent you from doing something."

"My doing to others is pretty much in the distant past,
as I've told you. And I have no future plans other than
to become increasingly retired, which I cannot see as a
threat to anyone."

"Can you think of anyone who suffered an injury from
you long ago, but who's been prevented until now from
getting back at you? Someone who's been in jail, maybe,
and has only recently gotten out. Or someone who's been
out of the country for a long time, and has just returned.
Someone like that, with a long memory and a grudge."

Marcus's eyes widened, but he shook his head. "I can't
think of any such person. Thomas?"

"No," said Decker, after a moment of thought.

"No," echoed Marcus.

"Another question, then. Who knew you were going
to attend the opera that afternoon?"

Marcus's eyes were cold. "Thomas and I have wondered about that. It was no secret, but at the same time
it wasn't knowledge that was widespread."

"Who knew?"

He spread his hands. "Thomas; the staff here at the
house; Angela, of course; the people in Boston who sold
me the tickets. My family, friends, and acquaintances
know I enjoy opera, but I don't recall telling any of them
about my plans to see that production of *Carmen*." He
looked at me. "I'm afraid I haven't been of much help to
you."

"You never know," I said. "One last question. Why do you have a bodyguard?"

The cold eyes stared at me. "I will tell you what I told the Boston Police when they asked me the same question. I'm a wealthy man. When I travel, I sometimes have large amounts of money with me. Thomas travels with me to give protection to my person and property."

I tried to read his enigmatic face. It was possible that he was telling me the truth. I looked at Decker. "I guess it's time you and I discussed the business end of things."

"I'll leave you alone, then," said Marcus, rising. "These days I prefer my books to matters of business. We'll all have a drink before you leave." He went out into the hall, and shut the door behind him.

"He trusts you a great deal," I said to Decker.

"And not without cause," said Decker, walking around to the other side of the desk, sitting in Marcus's chair, and taking a folder from a side drawer. "Here. He trusts you a great deal, too. This is a summary of his business interests. I'll answer any questions that I can."

An hour later, I looked at the last page of the folder. Marcus had not exaggerated when he'd said his business interests were extensive. They ranged from Marcus Import and Export, headquartered in New York City, to holdings in a variety of companies and businesses. He owned trawlers in New Bedford and Provincetown, a South Carolina trucking firm, a considerable interest in a Gloucester canning factory, shares in several newspapers, a paper mill, and a dozen other enterprises. I handed the folder back to Decker.

"He's got an eye for business. Not many losers listed here. He's had most of this stuff for a long time."

He nodded. "The canning factory up on the north

shore is new for him. And the fishing fleet. He didn't really get interested in that business until he got his own boat and found out he liked to fish himself. And after he got the trawlers, he thought he should have a canning factory, too, to process the fish he caught with his boats. The rest of the businesses he's had for years. He likes to be in things for the long haul, and he's got enough money that he can ride out slumps and wait for things to get better. So far, they always have. Nowadays he's got managers running things, and his two boys are taking over more and more. If they do as well as their father did, things will be fine."

"And as far as you know, none of these businesses has generated an enemy mad enough to take a shot at your boss."

"Your boss, too," said Decker. "No, not that I know of. As you learned yesterday, we have private detective agencies investigating that possibility. So far, they haven't come up with anything. If they do, we'll let you know."

"Fine. There's another thing. I thought I'd ask you first, and Luciano second, if I need to."

His eyes became hooded. "Ask."

"Cherchez la loot," I said. "Look for the money. Who benefits if Luciano dies? Who inherits?"

He stared at me.

"You usually don't get killed by strangers," I said. "Your friends and your family members are more likely to do it, and one big reason they do it is because they want your money."

Decker leaned forward. "Look. I've been with Luciano for a long time. I owe him, and I do what he says, and I take care of him. He trusts you, but that doesn't mean I do. You want to talk about who's in his will, you talk to Luciano, not to me." His voice was like the ice in his eyes.

For a while we stared at each other. No one blinked. Dueling eyeballs. "You talk with him about it first," I said, "and I'll come back later to hear what you both have to say." I got up.

Decker took a breath and sat back. "What will you do now?"

"See if I can find Joe Begay. Luciano seems to think he's surrounded by hostile Indians, so I thought I'd go have a talk with some of them."

"Ah," said Decker. He put away the folder, and we went upstairs.

9

Gay Head is not the easiest place to locate people, but when I stopped at the police station and asked where I could find Joe Begay, a young cop told me where he lived. They apparently didn't get many six-foot Navajos in Gay Head, so Begay had attracted some attention among the locals.

"He just got married to Toni Vanderbeck," the young cop explained. "I been out with her sister, Maggie, once or twice. Before Toni got married, her and Maggie lived together. Of course, now Maggie's got her own place." The idea seemed to please him.

I thanked him and drove until we found the right house. It was down a short, sandy driveway, not far from the sea. The house was a smallish cedar-shingled structure, with gray-painted window frames and eaves. There was a garage out back. In the yard were two cars: a middle-aged Plymouth sedan and a newish Dodge four-by-four with this year's Arizona plates. Joe Begay hadn't gotten around to registering his truck in Massachusetts yet.

I parked beside the Dodge, and we got out. The smell of the ocean washed over us, fresh and clean, blown ashore by the southwest wind coming around the cliffs.

The door of the house opened and a bronzed young woman stepped onto the porch, and looked at us, smiling. "Hello."

She was the woman I'd seen through the binoculars yesterday.

"Mrs. Begay?"

She smiled some more. "Yes. I'm Toni Begay."

"I know your sister," said Zee, as we came up to the porch. "I'm Zee Jackson. I work at the hospital. This is my husband, Jeff."

"How do you do?"

"I'm well," I said. "I'm looking for your husband."

"You've come to the right place," said his wife. "Come in."

We went in, and there was Joe Begay.

He flowed up from the chair he'd been sitting in, no less lithe than I remembered him from two decades before.

There was a faint scar on his forehead, a souvenir of that last patrol we'd taken, and there were lines on his face that had not been there before. But the bones of his face still had that chiseled look, his deep-set eyes still hid under black brows, and his hair was as black and straight as before.

"Young Mr. Jackson," he said. "And Mrs. Jackson." He shook my hand. "You've filled out a little in the last twenty years."

"You've added a pound or two yourself, Sarge."

He slapped his belly. "Solid muscle. Mostly." He turned to Zee. "As you no doubt know, Mrs. Jackson, I stopped briefly at your wedding. Your husband is a most fortunate man."

"Thank you. You should have stayed for the dancing."

"I didn't have an invitation. I just went by to see if the J. W. Jackson my sister-in-law said was marrying her friend Zee Madieras was the same J. W. Jackson who saved my ass in Nam. Once I saw that it was, I pulled out."

She shook his hand. "Jeff told me that you were the one who saved his life, not the other way around. Which one of you is the real hero?"

Begay and I looked at each other. "Probably neither one," said Begay.

Zee looked at Toni Begay. "Did he ever tell you what actually happened on that patrol?"

"No," said Toni, frowning at her husband. "He's never talked about the war. I did find some medals in a shoe box he brought with him from Arizona, but he said they were nothing."

"I think you're in trouble," I said to Begay.

"Speak for yourself," said Zee. "I found some medals in the back of that drawer where you keep the socks and underwear that you think are too new to wear. I think it's time you guys try to tell us the truth, for a change."

"See what you've done," said Begay, giving me a wry look. "You get me in trouble in Nam, and now you get me in trouble in my own house."

"Never mind that," said Toni Begay. "We want to know the truth, and we want to know now. So sit down and talk. No, wait until I get us something to drink."

"Beer," said Begay, looking at her fondly.

Zee and I nodded, and Toni Begay brought out a half-gallon bottle of Ipswich Ale and four glasses. She poured, and I tasted. Not bad!

"I know a guy up on the north shore," said Begay. "He brings me a case of this stuff when he comes down."

"I've been through Ipswich," I said. "But I didn't know they had a brewery. Now that I do, maybe I'll go back."

"Enough beer talk," said Zee. "Who saved who?"

Begay looked at the floor. His wife looked at me.

"Well," I said, "like I told Zee, I met Sarge when I landed

in Nam. How many tours had you had by then, Sarge, three? Anyway . . ."

I told her about how, on that last patrol, we were dropped off in the bush, and how very soon we'd come under fire from mortar men or artillerymen who seemed to be waiting for us and who put shells right on top of us. As I talked, things I'd forgotten came back to me.

The noise was what had surprised me the most. Nobody had told me about that part of an action. It was amazing noise that rattled your brain. Lucky Joe Begay was an early casualty, taking shrapnel in his head.

"I was blind as a bat," said Begay, touching the scar on his broad forehead. "There were three men dead, and everybody else was hit, including the kid here. His legs looked like hamburger. How old were you, then? You looked like you'd never shaved in your life."

I shook my head. "Seventeen. I lied about my age. Anything to get out of Somerville. Teenage stupid."

"Amen to that," said Begay. "Anyway, Mrs. Jackson, your hubby here crawled to the radio and called in the gunships, and they blasted away at the area the fire seemed to be coming from long enough for us to get back to where the choppers could pick us up. And that was about it, wouldn't you say, J.W.?"

"Yeah, that's about it."

"No, it isn't," said Toni Begay. "You're leaving things out. What about those medals?"

"I should have thrown them out long ago," said Begay. "Medals don't mean anything, Toni. They give them away by the ton. All you have to do to get a medal is show up."

"None of that talk," said his wife. "You tell Zee and me what happened."

Begay looked at me, then back at her. "Well, hell. It was just that J.W. couldn't walk, and I couldn't see, so he was the eyes and I was the legs. He told me where to go, and I sort of dragged him along in front of the others until we got out of there. That's all there is to it."

The women looked at each other, and then at us. "So you saved each other," said Zee. "And the rest of the men. That's why you got those medals."

"After they got us to a hospital, they made a joke," I said. "Who has four arms, two legs, and one head? Mr. Jackson Begay."

"OR humor," nodded Zee.

"They could have added no brains," said Begay. "It seemed fairly humorous at the time. Then they split us up, and we didn't see each other anymore. They worked me over, and after a while I could see again as well as ever." He looked at me. "And I guess they got most of the metal out of you. How are the legs?"

"They won't win any prizes for looks, but they work okay. A little iron oozes out every now and then, but nothing serious." I spread my hands. "And there you have it, ladies. Now let's forget it. It all happened a long time ago."

Zee shook her head. "You two."

"So," I said, changing the subject to one women seem to enjoy talking about. "How long have you folks been married?"

Toni, who had been studying her husband, now smiled at me. "Six months, almost!" And she happily told us how it had all happened.

It was the strong bones and flat planes of his face that had first caught her attention when they'd met in Santa Fe. He had looked the way she had always thought an

Indian should look: as though he could cross the desert without water, or walk so softly that he could catch birds as they perched on twigs and sang. She had seen all of that in his face before she really even looked at the rest of him. When she did look at his body, it went with his face so naturally that she didn't even have to think about it. He was a whole person, so whole that she wondered if she'd ever seen one before.

Then Begay told his side of it. He had seen a girl from the East. Tawny-skinned, dark-eyed, Indian maybe, maybe not. Pretty, clean, slender. Staring at him, then looking away, then looking back.

They had been at the Governor's Palace, two more tourists looking at the jewelry and pottery spread out on the blankets. But when they saw each other, they had stopped looking at the arts and crafts, even though their eyes still seemed to be focused on them. They had moved toward one another, and when they were finally standing side by side, both were nervous but neither was surprised.

They had gone to a café and had coffee. She learned that he was from Arizona and was on vacation, and he learned that she was a Wampanoag from Martha's Vineyard, out West for the first time, on a buying trip for her shop on the Gay Head cliffs. They had spent the afternoon together, and had found talking easy although, had she noticed it, he learned much more of her than she did of him.

But her heart had learned what interested it, and for the next several days he had been her guide, driving her in his Dodge four-by-four up into the mountains to Bandelier National Monument, where he led her through the Frijoles Canyon ruins, and showed her the stone

lions crouched within their antler circle. She had never
seen such things, and marveled at them.

He had taken her to the pueblos in the area, and those
on southwest toward Albuquerque. She had bought jewelry, pots, and blankets at the pueblos with the help of
his gift of tongues, which had allowed her to speak,
through him, with the artists in those ancient cities. She
had returned to her hotel room with treasures she never
would otherwise have found.

They had seen much of each other, and when it was time
for her to return to her island, it had been agreed that he
would come there soon, so she could play guide and hostess in return for those roles he had played in New Mexico.

And he had come, and they had walked the Gay Head
cliffs and beaches, and sailed on Menemsha Pond in her
little Widgeon, and walked the streets of Edgartown and
Oak Bluffs, looking into the windows, and he had decided
that the island was a place where he could live, could settle down.

"And then he proposed!" Toni Begay's smile was wide.
"And of course I said yes, and of course everybody in my
family loved him, too!"

"How romantic!" said Zee. The women beamed at each
other.

"Actually," amended Begay, looking amused, "some of
her family weren't sure they totally approved until they
found out that I was supposedly a Navajo. Native American blood, you know."

"He's taking about Mom, of course." Toni took a deep
breath. "My mother, as you probably know if you read
the *Gazette*, thinks being a Native American is about as
important a thing as there is. She believes we all need to
fight for our rights."

That seemed like as good an opening as I was likely to get, but before I could raise the issue of the cranberry bog dispute, Zee began to tell Toni how we two had met. It turned into a two-beer story, since she remembered things I'd completely forgotten about. Having little to add, I sat back and listened. When, at last, Zee was done and Toni was telling her, in turn, how romantic our relationship had been and how nice it was to be married, I pointed out that in Zee's tale I sounded so much more wonderful than I knew I was that I wasn't sure Zee was actually married to me or to somebody else.

Zee sniffed and lifted her chin. "I was just trying to make you sound like a good catch. I take it all back."

"Come on, J.W.," said Begay, getting up. "I'll take you out for some air before your silver tongue gets you into more trouble."

"It's too late," Zee called after us.

As we went out the door into the yard, I could hear the running brook sound of the women laughing.

Begay walked to the Land Cruiser, and looked it over. Then he leaned against the front fender and crossed his arms.

"All right, J.W., what can I do for you? I don't think you came by just to talk about old times and the joys of marriage."

"Actually, I like the joys of marriage part. The old times I can do without."

"Ditto. But now the real reason."

So I told him about my job with Luciano Marcus.

When I was done, he nodded. "So Marcus thinks that maybe there's some Wampanoag mad enough at him to want to kill him."

"That's it."

A small, dry smile played across Begay's face. "Could be that he's right about that. I don't know if my mother-in-law would pull the trigger, but she wants that cranberry bog so bad that I don't think she'd shed many tears if your boss, Mr. Marcus, got run over by a truck. And she's not alone."

10

Begay took papers and a pack of Prince Albert out of his pocket and rolled a cigarette. He had good technique. I had rolled joints in my pot-smoking days back in the seventies, but even then I hadn't been particularly good at it, preferring a pipe.

Begay looked semi-apologetic. "I can't quite kick the habit, so I roll my own to make it harder on myself. And I won't smoke indoors." He lit up and inhaled and coughed. "It's dumb, but it's hard to quit."

How well I knew. My corncob pipe still haunted me, and I was ever on the verge of taking it up again.

"So your mother-in-law doesn't care for my boss," I said.

He looked off toward Noman's Land, where I could see a trawler working east, its outriggers spread like wings. "I think she's more worked up over that cranberry bog than she is about him personally. Sacred Indian ground, you know. Or traditional Indian territory, at least. He's the guy who's got it, and she wants it for the tribe." He tried a smoke ring, but the wind took it away half formed. "On the other hand, I can't see her hiring some gun to knock him off. She's more the type to do it herself, if she thought it needed doing."

"Any other mad Wampanoags that you know of?"

"There are a few. Some are on Linda's side, and others aren't. The feisty ones seem to spend more time picking on each other than on other people. Out on the res, we have the same thing. One faction lined up against another and nobody taking prisoners, when they'd all be better off getting along and ganging up on, say, you white eyes."

It was not an unusual phenomenon for partisans to hate each other more than they hated their common enemies. It happened in Africa, Ireland, the Middle East, and everywhere else. Why not in Gay Head?

"Leave us pale faces alone," I said. "We don't need you redskins wiping us out. We can do that by ourselves. I saw you and your wife wandering around down by Squibnocket Pond the other day, pretending to be bird-watching while you cased my boss's place. Just scouting?"

"You were up there, eh? They won't let me in, so I wander around the outskirts of the place, having a peek here, a peek there, and letting myself be seen doing it, just to let Marcus know that my mother-in-law is serious. Maybe you should meet her. She might know something about that business in Boston."

"Would she tell me, if she did?"

He dropped the cigarette and stepped on it, grinding it into the sand. "She's the in-your-face type, not much on sneaky stuff. If she likes you, you know it; if she doesn't, you know that, too. She's short on lying, I'd say, so if she knows something she might tell you what it is." He paused. "Of course, she might not, too. Nobody's honest all of the time."

"Except you and me."

"Yeah, except you and me."

"I think I'll take you up on your idea," I said. "You can introduce me to your mother-in-law."

"Better yet," said Begay, "I'll let my wife do it. Let's join the ladies."

We went into the house, and Toni Begay said, sure, she'd be glad to introduce me to her mother. But not today. Today, Linda was busy with meetings about tribal business. Would it be okay if Toni called when her mother was free?

It would be okay. I thanked her and looked at Zee.

"There are bonito waiting for us down at our end of the island. Maybe we should have a go at them while we've still got some daylight."

She got up and we said our good-byes. I shook hands with Begay. "Good to see you again, Sarge."

"He's gotten a promotion," said Zee. "Toni tells me that he's now a captain."

I looked at her, then at him.

The corner of Begay's mouth flicked up, then down again. "I've bought myself a boat. For pot fishing. I'm going to go into the conch business. Maybe do some lobstering."

"It's not the easiest way to make a living."

"That's what Buddy Malone, the guy who sold me the boat, said. He went broke. But he's going to show me the ropes."

"He's got two kids in college, and bills like everybody else," said Toni. "Nice people. I know his wife. He's going to try getting on as a carpenter, but I'm afraid they're in trouble."

Not too many of the tens of thousands of tourists who pour onto the Vineyard every summer realize that the island's permanent population is one of the poorest in Massachusetts. Vacationing mainlanders rarely see much other than the yachts, the golden beaches, the fashionable shops, the quaint streets, and the fine restaurants. They see the great houses of the whaling captains, and the flowered gardens of Edgartown, the gingerbread cottages of Oak Bluffs, and the lovely farms and winding roads of West Tisbury and Chilmark; but they don't see the shacks buried in the woods, surrounded by the clutter that the poor always save just in case they might need it—rusty cars, rotting wood, broken tools, empty cartons. Nor do they see the winter lines at the unemployment office, or the social workers and police dealing with the violence that is rooted in perpetual and hopeless poverty. On Martha's Vineyard, the poor are poor in private. The island's public face is the one most people know.

"Fishing and farming," I said to Begay. "Two tough ways to make a living."

"Hey," said Begay. "Where I grew up, out by Oraibi, it almost never rained, and we used to plant corn with a stick. This can't be much tougher than that."

It was a blue sky afternoon. The only clouds in sight were those that always hang mistily over Cape Cod, across the sound. Near the horizon, the bright arc of sky became pale and hazy.

Zee and I headed for Edgartown. As I drove, she gave me a kiss. "One beautiful day after another on beautiful Martha's Vineyard, and tomorrow I go back to work indoors. Maybe I should give up this nursing stuff during the summer, and become a gardener or a groundskeeper. When it gets cold, I could do nursing again, back inside where it's warm."

"Makes sense to me," I said. "But who would take care of the moped drivers when they self-destruct?"

"Somebody else." She sighed. "But for the time being, I guess it's my job. Rats."

"On the other hand," I said, "consider my case: a grown

man wasting his life in an endless round of fishing and beer drinking. You've got it good, by comparison."

"Poor baby. Where are we going now?"

"I thought we'd drop the dinghy overboard in Oak Bluffs and fish by the ferry dock."

"Ah, the classic bonito location."

"I'm a classic kind of guy."

We drove down to Collins Beach in Edgartown to get the dinghy. The log chain I used to secure it to the Reading Room dock was still doing its job, and no young gentlemen yachtsmen had stolen the boat to row out to his own.

The all-male membership of the Reading Room, the clubhouse at the end of the dock, seemed to be tending to business. No one read there, of course, but so what? The guys drank and talked instead. And occasionally they even let wives and girlfriends inside as guests. Normally, according to rumor, the only women allowed there were waitresses and window washers.

Out in the harbor, boats of all sizes lay at their moorings. Other boats, sail and power, moved up and down the channel, heading outside or up toward Katama Bay. Across the water was Chappaquiddick, where, later in the summer, I would pick the beach plums I'd use to make the many jars of jelly I would then sell at outrageous prices to the farm stands that would in turn charge even more outrageous prices to the beach plum jelly fanatics who loved the stuff. My beach plum picking place is one of my most closely guarded secrets, one that I share willingly only with Zee. I have a couple of secret clamming places that I won't talk about, either.

I put the dinghy in back of the Toyota and we were about to climb back inside the truck when a police cruiser came down from South Water Street and parked in the Reading Room parking lot. I figured that there must have been police cars down there before, some time or other, but I couldn't remember seeing one. We paused and watched while the driver's door opened and the chief got out.

"Thought I saw you here," he said, bringing his pipe out of a pocket and tamping it with a tobacco-stained trigger finger while he dug out his Zippo lighter with his other hand. The chief liked his pipe. He lit up and the smoke blew gently toward the northeast.

"You don't need a boat," he said. "The bonito are all over Edgartown harbor. You can fish for 'em right off the town dock."

"Yeah," said Zee. "Shoulder to shoulder with a hundred other men, women, and children, most of whom don't have any idea what they're doing. No thanks. We're heading for O.B., where we'll have some space around us."

He puffed his pipe and looked this way and that, the way he almost always did. Not seeing anyone who needed to be arrested or rushed to the hospital, he took the pipe from his mouth. "Got a call from Boston yesterday. Detective named Gordon R. Sullivan."

We waited.

"He told me about what happened up there. How come you didn't?"

"It was in the Boston papers," I said. "I imagine the news even got to Martha's Vineyard."

"I missed the part about you two," said the chief.

"Good. Maybe everybody did."

The chief puffed a few more times. "If they think you two can ID them, they may come down here looking for you."

"I doubt it," said Zee.

His voice became slightly harder. He looked at me. "Lemme point something out to you, J.W. You're not just a single guy anymore. If you were, and if it was only your neck that was in a noose, I'd walk away right now. But you aren't a single guy anymore. You have a wife, and it's Zee's neck, here, not yours, that could be under the ax. You should have told me about this."

I felt a little flush of color. I didn't like being told I was wrong. Especially when I was. But before I could speak, Zee did.

"Now, you just hold it right there, chief! Don't try to ignore me and feed that protect-the-little-lady line to Jeff! He's just macho enough to take you seriously! If you have something to say about us being in danger, you say it to both of us, not just to him! My God, you'd think this was the 1890s or something, and I was some sort of swooning damsel! If you think that, you just get the idea out of your head right now!"

The chief did not quite look abashed.

"Well, pardon me all to hell, Mrs. Jackson. And please take your finger out of my face."

I took a deep breath. "You're right," I said. "I should have told you."

He feigned shock. "My God! Let me get out my pocket calendar and make a note of this. J. W. Jackson admitted he was wrong and I was right. Mrs. Jackson, you're a witness."

"What did Sullivan tell you?"

The chief spelled it out. It was the story as it had happened, plus one thing new: Sullivan had traced the shotgun.

"Belonged to a guy up in Vineyard Haven," said the chief. "Stolen in a housebreak last spring." He knocked the dottle out of his pipe, blew through the stem, and stuck it back in his pocket. "Interesting, eh? Gives an island spin to things."

It did, indeed. I looked at Zee. Her anger was gone.

"That changes things a little," she said.

He nodded. "Yeah. Well, I don't have any brilliant ideas about what we can do, but I'll let the other police on the island know about what happened up in Boston. They'll keep their eyes and ears open, and maybe they'll see or hear something. You two start being careful. If anything happens that worries you, let me know."

"You can count on it," said Zee, taking my arm.

"I'll ask the OB police to keep an eye on you while you're at work, Zee, and I'll have my own people come by your place now and then. And we'll all keep our ears open in case anybody's asking about where you live or anything like that. Anybody call you and not give a name, anything like that, you let me know. In case I'm not in, you can call Dom Agganis or the sheriff. Keep in touch."

He got into the cruiser, turned around, and drove back into town.

The day didn't seem as nice as it had when I'd left the house. The same blue sky arched from horizon to horizon, the same gentle southwest wind flapped the yacht club flags and filled the sails of boats coming in and going out of the harbor, the same sun shone bright.

But it seemed colder and darker to me.

And that night, late, I suddenly awoke to some sound out by my shed, and knew that Fred Souza was prowling around, up to no good. I eased out of bed and threw on the yard light. No one was there, and after a while I went back to bed, where I finally slept again.

The next morning, after Zee left for work, I drove to Manny Fonseca's woodworking shop.

Manny Fonseca was not only a fine-finish cabinet-maker, but one of the Vineyard's prime gun aficionados and a crack pistoleer. Once he'd thought of himself as a frustrated frontiersman, born a hundred years too late to tame the Wild West as surely he'd been created to do; but then he had discovered (initially to his horror) that he had just enough Wampanoag blood in him to qualify as an official member of the tribe, and since then had reversed his position and argued that the real tragedy of his life was that he'd been born too late to stop the Europeans from taking the country away from his ancestors.

He was the best shot I knew, and he bought and sold guns as fast as new ones caught his fancy and older ones bored him. He had all of the gun dealer's licenses that you can have, up to and including the right to handle machine guns.

I wasn't interested in a machine gun, but I did want to see Manny, so I went right into the shop, which smelled of sawdust and the oils and stains of Manny's profession. Manny was gluing a chair together. He looked up as I came in.

"Hey," he said, smiling. "How's married life?"

"The one smart thing I've done."

"You got it," said Manny. "What brings you down here this time of day. I'd have figured you to be fishing for bonito."

"You're right. I should be fishing. But something's come up."

"What?" He put a last clamp on the chair and capped the jar of glue.

"I want you to find a pistol for Zee and teach her how to use it."

He looked at me. "Zee? You're kidding me. Zee hates guns. She wouldn't take one if Jesus gave it to her."

"Well, you have to do Jesus one better, then. I want her to have a handgun and to know how to shoot it, and I think you're the man to teach her."

"Let's go up to the house," said Manny, giving the chair a final approving look. "When we get there, you can tell me what's going on."

— 11 —

In the basement gun shop at Manny's house, I told him about the incident in Boston and the news that the shotgun was from Vineyard Haven.

Manny whistled. "I see why you want Zee to carry. I tell you something, J.W., if more women learned how to use guns and carried them, they'd be a lot better off, no matter what these blamed bleeding heart liberals say. My wife knows how to shoot and I told her that if I ever go off my rocker and start beating on her, she should put a slug right in me and never hesitate!" He handed me a pistol.

I couldn't see Helen shooting Manny without hesitating, but I was pretty sure that's what he thought she should do.

"What is this?" I asked, turning the semi-automatic in my hand and looking at it.

"Beretta 84F. .380. Thirteen rounds, double action. I put the wood grips on it. Plenty of whack at close quarters. It'll fit Zee's hand, too, and won't kick too much. She don't like it, we'll come up with something else. Important thing is that she knows how it works, isn't afraid of it, and can hit what she aims at."

I pointed the pistol at a wall and sighted down the short barrel. Like Scarlett O'Hara, I could shoot pretty well if I didn't have to shoot too far. "The problem will be getting her to learn that stuff," I said. "She's pretty hostile to guns."

"Yeah, I been thinking about that," said Manny. "I think it'd probably be best to go the sporting route. Target shooting for family fun, and like that. She might go for that when she wouldn't go for the self-defense bit. What do you think?"

I thought we'd still have problems. "How much you want for this thing and some bullets to go with it?"

He told me.

"You willing to be the instructor?" I asked.

"Sure. Be glad to. Don't want no Boston hood coming down here and finding Zee unarmed."

Good. Not only was Manny a better shot than I was, he was an excellent shooting instructor. There was no doubt he'd have a lot more success teaching Zee how to use the pistol than I would. Even so, I knew I wouldn't be surprised if, after dutifully learning all Manny could teach her, Zee would then hide the pistol away and never use it. I decided not to tell Manny that, though.

"I'll take it," I said.

"Fine. You decide you don't want it, I'll buy it back. Something else. Woman needs a gun, she doesn't want it in her purse where somebody can grab her purse and gun and all. She wants it on her belt where she can get at it if she needs it. They got some rigs that are good for women. After Zee learns how to handle this pistol, I'll come up with some leather for it, so she can have it with her. Like they say, it's . . ."

"I know," I said, quoting the ancient dictum: "It's better to have it and not need it than need it and not have it."

Manny nodded. "You got it, J.W. When you want Zee and me to get started?"

"Tomorrow," I said. "After work."

"Meet you at the club at five-thirty," said Manny. "Tell

you what. I'll have Helen come along. She likes to target shoot, and Zee won't feel so much like she's being turned into a Joan Wayne."

Joan Wayne. I hadn't heard that one before.

I took Zee's new pistol and a box of bullets and went home. I tucked the weapon and ammunition into the drawer of my gun cabinet, and set about making a supper that would soften Zee's resistance: pork saté, a nifty Indonesian barbecue that can set your taste buds singing. The secret is in the marinade, of course.

I melted a quarter cup of butter in a saucepan, then mixed in a tablespoon of lemon juice, a bit of grated lemon rind, a little Tabasco, some onion and brown sugar, a tablespoon of coriander, some cumin, ginger, salt, and pepper, a crunched garlic clove, and about a half cup of teriyaki sauce.

I mixed all of that up, and let it simmer five minutes. Then I cut the fat and sinew off the pork tenderloin, sliced the meat into three-quarter-inch cubes, stirred them into the sauce, and put everything into the fridge to marinate.

By the time Zee got home, I had the meat on skewers, the grill going out back, rice ready to cook, and a fresh spinach salad in the fridge. And of course I had the chilled martini glasses in the freezer beside the bottle of Lukusowa.

We went up onto the balcony with our drinks and looked out toward the sound. The slanting evening light passed over our shoulders, over the garden, over Sengekontacket Pond, where a few die-hard tyro surf sailors were still learning to play with their boards in the falling wind, over the road and beach beyond the pond, out over the sound, and on over the Atlantic, where, just beyond the horizon, darkness was rolling toward us.

After supper, accompanied by the house cabernet sauvignon, Zee sighed and patted her belly.

"I think I can make some money by renting you out to train husbands who don't know how to welcome their wives home in the evening."

"Let me chose the wives, and it's a deal."

"On second thought, forget the whole thing."

After cognac I told her about my purchase.

"I don't want anything to do with it," said Zee, shaking her head. "I know there's some chance that those guys in Boston may come down here, and I know that the gun being stolen in Vineyard Haven probably makes it more likely that somebody down here is tied into the shooting, but I have no desire at all to learn how to shoot a gun. Forget it."

"Helen's going to be down at the club with Manny tomorrow, after work," I said. "They'll be doing some target shooting. I'm not very good at it, compared to Manny, but it's fun sometimes. I'd like to have you come along."

"No," said Zee. "I don't like guns."

"Neither did Sam Spade, but he knew how they worked. You should know, too, because we're going to have them in the house, and the more you know, the safer you'll be."

She thought about that.

"When we have kids," I said, "The guns will still be there. They'll be locked up, but they'll be there and I'll want to teach them how to use them correctly. It'll be better if you know about them, too."

"That's a pretty low road you're taking, Jefferson. Waving our children at me before we even have them."

"You don't have to shoot if you don't want to, but I'll feel better if I know that you can if you wish, and that you'll be safe while you're doing it. Guns are very dangerous, especially if you don't know anything about them."

"I'll take my chances."

"Will you come down to the club and watch Helen and Manny and me shoot?"

"Sure."

That was as much as I was going to get out of Zee.

"Good," I said. "Maybe once you get there, you'll change your mind."

"Maybe," said Zee. "But don't count on it."

Later, in bed, she poked me in the ribs with her finger just as I was sliding off to sleep. "I don't need a gun to protect myself. I don't."

"Maybe you're right."

"I am. So forget the whole idea."

"There's me, too," I said.

"What do you mean?"

"I mean that I'd like you to be able to protect me, too, if I need protection."

She lay silent for several minutes. When she spoke, her voice was touched with anger. "You sure can walk the low road when it suits you. First it's our children who need me to know about guns, and now it's you."

"I'm shameless," I said. "I admit it."

"Shameless, and disgusting, too."

"Shameless and disgusting and lower than a snake's belly."

"Worse than that, even. You don't deserve to be protected."

"You're probably right, but I'm so rotten that I want you to protect me anyway."

"This is a cheat, you know. You're making me do something I don't want to do."

I sat up in bed and turned on my reading light. Zee stared up at me from her pillow. I looked down at her. "No," I said. "I would never make you do something you don't want to do. If you do this thing, it has to be because you've decided it's the right thing to do. If you don't think it is, don't do it."

Her hair was like a black nimbus around her face. Her eyes were huge and dark and deep. "You think we're in danger, don't you?" she asked.

"I don't know if we are or not."

"But you think we might be."

"I think we should keep that possibility in mind. I don't think we should start jumping at shadows, but I think we should be careful."

"So careful that I have to carry a gun?"

My heart turned over as I looked down at her. I touched her lips with my finger and then pushed a strand of raven hair from her forehead. "Not if you don't want to. It's just that I might not be there if you need help. You'll have to help yourself."

"I'll have to think about it." She stretched her arms up toward me. "I love you, you know."

"Yes." I sank down toward her. When people love you, you can manipulate them even when they know you're doing it.

The next evening, after Zee got home from work, we got into my old Toyota Land Cruiser and drove down to the Rod and Gun Club shooting range.

Manny and Helen Fonseca were already there, with Manny's normal piles of shooting gear spread out on the twenty-five-yard table. He was also wearing his weapons belt, complete with holstered side arm, extra clips, and pouches holding who knew what. I carried the

Beretta 84F and its bullets in a paper bag, along with my earplugs and shooting glasses. I put the bag on the table.

Helen and Manny had set up the targets, and I noted with satisfaction that they were using the ringed ones instead of the man-shaped ones. Zee would be more likely to shoot at the ringed ones.

Zee and Helen embraced, and Manny shook our hands, and looked at Zee. "You want to watch for a while?"

"Yes."

"Fine. It's pretty noisy, so you'd better wear these." He handed her some earplugs. "What we're going to do, Helen and me, is shoot from here first, then move up and shoot from about ten yards. It's pretty close, but if we were shooting at, for instance, somebody who was shooting back, the chances are we wouldn't be doing it at long range anyway. The idea here today is just to have some fun and see how good or bad we are." He gestured at the table. "I got several guns here, and we'll shoot 'em all. Some are revolvers and some, like this one here on my belt, are semi-automatics like the one J.W. brought along. I'll shoot first with this here Colt .45 Double Eagle, and Helen will shoot with her Smith and Wesson Lady Smith .38. You won't have any trouble telling them apart. Mine makes the biggest noise." He grinned. Nothing made Manny happier than shooting pistols and talking about them.

Manny shot two clips through his .45 and blew the center out of every target he shot at. Helen, reloading between targets, fired her little .38 first with one hand, then the other, then with both, getting the bullets all in the targets, but not so centered as Manny had done.

"Why do you shoot with each hand?" Zee asked Helen, as the shootists paused and targets were being replaced.

"It's just for fun here," smiled Helen. "I'm really not good at all with my left hand, and I'm only so-so with my right, so if I really want to hit anything I have to do it with both hands. But if I was, say, a police officer and I got shot in my right hand, I'd need to be able to shoot with my left one."

"Oh," said Zee.

"Manny's good with either hand," said Helen with a bit of pride in her voice. "Manny, shoot with your left hand, so Zee can see how it should be done."

"Sure," said Manny. Shooting southpaw, he promptly blew the centers out of more targets.

"Manny's got the touch," said Helen, nodding. "I'll never have it, but he's got it. He's a natural shooter."

Manny was pleased about his skill, but not vain. "It's a gift," he said, "like some people have perfect pitch. Me, I couldn't carry a tune in a bucket, but I can shoot pretty good if I stay in practice. I can't teach anybody else how to be a great shot, but I can teach them how to shoot well. Helen here could be a lot better if she'd practice, but she's got other things she likes to do better, so she's not as good as she could be. Her and me are going to shoot with some of these other pistols now. Each one's a little different, but the principle is the same with all of them." He smiled and I knew his favorite wisdom was coming: "The secret is to stand in back of the gun when you shoot it."

Zee gave him enough of a smile to make him feel good, and he and Helen blazed away some more, shooting with first this and then that pistol in Manny's collection. The calibers ranged from .45 to .22, and the noises produced made me glad to have earplugs.

"Now, then, J.W., let's try out that .380 you have in

that lunch bag." Manny got the Beretta out of the bag, checked it for safety, and slipped the clip into the handle. He glanced at me. "You mind if I shoot it first?"

I didn't mind, and Manny, squeezing off the shots, blew out the bull's-eye of his first target, then that of his second. He popped the clip and reloaded it.

"Nice little gun," he said, handing clip and pistol to me.

I put on my glasses, assumed the two-handed stance he'd taught me, and emptied the clip into a target. The first shot went high, but the others were all on the paper. Not bad. If that had been a man out there, he'd have been pretty leaky by the time my clip was empty.

"Thirteen rounds," Manny was saying to Zee. "That's a lot better than the six rounds in Helen's Lady Smith, but Helen likes the revolver and doesn't like a semi-automatic."

"I can figure out how my Lady Smith works," said Helen, "but I'm never sure what's going on with those semi-autos. I don't feel comfortable with them."

"That's right," said Manny. "When they were thinking about bringing out a pistol for women, Smith and Wesson did a study about what the ladies thought about guns. They found out that women thought semi-automatics were too complicated, and that they didn't think anything smaller than a .38 would stop a rapist. So the Lady Smith is a .38 revolver, and Helen likes it better than the other guns here. It's not too big and it's not too little, it's got a good trigger pull, and it's got stopping power."

"Then how come you talked Jefferson into taking this Beretta?" asked Zee.

"You get six shots with the Lady Smith and thirteen with the Beretta. Six should be plenty, but thirteen is seven more than plenty, in case you miss the first six times. Besides, the new autoloaders are just as safe as any revolver and just as trouble free. More gun for your dollar, I think. And so do most police and military agencies I know of."

"Then why is Jeff's police gun a revolver?"

"Because he was too cheap to buy an autoloader, I guess. A few old-timers still carry those police specials, but most law officers are wearing autoloaders of some kind these days. Just a matter of firepower. You don't want the bad guys to have better weapons than you do, like happened down in Waco with that wacky religious guy and his gang. Say, would you like to take a few shots with the Beretta?"

Zee hesitated, and I wondered which way she would go. I was pleased to discover that I really didn't care. Then she nodded. "All right," she said. "I'll try it."

"Good girl," said Manny. "I'll show you some things about the weapon, and then we'll fire some rounds. I think you'll have fun shooting this gun. It's a nice little piece."

I felt glad and sad at the same time, as they began to talk.

12

When Zee and I got home later that evening, she wasn't in the grumpy mood I'd half expected. Instead, she played with Oliver Underfoot and Velcro, and was thoughtful and quiet for the most part, although an occasional frown crossed her brow.

I had anticipated a more irritable disposition, and had planned a counterattack at the supper table, since Zee, for all her sleek slimness, could probably eat a horse if she tried, and found it hard to be in a bad humor when she had a full belly. I wasn't serving horse, but something better: the Scandinavian fishbake that both of us could eat seven days a week without complaint. I made mine with cod this time. Delish, as always.

Zee was properly impressed, and almost her normal self as she drank the last of her wine and wiped her lips.

"Now I know why I married you, Mr. Jackson."

"Since we're hitched, you can stop that Mr. Jackson stuff and just call me J.W."

After supper, while I washed and stacked the dishes, Zee made a phone call. As I hung the dishcloth over the spigot and dried my hands, she came into the kitchen.

"I just talked to Manny. We're going to shoot again tomorrow evening."

I was surprised. "Fine. That gun is yours, by the way."

"I don't want it! I don't know if I'm going to go on with this."

"You don't have to if you don't want to. Manny will buy the gun back if you don't want it. I'm not going to say any more about it."

"I know. But you'll be thinking about it."

"Maybe."

"It's all right," she said. "I'm thinking about it myself."

"Okay. The thing is, what I think about how you should live and what you should do doesn't make any difference. It's what you think that counts." I poured coffee and carried two cups out onto the porch where we could watch the fireflies flicker across the garden and through the trees. "Of course, I reserve the right to give you wise advice."

"Which I don't have to take."

"Or even consider. You're a grown-up person. You get to decide what to do with your life."

We sat and looked up at the stars through the screen that held the mosquitoes at bay. The fireflies sparked and gleamed in the darkness.

"I think you should know," said Zee, "that sometimes I want to be given wise advice. Sometimes I probably even want to be told what to do."

"Yeah. Me, too."

"And I guess I want you to be the one to do that, sometimes."

"Yeah. That's what I want you to do, too, sometimes."

She took my arm and put her cheek on my shoulder. "Of course, I reserve the right to ignore your advice whenever I want to."

"Well, of course."

"And to tell you what I think about things whether you want me to or not."

"I'm sure that was in our wedding vows somewhere. An ancient, sacred, wifely right."

"I distinctly remember it because there wasn't any corresponding ancient, sacred, husbandly right."

"I think I noticed that, too."

I was in a good mood when we went to bed, but before I got to sleep Freddy Souza slipped into my head, and I found myself listening for odd night sounds and sometimes thinking I heard some. I made myself stay in bed, and finally got to sleep.

I had plans for the next day, but as the poet noted, the best-laid schemes gang aft a-gley. As I was right in the middle of washing the breakfast dishes next morning, the pump in the well stopped working and I was abruptly waterless. I tracked the problem down to the switch on the pump itself, which was ancient and had long since been functioning more because of the grace of the water gods than my maintenance efforts over the years. So things go in the investigation biz, as in all other work. Instead of solving the riddle of who wanted Luciano Marcus dead, I went to Vineyard Haven to buy a new switch.

I found one at a plumber's supply place, then drove down to the Dock Street Coffee Shop in Edgartown to have a coffee and Danish to build up the strength I'd need to do the repairwork. I had just come out onto the street again when the chief met me. He pointed at my rusty Land Cruiser, which was parked in the lot across the street in a spot that had miraculously opened up just as I'd arrived.

"You know, there's a petition being circulated to prevent you from parking that bucket of bolts inside of city limits between May and October. The argument is that the tourists take one look at it and cancel their hotel and restaurant reservations and go vacation on Nantucket instead."

"And property values plummet. I've heard it all before."

We looked across the parking lot. Out in the harbor beyond the yacht club, boats were hoisting sail, catching the morning wind, and heading out of the harbor. At dockside the charter fishing boats were loading clients aboard for the day's excursions to the bluefish and bass fishing grounds, and a couple of pot fishermen were already unloading their catches.

The streets were crowded with brightly dressed tourists who didn't seem to understand that these were actually real streets and not just wide sidewalks, and the summer cops were doing their best to keep them from being run over by the cars that a lot of walkers apparently thought were just make-believe. Overhead, the blue sky was clear and bright, and the sun was golden and warm.

The chief was looking at the boats unloading conchs. He shook his head.

"Hell of a way to make a living. Makes me almost glad I'm a cop."

Actually, the chief liked being a cop. Like most cops, it made him feel good when he was able to do something that helped people out. But like most cops, too, he had to put up with a lot of grief from the very people he was paid to serve. I'd liked the helping part, too, but the grief had become too much for me, so I'd become a civilian again.

The chief was still going on. "Boats that leak, pots lost, cranky engines, bad weather, bad prices; you name the trouble, they have it. It's a wonder more of them don't give it up."

"Why don't you give one of them your job?" I asked. "A lot of people here in town think you should have retired years ago. You're too grouchy, and all you do is drive around in that cruiser and give people like me a hard time."

"It won't be long," said the chief. "I'm going to hang up this badge and go to Nova Scotia every summer. Get away from these damned crowds. Come back down in time for scallop season. Live like a human being for a change."

"Sure. How long have you been threatening to do that? You're all talk."

He nodded at the boats. "Jimmy Souza, there. Drunk already."

I looked and saw Jimmy helping Albert Enos unload his catch. Jimmy swayed while he worked.

"He's a nipper," said the chief. "Keeps nips of vodka in his pockets. Expensive way to drink, but he thinks the vodka isn't on his breath and that if he sticks to nips nobody will ever know he's drinking at all."

Over on the dock, Jimmy Souza tried to swing a gunnysack of conchs up into Albert's truck, but couldn't manage it. He dropped the sack and swayed toward the water. Albert caught him and put him into the passenger's seat of the truck, then put the sack of conchs into the back.

"Jimmy used to be a good man," I said.

"Maybe he will be again. Meantime, though, his house is up for sale and his kid can't afford to stay in college. Booze is bad for some families."

I decided not to comment on that one. "While you're here," I said, "tell me more about that stolen shotgun. I'd guess it wasn't sawed off when it left the island. Who did it belong to?"

"Guy named John Dings. Lives off Lambert's Cove

Road. Somebody got in to his place last spring, when he and his wife were out for the evening. Didn't steal anything but that shotgun. They figure thieves came in a back window that was open. They didn't take a lot of stuff that a pro would have gotten, and they didn't vandalize the place, either. Odd case."

"Didn't take the CD player or the family silver?"

The chief shook his head. "Just this shotgun that ended up in Boston. I hear that Dings was pretty upset when he learned that somebody had cut his favorite 12-gauge in two. Bad enough to have it stolen, but sacrilege to have it sawed off like that."

"Any idea about who did the job?"

Again the shake of his head. "Happened before most of the summer people get down, so I'd guess it was probably some island guys. We got our share of that kind. Kept an eye his place, and when he and the wife went out, they went in. Something like that. So far, nobody's talked about it, but usually, sooner or later, somebody will. When they do, we might be able to nail them. You were a cop. You know how it is."

I did. If criminals could learn to keep their mouths shut about their work, cops would catch a lot fewer of them. Instead, they just can't keep from confessing or bragging, and sooner or later they do it to the wrong person, and that person tells it to somebody who tells the cops. It's a fact that criminals, as a class, are not too bright.

"Maybe I'll go talk with John Dings," I said.

"Why would you want to do that?" asked the chief, looking up Main Street.

I told him about the job with Luciano Marcus. He sighed.

"You don't have any PI license that I know about."

"If I did, you'd probably try to take it away from me."

"I'd be doing everybody a favor, if I could. Just make sure you don't get yourself tangled up in the official investigation. You might get in trouble."

"I don't know of any laws that keep honest, upright citizens from asking questions."

"I don't even know many honest, upright citizens," said the chief. "Look up there. That lad at the four corners was doing real well when we started talking. Now he's got traffic backed up beyond the courthouse. I've got to go save him and the citizens. You find out anything about this shooting business, you let me know. And be careful." He walked up toward the traffic jam.

Across the parking lot, Albert Enos had finished loading his sacks of conchs into his truck. He got into the driver's seat beside Jimmy Souza, and pulled out of his parking spot. He paused when he came alongside of me. Beside him, Jimmy was bleary-eyed and smelled of vodka.

"I'm taking him home and paying him off," said Albert. "Gotta find myself a new crew."

"Things don't always work out," I said. "But you have to do what you have to do."

"No, you don't," whimpered Jimmy.

"Yeah, you do," said Albert. He drove away, looking unhappy.

I went home, and while I replaced the old switch with the new one and got the water running again, I thought about poor, ruined Jimmy, and angry Fred, and listened to the sound of gunfire coming from the Rod and Gun Club. Some shooters besides Manny and Zee were burning powder. They were still at it when I finished the morning's dishes, and still at it when I made ham and

cheese sandwiches for lunch. I was on my second Sam
Adams when the shooting finally stopped. I took the
sandwiches and beer out to the table on the lawn, set
Jimmy's troubles and his son's threats aside, and worked
on my beer while I thought about other things. When
the beer and sandwiches were gone, I drove to Vineyard
Haven for the second time that day.

John Dings lived at the end of one of those narrow
dirt driveways that leads from the lower part of Lambert's Cove Road off toward Tashmoo Pond. It was a
modest house with a million-dollar view, looking across
the pond. There were two cars in the yard, and a dock
at the foot of a flight of wooden steps leading from the
back of the house down to the water. Tied to the dock
was an outboard motorboat about twenty feet long. You
see boats like that all around the island. In anything like
decent weather, their owners go out and fish just off
shore. John Dings, I guessed, went after cod, blues, and
bass out in Vineyard Sound.

I knocked on the door and a woman opened it. She
looked to be about forty years old.

"Mrs. Dings?"

"Yes, I'm Sandy Dings." She looked at the Land
Cruiser, then back at me.

I told her my name, then put on my winning smile,
and said: "I just talked to the chief of police down in
Edgartown. He told me that a shotgun recently used in
an attempted crime in Boston was stolen from your husband last spring. I'd like to talk with you about the
theft."

She hesitated. "Are you a policeman?"

"No. But I'm investigating the incident for a client."

"What client? Are you a private detective?"

"No, but I'm making inquiries. My client has a considerable interest in the case. You may be able to help us."

She looked doubtful. "Just a minute," she said. She turned and said in a loud voice. "Jean! Jean, you're going to be late to work! Hurry up!" She turned back to me. "That girl. She'll be late for her own funeral, I swear. She's late for classes, her dates have to wait for her, and she'd be late for work every day if I didn't build a fire under her."

A college-aged girl appeared in the door behind her. She was wearing a waitress's uniform. "Here I am, Mom. Who's this?"

Mom had already forgotten my name.

"J. W. Jackson," I said. "I'm making an unofficial investigation of a shooting in Boston that involved a shotgun that was stolen from this house last spring. I'm hoping that you folks can be of some help."

"You won't get any from me," said the girl. "I was out that night. When I got back, it was all over." She kissed her mother on the cheek. "Mom, I've got to run! Nice to meet you, Mr. Jackson." She went out to one of the cars, got in, and drove away, throwing up gravel and dust behind her.

Her mother looked after her, and sighed. "She's always been like this. If she's an hour late, she thinks she can still make it up in the last half mile."

"Well," I said. "She hasn't been fired yet, so they must like her."

"Oh, she's a sweet girl. And she's got to work to help put herself through UMass," said Sandy Dings. "College costs so much these days."

"Yes." It was true. I didn't know how anybody could afford to go to college anymore. It had been bad enough when I'd gone, and I had the GI Bill to help out.

Sandy Dings abruptly pulled the door open. "Well, come in, Mr. Jackson. I don't know what I can tell you, but I'll do my best."

We went in and sat down. It was a comfortable, middle-class sort of house, clean and modest, and unassuming. Mid-century Sears Roebuck decor.

"If my husband were here," said Sandy Dings, "he could tell you more about the shotgun. I'm afraid I don't know much about them except that the one they stole was his favorite, the one he used when he and Jimmy went duck and goose hunting. I guess it had sentimental value, too. If a gun can have sentimental value."

She looked at me in sudden irritation. "You know what the worst thing about it is? It's not that they stole the shotgun, although that's maddening, too; it's the feeling you have of being violated! It's almost like being raped! Somebody comes right into your house and takes your things! It's scary and it makes you mad! You think that if it happened once, it can happen again. You begin to wonder who it was, and if you know them, and if they know you."

"Where did they get in?"

"Probably a back window. It was open a crack so the wind would bring in some fresh air. There was a northeast wind that night, and I wanted to air out the house. I don't even leave any windows unlocked anymore unless somebody's here. That's what a thing like this does to you."

I got up and looked out the window. It offered a nice view of the pond. Not far from the window there was a back door that led out onto a deck. I went out the door and walked to the railing on the far side.

To my left I could see the opening where the pond

was tied to Vineyard Sound. On the far side of the sound was Cape Cod. On the water, about halfway across, one of the island ferries was headed toward Woods Hole.

On the other side of the pond there were houses with docks. There were small boats on moorings, and others pulled up on the shore. It was a peaceful scene.

Sandy Dings came out and stood beside me.

"It's very beautiful." I said.

"Yes. We love it." She pointed across the pond at a house almost hidden in the trees. "That's where we were that night. At my sister Lillian's place, playing cards. And while we were there, they were here." She shook her head.

"Your daughter said she was out that night, too."

"Yes. She and my sister's boy and some of their friends were down for the weekend. All of them from UMass Boston, you know. It was such a pretty April, they all came down a couple weekends that month. Anyway, they went down to Edgartown together, I think. You want to hear something ironic? It's that I told Jean that since we were going to be out, she and her friends could have their party here at the house. If they'd done that, there wouldn't have been any robbery. But they already had plans to go to Edgartown, so that's where they went."

"Where did your husband keep the shotgun? Did he have a gun cabinet?"

"Oh no. He just kept it in the hall closet. He only used it to hunt duck and geese, and when he was through shooting, he'd clean it and put it back in the closet."

She led me into the hall and showed me the closet.

"Who knew it was there?"

"The police asked us that, too. I don't know who knew. Anybody, I imagine. It wasn't a secret, or anything like that. I imagine there are a lot of guns in closets here on the island. Wouldn't you think so? I mean, if I was looking for a gun, I'd look in the closet. Wouldn't you?"

"I guess I would. Is Jean your only child?"

"The only one still more or less at home. Her brother lives in Pittsfield with his girlfriend." The way she said "girlfriend" suggested that she did not approve of the alliance. Then she clarified her meaning: "I wish they'd get married. I just don't understand these young people these days. When I was her age, John and I got married. What's wrong with that?"

I showed her my wedding ring, pleaded ignorance, and left, wondering if I'd learned anything useful.

At home I decided that reheated pork saté would be just fine for supper, set the table, and waited for Zee to get out of work. She drove down our long, sandy driveway about half past five, gave me a kiss, declined my offer of a pre-target-practice martini, changed clothes, got her paper bag of gun, ammo, glasses, and earplugs, and asked if I wanted to go watch her and Manny shoot.

I said yes, and we drove off to the Rod and Gun Club. There, while I watched, she and Manny talked and shot and talked and shot some more. I stayed out of it. Finally, they were done.

She and Manny had a last chat while they packed up their gear, and then we went home. While Zee cleaned her Beretta, I fixed up martinis, cheese, crackers, and bluefish pâté. We then went up onto the balcony. There, for a time, there was little talk. The night came gently down.

"You seemed to be popping away pretty well tonight."

"Yes," said Zee. She sipped her drink. "Manny Fonseca loves to shoot. He really knows what he's doing." She paused, then gave me a long look from under her dark lashes. "It's a funny thing," she said. "You know how I don't like guns . . ."

"Yes." Zee was a nurse, a healer.

"Well, I don't know how to explain this, but . . . I like shooting with Manny. At targets. I didn't like the idea of doing it, and I expected to hate it, and I would never have done it if I hadn't known that you wanted me to, even though I knew you wouldn't ever talk about it again. But yesterday, when Manny showed me how the pistol worked and taught me how to hold it and aim it and shoot it, like you might teach somebody else how to hold and shoot a basketball, or hit or pitch a baseball . . . it was exciting to shoot and hit what I aimed at. To feel that I was the master—not yet, not really, but some day, maybe—that I was the master of the pistol, and that it would do what I wanted it to do. I'm not a rider, but I've seen women on horses, and I've thought that part of the reason they love riding is that they're mastering a huge, powerful, dangerous, beautiful animal. That they have all that power and beauty and danger under their control. That's what, all of a sudden, when I was finally honest with myself, I felt yesterday when I started to shoot the pistol pretty well. Last night I thought about it, and it worried me, and I didn't know what it meant and wondered if it would happen again. I didn't know whether to hope it would, or hope it wouldn't, but I had to find out, so I phoned Manny, and this evening I felt it again. It was like I felt the first time I helped with an open heart surgery: like I was doing something powerful and beautiful, that didn't need any justification because it was right in itself."

I had done some shooting, but I'd never felt anything like that. For me, shooting was just a way of getting a job done. When I'd been a soldier and later a cop, weapons had only been the tools of my trade, and tools of last resort, to boot. Now Zee looked at me, and her eyes were dark and glowing and perhaps a little worried.

"Another thing," she said, with a strange smile on her lips. "Manny told me something . . ."

"What?"

"He said I'm a natural."

13

The next morning the first thing I did after breakfast was put aluminum sulfate on my new hydrangea bush. Two ounces mixed with a couple of gallons of water every couple of weeks was going to turn its flowers into the deep blue color that I prefer hydrangeas to be. Or so the aluminum sulfate package said.

Zee had gone off to work, leaving her pistol at home. She had met my objections to this idea by explaining, one, that she didn't like the lump it made in the waistband of her uniform; two, that she wasn't going to wear sloppier uniforms just so her hardware didn't show; and three, that just because it seemed that she was a natural pistoleer who could pop targets with either hand, she still had no intention of shooting any human beings, not even hooded hoods from Boston.

I was putting away my watering can when the phone rang. For not the first time I wondered if I might not be smart to get one of those portable phones you can take out to the garden with you. I made the run to the house. It was Toni Begay.

"Hi," she said. "You wanted to meet my mom. Well, today's the day, if you're free. We're going for a walk together after lunch. My uncle Bill will be there, too. As a matter of fact, why don't you come up before noon, and we'll have lunch together?"

"I'll bring the beer. Eleven-thirty or so?"

"See you then."

I wondered if I should take my old police revolver with me. The idea made me feel silly, but if I really thought Zee should carry, maybe I should do it myself. I ended up putting the gun into a paper bag, and putting the bag under the seat of the Land Cruiser. While I drove to Al's Package Store for a couple of sixes of Molson, then went on up to Gay Head, I thought about the Marcus case.

There is an operating principle in criminal affairs: Often the person you think is the most likely suspect actually did it. Not always, but often enough. Thus, experience has taught cops to always look first at friends and family when somebody gets beat up or robbed or raped or killed. They know that the most dangerous people in our lives are not strangers or muggers or hired killers or professional criminals; they're the people we live with or hang around with. The people we most trust.

Once they know that kin and comrades aren't the bad guys, cops look at the next most obvious suspects: avowed enemies of the victim. If someone says he's going to kill you, and then you end up dead, the cops are going to want to talk to the guy who threatened to do the job.

Thus, it was logical for me to talk with Linda Vanderbeck, who was apparently open in her hostility to Marcus. And even if it turned out that Linda had nothing to do with the shooting, it was a pretty sure thing that she had allies who might be even madder than she was, and who actually might have done the deed. Through her, I might find the actual shootist.

Probably not.

But maybe.

Before meeting her, though, I'd stop at the Marcus estate, and ask the inheritance question.

Turning into Marcus's driveway, I was impressed once again by how innocuous an entrance it was to so palatial an estate. No one who didn't know where the driveway eventually led could guess the truth from the narrow lane and battered Gubatose mailbox. Nifty.

Many of the island's largest houses lay at the ends of such nondescript roads, and their owners, who like Luciano Marcus placed high value on privacy, made sure that their driveways were never improved enough to catch the eyes of tour bus drivers or vacationers curious about the lives of the rich and famous. On Martha's Vineyard, the rich and famous preferred to be unseen, except by each other.

I drove up to the house past a groundskeeper who this time looked at me without a frown before taking his transmitter from his pocket and notifying the house of my impending arrival.

Thomas Decker met me at the door and took me up to the veranda, where Luciano Marcus put aside his book and rose to meet me.

"You have news, Mr. Jackson?"

"Not much, but it's interesting." I told him about the shotgun having been stolen from John Dings, and of my visit with his wife.

He listened, expressionless, then said: "So the gun was an island gun. What do you make of that?"

"It makes it more likely that there's an island connection. It also makes it more important that you get a professional investigator to work here on the Vineyard."

"You may be right," he agreed. "If I decide to do that, I'll let you know. Meanwhile, what can I do for you?"

I thought he knew what he could do for me. "May I be frank?"

"I prefer it."

"All right." I went over the theory that family, friends, and announced enemies are usually the causes of our troubles, and that family came first, because even if you didn't have any friends, you almost always had family. "And what I really want to know," I concluded, "is who profits if something happens to you. Who benefits."

He gave a small smile. "Yeah. That cherchez la loot bit. Thomas told me about that. That's cute. I never heard that one before."

"The old money trail theory," I said.

He nodded. "And you want to know who'd get rich if I get dead."

"Yes."

"Like Thomas here."

I looked at Decker. "Maybe. I don't know. Is Thomas going to inherit enough to make him want you dead? But I'll tell you: I might make an exception for Thomas. I saw how he acted in Boston. I don't think he would have tried to get between you and the shooter if he'd been the one who hired him for the job."

A thin smile flickered across Decker's face. "Thanks. I think."

I kept looking at him. "Of course, you might have just been pretending to get in front of the shotgun. Maybe you were going to wait until the kid took out Luciano and then you were going to take out the kid so he couldn't finger you as the mastermind."

Decker's little smile got smaller. "What a clever guy I am to have thought of that. Who would have suspected me?"

"Afterward, probably nobody. Since the shootist messed up, I'll bet that it crossed your boss's mind. I know it crossed mine."

"A rather Byzantine theory, Mr. Jackson." Decker didn't look at Marcus.

"Too Byzantine for me," I said. "My experience with crime is that it's usually pretty straightforward. Somebody wants you hurt, they hurt you right then and there with whatever's available for the job. If he thinks far enough ahead to hire somebody to do the job for him, he stays well away precisely because he doesn't want anybody to know he's involved. As far as I'm concerned, Thomas, you're pretty low on my suspects list. And I don't even know if you're in the will."

"I'm greatly relieved," said Decker, his eyes hard.

"While you're feeling relieved, you should feel relieved that the guy with the gun was an amateur. A pro would have dropped you first, then dropped Luciano after there was nobody around who could shoot back."

I turned back to Luciano Marcus. "What about the other people who work here? Do you trust them all? Do any of them have a reason to want revenge? Disgruntled employees have been doing a lot of killing lately. Have you fired anybody recently, for example? Have there been any disputes over work or wages or anything like that? What about Vinnie, for instance? Could he have been in on this business in Boston?"

Marcus raised his hands. "Come over and sit down, and we'll have some coffee. Thomas and I have gone over all this. We'll tell you whatever we can." He gave Decker a quick look. "Come on, Thomas. Sit down. I think J.W. here was only, like he said, being frank."

"Yeah," said Decker, and I saw that the ice was still in his eyes. I decided that I would not like to go up against him. He was too cool, too professional, not quite as human as I prefer people to be.

Priscilla brought coffee, and Marcus and Decker discussed the staff person by person. Priscilla, her husband, Jonas, Decker, and two of the groundskeepers had been with Marcus for years. The other groundskeepers were islanders who had been employed when the estate was first built, and who went back to their houses when their daily duties were ended. Marcus paid well, and there were no known hostile feelings among the staff.

When they were finished with the staff, they both paused. I pushed on: "What about family? I've seen the file on your businesses. Somebody's going to inherit a lot of money when you die, Luciano."

Luciano tried a joke: "You can talk this way to me and Thomas about family, but don't you try it with Angela! She won't stand for people to think bad things about the family! She'll hit you with a cabbage!" He put a smile on his face.

"Maybe we could start with Vinnie," I said. "He's staff, too, as well as family."

The smile left the old man's face as he spoke of Vinnie. Vinnie was Luciano's oldest grandson, his daughter's eldest, a personable, good-looking lad who loved and was brilliant with cars, was fond of girls and spending money, but, frankly speaking, probably not destined for work requiring lofty intellectual accomplishment.

"Not a bad boy," said Marcus. He paused and looked at Decker. "Wouldn't you agree, Thomas?"

Decker looked back at him and then at me. "Luciano has influence with UMass Boston, and got Vinnie admitted there. Vinnie was a party guy, and flunked out after one semester. Then he met people outside of college, and began to make his mother unhappy, so Luciano brought him down here. To separate him from those, ah, companions, you understand. He's not what you call happier here, but he's out of trouble and he has fun when the college girls come home for the summer."

"What sort of things did he do that made his mother unhappy?" I asked.

Decker made a small gesture. "The sort of things young guys do when they have time on their hands. Misdemeanors. Nothing serious." He paused and I waited. He looked at Luciano and shrugged. "Vinnie always needs more money that he has, so he began to run numbers that semester he was at college. Nothing big, you know, but big enough to get him into a little trouble with some people when he couldn't come up with money he owed them. Luciano bailed him out.

"Then Vinnie and a couple of his friends stole a car and got caught. Maybe it wasn't the first car they stole. It was very embarrassing to the family. Luciano arranged for the owners of the car to drop charges, and brought Vinnie down here to the island."

"Who were the two friends?"

"Just a couple of kids. A guy named Benny White and a kid they called Roger the Dodger. Benny was another UMass drop-out."

"Were charges dropped for the other two lads as well?"

"As far as I know."

"And now Vinnie's nose is clean."

"Yeah."

"And he's grateful to his grandfather."

Decker looked at me. "What do you mean?"

"I don't know what I mean. But when I first came up here, Vinnie called his grandmother Grandma, and he called his grandfather boss. I wondered why."

Luciano leaned forward. The corner of his mouth was

turned up. "I think I can tell you why. Angela slips him money, and I give him work to do. Vinnie likes her money more than my work. She spoils him, no matter what I say. Vinnie still has some growing up to do."

"And he's doing it?"

He chopped air with his hand. "He's not a bad boy. He's just lazy and young for his age."

"What about the rest of the family?"

Luciano clearly felt on solider ground with the rest of the family. I was assured that all other members of the family, the sons and the daughter in particular, were stable people, and all were profiting from his business interests, which, in fact, the boys were taking over, with Luciano's blessing. It was inconceivable to Luciano that any of them would hire someone to kill him.

Luciano seemed tired. He looked at Decker. "They don't have to do any of the stuff I did when I was young like them. They're all on the up and up, isn't that right, Thomas? No rough stuff at all."

"That's right," said Decker. His eyes flicked from Luciano to me. "I think that's enough family talk for now. You have any other questions, you come back and talk to me later."

It had probably been inconceivable to Abel that Cain would do him in, but I didn't offer that thought to Luciano and Decker. Instead, I asked for the addresses and telephone numbers of Thornberry Security, up in Boston, and Aristotle Socarides, over on the cape. When I got them, I said I'd stay in touch, and drove to Joe and Toni Begay's house.

I arrived at eleven-thirty, on the dot, and the two Begays were waiting in the yard.

"Get back in," said Toni Begay, as I stepped out of the

Land Cruiser. "We'll go with you. We're going to eat at Uncle Bill's house."

Her husband put a picnic hamper in the backseat, and he and she climbed in beside me.

"No need to take two cars," said Begay. He popped three bottles and gave a Molson to each of us. "Warm day."

"They call Uncle Bill a shaman," said Toni Begay. "But to me he's just Uncle Bill. He just got back to the island after being away a long time. Out West somewhere. I don't know just where." She looked up at her husband. "Hey, maybe he was out there in your country, on the reservation. Did you ever run into Uncle Bill out there?"

"If I'd run into Bill Vanderbeck, I'd have remembered," said Begay. "I haven't been out there too much of the time in the past few years myself, so he could have been there and I wouldn't have met him."

I wondered where Begay had been, if he hadn't been on the reservation.

"You'll like Uncle Bill," said Toni Begay to me. "I'm taking him a dream catcher." She showed me a small circle made of bent willow. There was a woven net inside it, and it was decorated with feathers, leather thongs, and tiny shells. "These catch the bad dreams before they get to the sleeper," she said. "They're really part of Oneida mythology, but since I'm making them, they're also genuine Wampanoag craftsmanship, and I'm going to sell them at the shop. I think a shaman might like a dream catcher."

"I didn't know we still had shamans," I said.

"I've seen some," said Begay. "Down in some of those countries south of Mexico. Or at least people said they were shamans. You find them when you get far enough away from the cities. The farther you go, the more there are. You could probably find them in the cities, too, if you knew where to look." He smiled down at his wife. "But I didn't know they had them on Martha's Vineyard."

"Well," she said, "we have one, at least."

"I thought you were supposed to be a true-blue Christian," said Begay, good-naturedly. "I doubt if Father What's-his-name who married us would approve of you believing in medicine men who can influence the spirits. The good father is a twentieth-century priest, not a medieval one. I doubt if he even believes in spirits."

"When I was a little girl," said Toni Begay, "my sister and I used to go visit Uncle Bill. We'd go to his house and it would seem like nobody was there. Then, all of a sudden, there would be Uncle Bill. We used to say that he could make himself invisible. He made us laugh, anyway. I don't know if he can influence the spirits, and I don't even know if he's really a shaman. But some people say he is, and I know that he's my favorite uncle."

Uncle Bill lived down off Lighthouse Road, toward Lobsterville, at the end of a sandy driveway to the right that led through trees and scrub. The house was an old but well-maintained farmhouse. It had weathered gray cedar shingles and was trimmed with gray deck paint. Behind it was a small barn that now served as a garage. There was an elderly car parked in the yard, and beyond it was a good-sized vegetable garden, which was well hoed and weeded. At the moment, it was being watered by a sprinkler.

I parked in front of the house, and we got out and went up to the door. Toni knocked, then knocked again. There was no answer. We walked around to the back of the house. There was no one in the garden, either.

"Hello, Uncle Bill!" Toni called. Her voice seemed to disappear into a void.

We looked around. No one was in sight.

"Well, his car's here, so he can't be too far away," said Toni. She called again.

A voice behind us said, "Hello, Toni, my dear. How good to see you."

I barely kept myself from jumping, and was interested to note Joe Begay's right hand flash toward his left side, under his arm, then pause and fall back. I felt a shiver go up my spine.

. We turned and I saw a man standing where, I could have sworn, no man had been only seconds before. He was a man of indeterminate age, somewhere over fifty, I guessed. Or was he younger? I suddenly wasn't sure. He had a head of thick, black hair that was touched with gray, and he wore jeans and a short-sleeved shirt bearing the logo of the New England Patriots. He was smiling at his niece.

"Hi," said Toni. "I knew you had to be here somewhere."

Uncle Bill nodded and gestured vaguely toward the trees behind him. "I was out there when I heard you drive in. Come inside and get something cool. Ah, I see you've brought lunch and your own beer. Fine, we should have plenty for all." He put out his hand to Begay. "Hello, Joe. Good to see you again." Then he looked at me, and again put out his hand. "Hello. I'm Bill Vanderbeck."

"J. W. Jackson."

His hand was brown and rough. "I remember seeing you up at the Marcus place," said Uncle Bill, with a smile. "You were looking at Joe and Toni here, while they were supposedly birding down by Squibnocket."

I suddenly remembered the flight of birds that had flown from the bush halfway down the hill.

"I didn't see you," I said. "But I saw the birds."

His smile grew wider. "Some people used to say that I could walk through walls, but it was never true. Come on in."

We followed the shaman into his house.

— 14 —

The inside of Vanderbeck's house was as commonplace as
the outside. I had somehow expected something unusual,
something more shamanlike, whatever that might be.
Maybe a mandala on the wall, or an African mask, or even
one of those sand paintings that the tourists buy out
West. Maybe a copy of some cabalistic tome lying open on
a table. Instead, the inside of the house was just slightly
shabby, ordinary New England. There was a fireplace,
there were comfortable pieces of furniture that weren't
particularly old or particularly new, there were worn
throw rugs of traditional design and size—none of them
Navajo. The kitchen was the usual sort, housing a stove,
sink, refrigerator, counters, and shelves. Maybe the
shaman stuff was in some other room.

"Look around while Toni and I get the food on the
table," said Vanderbeck, seeming to read my mind.

Begay grunted, and he and I wandered through the
house, our hands in our pockets. Besides the kitchen
and living room, there was a small dining room, a bath-
room with a claw-footed tub, and what might once have
been a nursery but was now a small sunroom with a large
window overlooking the vegetable garden. A stairway
led down to a basement and another led up to what I
supposed were bedrooms (and maybe the room with the
shaman stuff in it; the pentangle on the floor, or whatever). We decided not to go down or up, but instead

strolled back into the living room and found Toni and her uncle already plunked down in easy chairs and sucking on bottles of Molson.

"Nice place," I said, sitting down.

"Been in the family for a hundred and fifty years or so," said Vanderbeck. "When I go, Toni here gets it. Good place for kids. Mine are all grown up and gone away, but maybe these two will hatch some."

Toni smiled at this idea, and Begay smiled, too.

"I see you had a nursery," I said.

"Ah," said Vanderbeck. "You noticed that, did you? Yeah, that's what that sunroom was. The kids' room, when they were little. We'd put them in there with their toys and blankets, and they'd play or sleep till they got tired of it. How'd you know it was the nursery?"

"I don't know," I said, my mind racing. How *had* I known?

"Maybe he's just intuitive," said Toni to her uncle.

I didn't think of myself as intuitive. I preferred to think of myself as being very rational and cool-headed, and only believing things when I had enough evidence. But maybe Toni was right, maybe I was intuitive sometimes. Probably everybody is. For sure, I couldn't figure out why I'd thought the nursery was a nursery.

"He just got married," said Begay. "Maybe he has babies on his mind."

"There are worse things than that to have on your mind," said Vanderbeck. He finished his beer. "Let's eat."

We followed him into the kitchen, got more beer, and sat down to sandwiches and chips. Vanderbeck looked at Begay.

"Toni tells me you've decided to stay here on the island," he said. "Long way from the res."

"Yes, sir," said Begay. "In more ways that one."

"Call me Bill," said Vanderbeck. "I'm not a sir."

"Yes, sir," said Begay. Everybody laughed.

"The fishing business is tough," said Bill.

Begay chewed for a while, then swallowed. "How'd you know I was going into the fishing business?"

Bill waved a vague hand. "No secret. People talk. Lotta guys going out of business, others coming in. You know anything about pot fishing?"

"Buddy Malone's going to show me the ropes," said Begay. "I have some savings to keep us going if we need it. If I have to, I can always go back to my old job, and I can do it living here as well as I can living anywhere else, as long as I'm willing to travel."

"He was a rep," explained Toni. "He represented different people and products, and got the ones who wanted things together with the people who could produce them, and vice versa."

"Ah," said Vanderbeck. "A middleman."

"That's it," said Begay. "You need gidgets, I'd put you in touch with a gidget maker. For a fee, of course."

"Any particular kind of gidgets?" asked Vanderbeck. "Did you specialize?"

Begay drank some beer. I had the impression that he did that to give himself a moment to get his story together in more detail. "No specialization," he said. "The process is the same no matter what the gidget. Firm I worked for handles all sorts of stuff, here and abroad. Anytime a ship goes from one port to another, there's a chance that some of their gidgets are on it."

"Big outfit, then?"

Begay had some chips. "Medium size," he said. "Big enough to keep busy. They have a lot of connections, and they do a good job, so they get as much business as they can handle. It's not very romantic work, but there's money to be made."

"I'd think that you'd probably end up dealing with some kinds of things more than others," said Toni's uncle Bill.

"Well, I guess we probably move more of some kinds of stuff than others. We handle a lot of kitchen appliances and farm machinery, for instance. And industrial piping. Valves and joints and that sort of thing. I didn't know much about a lot of the stuff. I just got the interested parties together."

"Toni says you were good at your work."

"Well, I guess so. I haven't missed any meals yet anyway."

"I'm sure she's right. Otherwise you wouldn't be going fishing."

Begay smiled. "How do you figure that?"

"Theory of Occupational Compensation," said Vanderbeck.

I looked at Vanderbeck's eyes and wasn't sure whether I saw laughter or solemnity.

"I'm afraid I never heard of that one," said Begay.

"Not surprising," said Uncle Bill Vanderbeck. "It's my private, unpublished theory. Vanderbeck's Theory of Occupational Compensation. Some day I'll write it down and send it to somebody to publish, so I can die knowing that I made a real contribution to social science.

"What this theory does is explain why people enter professions, and why some people stay in them and others leave. The first part of the theory says that each person enters a profession that forces him to compensate for his primary sense of inadequacy. For instance, when you first go to college it doesn't take you any time at all to figure that psychology majors are all a little wackier than other students, or at least are afraid that they are. They're more nervous and spooky and obnoxious. You remember?" He looked now at Begay.

"I remember," said Begay, and so did I.

"That's right. Those people all wanted to be the future shrinks of America to compensate for their fear that they themselves were crazy. You also noticed that the college jocks were flexing their muscles to compensate for their fears that they weren't manly enough, and the ROTC guys were going through all that military stuff to compensate for their fears that they were afraid of combat. You get the picture."

I got it. "You mean the same thing's true right across the board, in college: the English majors are all worried about not being literate enough, the Business majors are all scared stiff about being economic failures, the Social Work people are afraid they're not humane enough, and all like that?"

"That's it. And after I noticed all that in college, I took a look at the professions people enter, and by God the same rules apply.

"But there's more: just because a person feels inadequate doesn't mean that he actually is inadequate. When you enter a profession you discover one of two things: that, in fact, you are inadequate, in which case you stay in the profession, continuing to compensate; or that, in fact, you're not inadequate at all, and don't have to compensate, in which case you leave the profession." He laughed.

Begay nodded. "Which explains why all professions are filled up with inadequate people."

"Highway engineers are a good example," said Toni.

"Okay," I said, "but what happens when you leave your profession?" I had left a few myself, after all.

Uncle Bill handed me another beer. "Well, what you do then is enter another profession that forces you to compensate for your secondary sense of inadequacy. We all have more than one sense of inadequacy."

Begay was smiling. "And if your new profession proves to you that you really are inadequate, you stay; but if you find out that you can do it, you leave the second profession and enter a third. Right?"

"Etcetera, etcetera. It happens every time." Uncle Bill looked at Begay. "And now you know why I said you were probably good at your business."

Begay thought back, and remembered. "Because if I wasn't, I'd still be doing it?"

"Right." Vanderbeck nodded.

I looked at him. "And what do you do?" I asked with an impulsiveness that surprised me. "What's your profession?"

The shaman smiled at me. "I'm retired. I don't do anything. I'm like you."

How had he known that I didn't have a regular job? I felt frustrated by him, and the frustration drove another question out of my mouth.

"What were you doing there on Luciano Marcus's land?"

"Oh," said the shaman. "I go by to look things over now and then. I take it that you're working for Luciano Marcus for the time being. Well, I'm working for Linda, my sister-in-law, for the time being. Next time you see your boss, tell him I'll be along for a talk one of these days. We should try to get this cranberry bog business settled out of court, if we can."

"Marcus has men all over the grounds. How come nobody saw you and stopped you?"

The shaman drank his beer. "Beats me," he said. "I've never understood why people ignore me as much as they do. Say, Toni, I think it's time for us to meet your mother for that walk. Let's get going."

Joe Begay and I exchanged looks, got up, and followed his wife and her uncle out of the house. As we did, I said, "Someday maybe you'll tell me what you used to do when you weren't arranging for gidget sales."

"Maybe," he said. "But not right now."

15

We met Linda Vanderbeck back at the Begays' house. I had seen her picture more than once in the *Gazette*, accompanying the ongoing stories about the Wampanoags' internal conflicts and efforts to influence Gay Head politics. She was an attractive woman, but not one who apparently tried to be. And she was full of vim. Her skin was tawny and her hair was long and black and tied back with a silver clasp that looked Southwestern to me, Navajo, maybe, or Zuni or Hopi. I could never remember which designs were from which people out there.

She had a firm handshake. "Toni says you wanted to meet me. We can walk and talk." An elderly man came out of the house, followed by a younger version of Toni Begay. "This is my father, Charlie Pierce. Dad, this is Mr. Jackson, from Edgartown."

"Howdy," said Charlie Pierce, shaking my hand. He barely filled up his clothes, and looked as if he were made out of leather. His hair was gray, but his eyes were bright.

"Call me J.W." I said.

"All right, J.W. You call me Charlie."

"And this is my daughter Maggie."

"Hi," said Maggie. "We met at the wedding. Zee's beautiful! You're a lucky man."

"Yes."

Charlie took a stick that was leaning against the house. "Where we walking today, Linda?"

"Along the beach," said Linda, and we set off along a path leading there. I fell in beside her. She glanced up at me. "Well, what can I do for you, Mr. Jackson?"

"Call me J.W. Everybody does."

"What can I do for you, J.W.?"

"So you won't think I'm sneaking up on you, I'll do the first telling. I just took a job with Luciano Marcus."

She didn't quite miss a step, but she almost did. "Go on."

I told her about the incident in Boston, about the job Marcus had offered, and about the shotgun being stolen from John Dings.

"So I'm looking for anything that might help me figure out who done it," I said.

"And you figure it was some Indian," she said with a steely voice.

"I don't figure anything yet. But you and Marcus haven't exactly been hugging and kissing lately."

We came out onto the beach. "I don't like this," said Linda Vanderbeck. "I don't like being called a killer, or even being suspected of being one, and I don't like anyone who even thinks such things. I don't think I have any more to say to you. I think you should get away from me!"

But I didn't leave. Instead, I said: "I've seen the names some of your rival Wampanoags have called you in the letters they write to the *Gazette*. Compared to them, being a mere murder suspect seems pretty tame. You aren't just being tender-skinned about this because I'm not a member of the tribe, are you?"

"Jesus Christ! The old reverse racism argument. No, I'd feel the same way if you were a full-blooded Wampanoag."

"Well, I'm not a full-blooded Wampanoag or a full-blooded anything else, and I'm not calling you a murderer. Not yet. What I see in you is somebody with a motive, and somebody who probably knows other people who might be glad to see Marcus dead. None of that means anything yet, but all of it might mean something."

"Have you got a badge of some kind, Mr. Jackson?"

"No."

"Then why should I talk to you?"

"So some guy with a badge doesn't?"

"Bah!"

We were approaching the foot of the many-colored clay cliffs of Gay Head, the westernmost point of Martha's Vineyard. A century before, in a winter storm, the *City of Columbus*, running between New York and Boston, had wrecked on Devil's Bridge and spewed its human cargo along all the beaches of western Martha's Vineyard. Linda Vanderbeck's forefathers and many another Gay Header had exhausted themselves dragging the icy corpses, gear, and the occasional rare survivor out of the surf in the hours after that fabled wreck.

But today was another sky blue day, with no suggestion of a brewing storm except in Linda's face and voice.

"We don't have any killers in Gay Head. Our fight with Marcus is about the law. He's got land that belongs to my people, and we want it back. We'll beat him in the courts, if we have to. We don't need to shoot him. Besides, he's an old man, and he's got a bad heart. He could die any time. It would be stupid to shoot him, and we're not stupid."

"Even Gay Head has its stupid people," I said. "Its hotheads. Its stupid hotheads."

She gave a bitter smile. "Yeah. Some of them wrote those letters you talked about. You should go talk to them, not to me."

"But some of the hotheads in the tribe are with you on this issue. Can you give me the names of any people I might talk to?"

She shook her head. "You won't get any names from me. I don't know any murderers."

"Most of us probably don't, but none of us really knows. Almost every time a killer gets nailed, you can find some neighbors and family members who say he was a real nice guy, and that they couldn't be more surprised."

"If you find a killer in Gay Head, I couldn't be more surprised. Your would-be killer up in Boston ran away. What I do, I do in the open. I don't think I can help you, Mr. Jackson." She paused and her father and Bill Vanderbeck came up to us.

"I like being under these cliffs," Bill Vanderbeck said to me, as we began walking again. "When I was a kid, my friends and I used come down to fish or take mud baths made out of the clay." He smiled at his sister-in-law. "Now Linda and her friends frown on the mud baths"

"They're harmful to the cliffs," snapped Linda.

His smile was unchanged. "But people still sneak down here and take them anyway. I'm sort of on their side."

Charlie Pierce nodded and muttered something that caused his daughter to give him an annoyed look. Then she turned back to her brother-in-law.

"You always were obstinate," she said. "Worse than your brother, when he was alive, and he was stubborn as a mule."

"You were a well-matched team," said Bill, agreeably. "Likes attract, they say." He looked out to sea.

"I have to be stubborn," she said. "If I wasn't, the Luciano Marcuses of this world would take everything our people own. You don't give a damn about what's good for the tribe."

"Maybe I'm just not as sure as you are about what that is."

"You can go places other people can't go. You can help us."

"Maybe."

"Did you get a look at the place, like I asked?"

Vanderbeck nodded. "I did."

She was impatient. "And?"

"Fence all around the estate. Six men working the grounds. I'd say they were sort of combined grounds-keepers and security people. Marcus likes his privacy, like you said. One road in. Gate. NO TRESPASSING signs. Some sort of camera pointed at the driveway. Up in a tree. Two more cameras farther along, so anybody driving in can be seen. If anybody is watching the screens, that is, and somebody probably is, part of the time, at least. Dogs let loose at night.

"I didn't go up to the house, so I don't know about that. Lots of walking paths. Flowers. Well-maintained place. Looks good."

"And nobody saw you?"

"Nobody stopped me, anyway."

"You've seen the maps. What do you think?"

"Joe and I have both looked at them. The place lies on the land you thought it did. On what they called Indian Land a long time back. The house in what one map calls Gay Head Farm. The cranberry bog and most of the blueberries aren't on that hunk of land."

"It's all on Indian Land," said Linda. "Sacred land!"

Charlie Pierce gave a disapproving grunt, and swung at a clod of clay with his walking stick. "Sacred land, my eye! Nothing sacred about it. Just a ploy so some people can try to get their hands on land that ain't theirs."

Vanderbeck's face showed no expression, but Linda's brows lowered. "Come on, Dad, you know as well as I do that we got robbed by the white men, and cheated out of that land. We intend to get it back for the tribe."

"I've said it before, and I'll say it again," said her father. "A lot of people up here in Gay Head didn't care if they was Wampanoags or not, until there was money in it. Till they found out they could get land and money by being Indians, they just wanted to be like everybody else. I don't think much of what that fella I met, that Manny Fonseca fella lives down there in Edgartown, used to call Professional Indians. Far as I'm concerned, all this stuff about the Wampanoags being a federally recognized tribe is just a way to get into the government's pocket and into some of our neighbors' pockets to boot."

"Dad, you're wrong as a bent nail. The Native Americans have got to fight for what's theirs, and I plan to be right there at the front of things while we do it!"

"And that's another thing," said her father. "This Native American stuff. Bunch of bullshit, you'll pardon my saying, if you ask me. Time was people didn't even want to be called Indians unless they had to be. Now Indian ain't good enough. An insult, they say. According to them damned Harvard Indians and their like, anyway. Rather be called the same as . . . what's that guy's name, Bill?"

"Amerigo Vespucci," said Bill Vanderbeck.

"That's the guy. Rather be named after some Italian sailor than be called Indians. Don't make any sense to me, daughter, nor to you, either, you think about it."

"Dad, I don't care if you call yourself an Indian or a Native American . . ."

"You won't hear me calling myself that!"

". . . or whatever. But you're a Wampanoag, whatever you call yourself."

The old man was as stubborn as his daughter. "You call yourself a Wampanoag, Bill? You call yourself a Native American?"

"I call myself a human being," said Vanderbeck, dodging the bullet.

The old man was on a roll. "And what does your son-in-law, Joe Begay, call himself, Linda? You ever catch him calling himself a federally recognized Native American or anything like that?"

Linda gave a great sigh. "I never asked him what he calls himself, Dad. The point is that . . ."

"The point is," said Charlie, "that Joe Begay never called himself any such thing. What'd he say he was? Part Navajo, part Hopi, and part everybody else that passed through? Half them people out there never heard of this Native Americans nonsense."

"The point is," said Linda, her voice rising, "that Luciano Marcus claims to own land that belongs to the Wampanoag people, and I intend to get it back. That cranberry bog is sacred and should be controlled by the tribe! And you know that, Dad, as well as anybody, so stop giving me a hard time. It's bad enough having the whites against us. We don't need to be fighting among ourselves."

"Hey," said Charlie cheerfully, pointing with his cane. "There's an osprey up there, over the cliffs. Pretty, ain't it."

I had been watching the hawk and feeling my heart stir for the brute beauty and valour and act, the falcon rung upon the rein of a wimpling wing in his ecstasy, rebuffing the wind, striding over the air.

I glanced down at Linda. She was looking along the beach and frowning as she saw some young people sitting in a bath of mud and seeming to have an enjoyable time. Vanderbeck smiled at her, and I saw some special fondness in his look. She was a tigress, burning bright. Did he love her? Had he loved her before his brother had married her, and did he still, in these years of her widowhood, after his own wife had passed on and left his house full of echoes?

Maggie Vanderbeck, also seeing the mud bathers ahead of us, trotted up and took her mother's arm, saying firmly: "Come on, Mom. Let's walk back. Otherwise you'll just get all worked up about those people and probably get in an argument with them."

Linda shook her arm free. "Well, they shouldn't be there."

"You're not a policeman, Mom. Help me out here, Uncle Bill."

"Like I say, I used to take mud baths myself," said Bill.

"Me, too," said Charlie Pierce, cheerfully.

"There," said Maggie. "You're outnumbered, Mom. Let's go back."

Linda shook her head. "No wonder I'm having such a hard time getting anywhere. Even my own family gives me grief." But with a last glance at the mud bathers, she turned, and we walked back whence we'd come.

Maggie Vanderbeck walked beside me. "Did you know that I've dated a guy who works for Luciano Marcus? Vinnie Cicilio. Do you know him? I met him up at UMass before he dropped out and came to work down here. Mom doesn't approve of him, as you might guess."

I said, "When you're old enough to go to college, you're supposed to be old enough to decide for yourself who you'll date."

She grinned. "That's the theory, all right. But Mom doesn't agree with it. She thinks anybody working for Luciano Marcus is off-limits."

"I hear that Vinnie isn't an upcoming Einstein, but that you're going to be a doctor. I take it then that your relationship isn't an intellectual one."

She laughed. "A marriage of true minds? No, not that. Vinnie isn't really island material, either. Some friends in Edgartown took him clamming down at the Eel Pond, but he didn't like digging in the mud. And Jean Dings talked her dad into taking him duck hunting once last fall, but Vinnie didn't like freezing out there in the blind. He doesn't like to fish, because he doesn't like to take them off the hook, and he doesn't even like mud baths here at the cliffs. What he really wants is to be back in the city."

"Doesn't sound like an ideal catch for an island girl."

"Hey, he's a good date. He's a great dancer, and he likes women to like him, so he works hard at doing what they want, and isn't afraid to spend some money, which is more than you can say for a lot of guys."

Including me. "Get 'em young and raise 'em the way you want them to be," I said.

She scuffed at the sand with her bare foot. "Like you say, he's no Einstein, but he'll open the door for the girl he's with. He likes me and my friends, and he's glad when we get back home from college, so we can all get together." She looked up at me, and smiled. "He's not somebody I plan to marry or get serious with, but he's a good date. If he liked spending money a little less and working for it a little more, he might be a catch for some girl."

I wondered how Vinnie felt about her. And I wondered how the young Gay Head cop felt about her and Vinnie. Maggie did not seem to be lacking for men, and I could see why. She was a young beauty. If I were fifteen years younger and had never seen Zee, I might make a play for her myself. As it was, I didn't feel quite like her father, but I did feel like, maybe, a big brother.

"So you and Vinnie aren't what they call an item, then?"

She laughed again. "No!"

"How about that young cop who's got the hots for you?"

"How'd you know about him?"

I created a conspiratorial voice. "I have my sources."

"Well, I'll tell you one thing, at least: He's a Wampanoag, so Mom doesn't give me any grief about him at all." She grinned up at me, and I had to smile back. Some women are born knowing how to juggle several men at once. It was a skill few of them declined to employ, and who could blame them for that.

I wondered if I was being juggled by Linda Vanderbeck.

16

On Tuesday, a morning of dim sun and an afternoon of warm drizzle, Zee finished her stint on the day shift. This gave her Wednesday off before she began the graveyard shift that night. The latter was an unfortunate name for a hospital working period, I suggested, not for the first time. Zee, who was used to jokes about grave matters, grave issues, and such, and who had, during the years we had known each other, been obliged to listen to most of my observations on life more than once, rewarded my wit with a small wifely smile.

"Let's go fishing in the morning," she said. "Just in case there are still some blues around. They'll be gone before long. Did you notice we have a leak in the porch ceiling?"

"Ancient wisdom has it that you can't fix a leak while it's raining, and you don't need to when it's not."

"We can fix this one when we get home from slaughtering the bluefish."

"You're on."

I was lying on the living room couch, reading a book. She swung a leg over me and knelt on my chest. "Now I am," she said, taking the book and dropping it on the floor.

The next morning, early, we drove to Edgartown, passed through empty streets down to Collins Beach, unchained the dinghy, and rowed out to the *Shirley J*. The rain had blown away in the night, the wind was now next to nothing, and the waterfront was barely coming awake. Out in the harbor, the yachts swung at their moorings, quiet but for the occasional sound of a halyard slapping against a mast. A few pot fishermen were busy on the docks, getting ready to head out into Nantucket Sound. It was already promising to be a hot and muggy day.

I cranked up the outboard, Zee loosed the bowline and hung it on the stake, and we motored out of the harbor past the lighthouse. To our right, the shore of Chappaquiddick curved toward the east.

Zee slid off the cabin into the cockpit, and stood with one hand on the crutched boom, a slim figure garbed in shorts, a shirt knotted around her belly, and a kerchief over her hair, as was her wont when she went fishing. She looked around, letting her eyes sweep the shore and sea. She looked happy.

At the Cape Pogue Gut, I put the boat's nose on the beach, and we got out with our rods. A pickup was coming along the inside of the elbow, bringing a fisherman or two to the gut, after the long drive from Wasque. A sure sign that fish were scarce all along East Beach.

But there were some at the Cape Pogue Gut, and Zee had one of them ashore when the pickup arrived, bearing Iowa and Walter.

Either would go fishing any time, any place, for whatever kind of fish were there. They fished for blues, bass, Spanish mackerel, and bonito; they fished for herring, cod, flounder, and scup; they fished for sharks; when there was ice on the ponds, they cut holes in it and fished; they jigged for squid. When there were no finny fish to catch, they raked for quahogs; they dug for clams; they tonged for oysters; and they scraped mussels off rocks and mud banks. Sometimes, for variety, if they could bum a ride, they would go out with the swordfish-ermen, or the conch fishermen, or the lobstermen. If it lived in the water, they hunted it.

"My God!" shouted Iowa, climbing out and glaring at Zee, as she cut the throat of her nice five-pound blue. "What are you doing here, woman? You're supposed to be home in the kitchen, not out here catching men's fish! Dad-blamed women getting uppitier and uppitier every day! Pretty soon there won't be any place left for a man to be alone!"

"Now, now," said Zee. "What would your wife say if she heard you coming on to me like that? Especially since I'm a married woman now."

"To hell with your husband," said Iowa. "He doesn't deserve you." They met and exchanged hugs, and he got his rod off the roof rack. "You leave us any fish?"

"Jeff's got one on."

"Well, if he's got one on, it means anybody can catch one. And look at that! While I gab with you, Walter's on already! Everybody's on but me!"

He hustled down to the water's edge and made his cast.

The fish were not there long, but at least there were fish. After they were gone, and the sun was climbing over the eastern clouds, we all stood and drank coffee beside Iowa's pickup.

To the west, sailboats and party fishing boats were beginning to motor out of Edgartown harbor and pass by us to the north. We watched Albert Enos, alone on the *Lucky Lil*, go east toward the conching grounds.

"Where's Jimmy?" asked Walter.

"Jimmy got through," I said. The island phrase "got through" is nice because it gives no indication of causality. The person may have been fired or may have quit; all the listener knows is that the person is no longer on the job.

Walter grunted at my news, but clearly was not surprised.

"Took a ride with Albert last week," said Iowa. "Guess there's money to be made in conchs, but you sure have to earn it. Latest thing is the government wanting to cut back on the pots you can have out. If it's not one thing, it's another. No wonder Jimmy Souza went broke, and him not the only one, either."

"Damned shame," said Walter. "Glad I retired before it happened to me. Hey, we're burning daylight. What do you say we switch to lighter tackle and go back over to the Jetties. Maybe some mackerel and bonito have showed up. Just because Dick Dirgins wasn't getting anything there when we came by doesn't mean he's not getting anything now."

"True," said Iowa, finishing his coffee. "So why are we standing here? Let's see what's happening under the lighthouse. We can do that on our way." Iowa emptied his cup, and climbed into the pickup. "You want to come with us, Mrs. Jackson? Hang around with a couple of real he-men instead of this yachtsman here?"

Zee took my arm. "No, I'm going to stay with Jefferson. We have to go home and try to find a leak in our roof."

"What ever happened to romance?" asked Iowa, and he and Walter drove off.

"Two of the good guys," smiled Zee.

Indeed they were.

We were home again well before the morning winds rose enough to hoist a sail. While I filleted the fish for smoking, Zee was up on the roof with a bucket of tar, trying to find and plug the pesky leak. In not too much longer, our work was finished, and Zee came down from the roof.

"The next time it rains, we'll know how well I did."

In the kitchen, we washed off the smells of fish and tar.

"And now the beach awaits," I said.

"I thought you were private investigating, these days."

"I'll private investigate tomorrow. Today, I'd rather be on the beach with you."

"No wonder you don't have a normal job," she said, shaking her head and putting her arms around me. "You can't keep regular hours. Okay, the beach it is. But I have to be home in time to go down to the club later. Manny's meeting me at five-thirty."

I wasn't sure whether I thought that was good or bad. I packed up lunch and beer, put our clamming buckets and gloves in the Land Cruiser, climbed into my bathing suit while Zee donned her red bikini, and we went off to the Norton's Point Beach. It wasn't yet noon, but already the July people were on the shore, topping off their tans for the last time before heading back over the sound to America, just as the pale August people were arriving.

"It's very odd," said Zee, later that afternoon, as she lay in the sun, looking warm and sleek. "I still really don't approve of guns and shooting. In fact, I think that most handguns should be banned, because they're really not good for anything but shooting people. But even while I'm not approving of them, I love to shoot them. And Manny keeps saying that I'm really good."

I understood. Similarly, neither Zee nor I approved of boxing, but we loved to watch a good match, especially in the smaller weights, where the guys have fast hands and can move. Ali was the only heavyweight who could fight like a middleweight. Other big guys might have bombs in their gloves and chins of steel, but none of them had Ali's fast feet and hands or his smarts and grace and humor. Now that we had Zee's little television in the house, we could occasionally see even a journeyman heavyweight bout that held our interest.

"You've got the right stuff," I said to Zee. "You're a born gun moll."

"You know," she said, "I actually think you and Manny may be right about that. I know I have a lot to learn and that if I really want to be good I have to practice all the time, but even being no further along than I am I somehow can pretty much hit what I'm aiming at. I don't know how to explain it. Except, maybe, that it's the feeling you have when you're casting really well. You don't know what's different about that day and your usual days when you may be casting well enough or even very well, but there is a difference. You can get your lure out there farther, and you can get it exactly where you want it, and you absolutely know that if there's a fish there that he's yours. It's like that. And you know what? I can do it with either hand." She actually shivered a little in the hot sun. "It's almost scary," she said.

But not so scary that she and Manny weren't going off to the shooting range again. I had been brooding about that since leaving home, and had decided that I was actually happy for them both. They had formed a bond that could be experienced only by people who shared a rare talent. Helen Fonseca and I might be married to the members of their small society, and might be invited to share their celebrations of their art, but we could never belong to their club because we lacked their talent. Helen and I could shoot, but we would never be shootists.

When the afternoon tide was low enough, we waded

out into Katama Bay, got down on our knees, and dug ourselves a good mess of clams.

As with quahogging, you can go clamming and think about something else at the same time. I thought about what I'd learned and not learned during my inquiries on behalf of Luciano Marcus. As sometimes happens to me, I suspected that I might know something that I didn't know I knew. But, if so, I had no idea what it might be.

Home again, we were well clammed and feeling warm and good. While Zee used the outdoor shower, the one we use three seasons of the year, I drove down to the Sengekontacket boat landing, got a five-gallon bucket full of salt water, and brought it back. I put the clams into it to spit out their sand overnight, and took my turn in the shower. I could hear the pop-pop of firing down at the club. Manny or someone else was already at the range. I looked at my nine-dollar waterproof watch. Almost five-thirty.

Zee came around the corner of the house, carrying her paper bag of shooting stuff.

"Blasting time," I said, drying off naked in the yard.

She paused. "You don't mind, do you?"

It was one of those questions women ask, but men usually don't. I was pretty sure that if I said I did mind, she would cancel the session with Manny.

I put my wet hands on her shoulders and kissed her forehead. "I don't mind," I said.

"Good." I got a kiss back.

She climbed into her little Jeep, and drove away. The Rod and Gun Club was only a few hundred yards from our house through the woods, but the woods were full of poison ivy, thorns, and the grabbing branches of scrub oak, so when we went there we usually drove: up our long sandy driveway, along the Edgartown–Vineyard Haven Road, back down Third or Seventh street to the boulevard and then into the club.

As I was getting supper ready a little later, I heard the sounds of bigger and then smaller guns firing from the range, and guessed that it was Manny with his .45 and Zee with her .380 popping away.

I had just finished setting the table, when I heard a car coming down the driveway. Our driveway is a narrow one, and clearly not a public road. On the other hand, I don't like signs that say "PRIVATE PROPERTY," "NO TRESPASSING," and the like, so sometimes a stranger comes motoring into our yard, discovers his mistake, turns around and leaves. Since Zee and I occasionally work on perfecting our all-over tans in the yard, now and then our visitors encounter sights they perhaps did not expect to see.

Generally, however, things being as they were, the few people who came down our driveway were not strangers at all, but people who knew us and wanted to see us.

Thus, I was not too surprised when a police cruiser came into the yard and turned around. Through the open living room door and the screened porch door beyond it, I saw the chief turn off the cruiser's engine, open the door, and step out. He closed the car door, and put an arm on the top of the car while he looked around and listened to the shooting from the club.

I went out onto the porch. "You on duty, or do you want a beer?" Not to my surprise, he declined the beer. When the chief is in uniform, he will rarely have a drink, so it was safe offering one to him. You got brownie points for free, just for appearing generous.

He came up onto the porch and took a chair. The wind was blowing down the driveway, making the porch the coolest place in Edgartown on this warm July evening. I went into the kitchen and came back out with iced tea. He sipped and nodded his head. "Nice place. Always was, still is. If I owned this place, I'd do like you do: hang out all summer and never go downtown till after Labor Day."

He dug out his pipe and lit up, then waved toward the Rod and Gun Club. "Just down there. Zee and Manny are popping a lot of caps. I'm sort of surprised, knowing Zee."

"Zee is sort of surprised herself," I said.

"She isn't doing too bad."

"So she tells me."

"Just talked with that detective, Gordon Sullivan, up in Boston. They think they've found the car. In a tow company storage lot. Stolen, of course, then abandoned and towed away. Found a box of double-aught shells under the seat. Just like the ones in the gun you took away from the guy."

"Any prints?"

"Too many. The owners, the tow company guys, the cops who finally found it, you name it."

"Our guy was wearing gloves."

"Just our luck."

I told him my theory that the shootist was an amateur, since a pro, having the time to do it, would probably have killed the bodyguard first, then killed Marcus at his leisure.

The chief grunted. "I'll drop that bug into Sullivan's ear, for what it's worth." He glanced around the yard. "Anybody hanging around here? Any odd phone calls? Anything like that?"

"Nothing."

"You see anything of Fred Souza?"

"No. They ever trace that sweatshirt?"

"You have any idea how many places there are in Boston that sell sweatshirts? More than there are tee-shirt shops in Edgartown, even."

"Wow!" I said. "That many?"

He got up. "I'll be on my way." He paused. "How do you feel about Manny teaching Zee to shoot?"

I hesitated. "I approve, on balance. I think too many people have guns, but I want her to know how to use one."

He nodded. "Yeah."

I watched him drive away. Behind me, the guns kept popping down at the Rod and Gun Club range.

Later, in bed, I listened to the sounds of the night: the odd calls of nocturnal creatures, the swish of leaves, the groans of tree limbs rubbing together. One or twice I thought I might be hearing unusual noises in the yard, but when I slipped out of bed for a look, there was no one there.

The next morning, when Zee was home from her graveyard shift and asleep in the bedroom, another car came down our driveway. I didn't recognize this one, or the two guys who got out of it. They were young, bronze-skinned guys with dark eyes and muscular bodies.

"You Jeff Jackson?" the first asked.

I had the garden hose, and was watering the flowers in the boxes on the front fence.

"That's me."

"I have a message for you," he said, coming up to me. "Stay out of Linda Vanderbeck's hair!"

And so saying, he hit me in the jaw with his right hand and followed with his left.

17

Real fights don't look like the ones in the movies. People don't land those spectacular blows that send their opponents through windows or over tables. Real fights are usually sloppy and badly done. And there are no fair ones.

So when the guy hit me on the jaw, he didn't do as good a job as he planned. I saw the punch coming and was moving back when it hit, and his following left went whistling through the air. Still, there were two of them, and two guys can usually beat the crap out of one guy, so I didn't stand my ground.

Instead, I hit the first guy in the eye with the nozzle of the hose I was holding, shot water into the face of the other guy, then dropped the hose, and ran away around the house. They came after me, but I had a good start, and while they were coming round the last corner of the house, back into the driveway, I had the door of the Land Cruiser open and had the paper bag full of .38 in my hands.

As they appeared, so did the pistol.

They stopped, wide-eyed and panting.

"I'm going to tell you something," I said. "It's dangerous to pick fights with people you don't know. It can get you killed. Give me your wallets."

"Our wallets?"

I cocked the revolver. "Your wallets. Toss them over here."

The first guy looked at the second.

"Do it," said the second guy.

They dug into the back pockets of their jeans, and brought out their wallets. They threw them at my feet. I picked them up and looked at the ID's, then tossed them back. They were two guys from Gay Head. Wampanoags on Linda Vanderbeck's side, for sure.

"Pick those up and go home. And keep in mind that I know who you are and where you live. If you give me or mine any more hard times, I'll give it back to you in spades. Does Linda Vanderbeck know about you two coming here?"

They exchanged looks.

"Well, does she? I doubt it."

They exchanged more uneasy glances. Then the first guy said: "No. But we heard about you and what you think. You keep your nose in your own business, not in hers. Not in ours, either."

I let down the hammer of the pistol, and lowered the gun. "You're a pair, you are. If Linda Vanderbeck ever finds out you came down here, she'll have your ears. She doesn't need the likes of you two defending her. Ye gods. Go home and grow up."

"You stay out of Gay Head," said the first guy, braver now that the pistol was pointed at the ground.

I looked at the second guy. "You better have a talk with your friend on the way home. Try to tune him in to planet Earth."

"Come on, Wally," said his friend. "Let's go."

"And don't come back," I said to Wally.

Wally and his friend drove away.

I put the pistol back in its bag and the bag back under the seat of the Land Cruiser.

When my hands stopped trembling, I went in and made phone calls. The first was to detective Gordon R. Sullivan in Boston. He was out, but would call back. Then I called Thornberry Security and asked for Thornberry himself. His cool-voiced secretary wasn't sure he had time to talk with me. I told her to give him my name. She did, and a moment later he was on the phone.

"Mr. Jackson. Have you decided to accept my offer of employment?"

Thornberry and I had left the Boston PD about the same time, one big difference between our departures being that he was retiring as a captain, to organize a private detective agency, and I was retiring on disability, with a bullet parked near my spine.

"Thanks, but no thanks, Jason. I'll stay a civilian. As you no doubt know, I'm working for Luciano Marcus, down here on the island, and I thought I'd touch base with you."

"Mr. Marcus told me he'd hired you. So you are an unlicensed investigator once again, eh? Very well, what base would you prefer to start on?"

I told him about my talks with Linda Vanderbeck, Joe Begay, and Sandy Dings, and about the two Gay Head guys. I gave him their names and addresses. He listened without comment. When I was done, he said: "And what do you want from me?"

"Anything you have. The shotgun is a definite Vineyard tie, so I'm looking for a link between somebody down here and the Boston shooting. I'm looking for motives and opportunities. Check out these two guys, for instance. And there's Thomas Decker. He carries a gun when he and Luciano travel. Luciano says it's because he sometimes has a lot of money on him, but that rings a little hollow with me. Why does Decker really feel a need to carry?"

Thornberry's smooth voice never hesitated. "Mr. Marcus has told you the truth. Many businessmen have bodyguards. Especially these days. And Mr. Marcus does often carry a lot of money. Mr. Decker has been with him for many years."

"I'm going to be talking to a detective named Sullivan," I said. "I'll be asking him the same questions I'm asking you."

"Detective Sullivan and I have talked to one another already. As you know, the confidentiality between our firm and its clients must be firmly maintained, else we'd soon be out of business. Detective Sullivan is not bound by such rules, so perhaps he'll be able to tell you something that I cannot."

I tried again. "What I want to know is whether Marcus has a past that's putting him in harm's way—something shady or maybe even criminal—that's catching up with him."

Thornberry's voice was like melting ice. "I can only tell you that our investigations have revealed no such information."

I decided that if I ever wanted a truly confidential investigation, I would hire Thornberry. His lips were vacuum-sealed. "How about his present business interests?" I asked. "Has he done anything to anyone lately that would inspire somebody to kill him? It might not take too much; a lot of killers have pretty short fuses these days."

"Indeed they have. I can tell you that so far our investigations have revealed no such evidence. Of course, we're still making inquiries."

I changed the subject. "What can you tell me about this guy over on the cape? A PI that Marcus hired named Aristotle Socarides."

"Mr. Socarides has the reputation of being too independent in his ways to work well with superiors. Thus, he operates alone. Not unlike you yourself if I may say so. Of course, Mr. Socarides has a license, whereas you do not."

"Is he any good?"

"He has that reputation as well," acknowledged Thornberry. "I believe that Mr. Socarides is looking into Mr. Marcus's business interests in Provincetown. I've received no reports from him as to his findings, if any. Perhaps he reports directly to Mr. Marcus." He sighed. "It would be better, I believe, if a single agency, ours in this case, was the recipient of all information from the various people employed by Mr. Marcus. But so far, I have been unable to persuade him of this."

I thought of how much information I'd given him, and how little I'd gotten in return, and almost smiled. Instead, I said: "If you learn anything that will help me out down here, let me know."

"Of course."

Of course.

I rang off and tried Gordon R. Sullivan again. He was still out, and would still call back. I called Aristotle Socarides. No answer. I was having a fine morning. I hung up, and the phone rang. It was Gordon Sullivan.

"You think of something, or come up with something, Mr. Jackson?"

"No. The chief down here tells me that you two have been in touch. I thought I'd tell you what I've been up to."

"Okay. You a licensed PI?"

"No. Strictly a civilian."

He thought that one over. Cops don't like to have citizens prowling around criminal cases, messing things up. On the other hand, there wasn't much I could mess up with this one.

"What do you have?" he asked, finally.

I told him what I'd told Thornberry, then asked him the same questions.

"Fact is," said Sullivan, "some state and federal people used to be pretty interested in Luciano Marcus. He is known to them, as they say in the papers. Got his start right after the war, the way I hear the story. He was a young guy then, just back from Europe, and out of the army, like a million other guys. Lots of ambition, and a pretty tough cookie, to boot.

"Started small, but grew fast. Stepped on a lot of toes. A few people disappeared or retired and he took over. A couple of arrests, but nothing stuck. No convictions.

"All that was a long time ago. The older he got, the further away from the rough stuff he got, the more legit. He may still have some ties to shady operations, but if he does, nobody's been able to nail him for it. Right now he's probably the deacon of his church."

"Anybody want him dead?"

"Somebody does, for sure, but we haven't found him yet."

I told him my theory that the kid was an amateur, and I could almost see him nod.

"Yeah, I been thinking about that, too. Usually these guys in sweatshirts kill each other over drugs or women or territory, or rob and kill some storekeeper to finance their habits. They don't hire out to assassinate old men coming out of opera houses. No, this has a different smell to it than most cases. It's not a professional job, and it's not robbery. It's something else. Something personal, I'd guess. The shotgun angle still interests me."

"You said there'd been a couple of earlier shotgunnings. Who were the targets?"

"Just a couple of toughs trying to be tougher. We won't miss either one of them, but we want the guys who got them."

"You have anyone in mind?"

"A lot of people are glad they're gone. We've been asking questions and talking to folks, but so far, nothing."

The police always have too much to do. "I'll stay in touch," I said.

"And I'll see if those two guys you mentioned are in our records anywhere," said Sullivan. "If they are, maybe we'll have something to work on."

"Maybe," I said.

I tried Aristotle Socarides again. He didn't answer again.

Ignoring Wally's warning, I got into the Land Cruiser and drove west, running things through my mind. It was a muggy day, with a misty sea, and a warm haze that made things seem more ethereal than usual. In Chilmark, when I crossed the bridge between Nashaquitsa and Stonewall ponds, Stonewall Beach, that thin spit of sand that usually keeps Gay Head from being a separate island, was only a dim line in a gray fog, and farther on the overlook, which on a clear day gives such a fine view of Menemsha and Nashaquitsa ponds, today gave only a fine view of gray mists.

The fog floated over the driveway leading into the Marcus estate, but as the road climbed, the haze thinned and then thinned some more, until it fell away behind me, and I drove into sunshine. The house on its high hill floated like a ship on an ocean of gray-white mist.

Priscilla opened the door when I knocked, and waved me toward Luciano's office.

"He's in the office, waiting for you."

Luciano's cameras worked in the fog, apparently. I went down the hall, and knocked on the office door. When invited to come in, I did.

Marcus was seated at his desk. It was covered with papers. He spread his hands. "It is a paper world we live in, Mr. Jackson. We can do nothing without letters, memos, forms, and bills. What can I do for you today?"

I told him whom I'd been talking to, and what I'd been told, and about the two guys from Gay Head. He listened without interruption, until I was done. His face betrayed nothing.

"So," he said, when I was through. "Two Wampanoag toughs, eh?"

"Two wanna-be heros, is more like it. Linda Vander-beck didn't have anything to do with it. They did it on their own. I don't think they will again."

"Do you think they're the ones who tried for me?"

"I doubt it, but Sullivan is checking to see if they have any Boston connections."

"Neither you nor detective Sullivan nor Mr. Thornberry see this as having to do with my business affairs?"

I nodded. "Neither past nor present."

"An amateur effort, you believe?"

"That's how I see it. It's worth remembering that most killers are amateurs, and that they can be as deadly as pros." I brought up the subject he was least likely to appreciate. "I asked you this before: Can you think of anyone in your private life who might be involved in this?"

"My family, you mean." His voice was hard.

"Who inherits, is what I mean."

"Everyone inherits."

"Cash or businesses or both?"

"My sons will control the businesses. There will be trusts. And there will be cash."

"A lot of cash?"

He shrugged. "What is a lot? There will be considerable."

"So everyone in the family has a motive."

He put a pill under his tongue. "I think you should spend your time looking someplace else. I don't want to talk about this anymore."

"Another question, then: When did you make arrangements to attend the performance of *Carmen*?"

He thought for a moment. "Late last winter. March, I believe. My wife doesn't care for opera, but I like it and Thomas goes where I go. I get mailings of upcoming productions in New York and Boston. I'm sure that I ordered my tickets at that time. Why do you ask?"

"The guy up in Boston knew you were going to be there. I want to know how long he had to find out."

He touched his chin with his forefinger and looked at me. "Four months," he said. "Quite a long time."

"Yes. I'd like to talk with Vinnie."

His eyebrows raised slightly. "Vinnie? Why do you want to talk with Vinnie?"

"There were three of you in Boston. I've talked with you, and I've talked with Thomas, but I haven't talked with Vinnie."

He frowned, but nodded. "Okay. You'll probably find him down at the garage."

"And some time or other I'd like to talk with your wife."

This time, his brows gathered together. "My wife? I don't think that Angela can help you."

"You're probably right," I said. "But I won't know that until I talk to her."

But now he was frowning even more. "I don't want Angela involved in this."

I stood up. "You're paying me to find out what's going on. As for not wanting your wife to get involved, she already is involved. She's been involved with you since you were married, and you've been married a long time. That's a lot of involvement."

His hand strayed to his chest. His frown didn't go away, but he nodded again. "All right. You can talk with her. But be gentle."

Like many men, he thought his wife was fragile, and needed protecting. I'd made the same mistake myself.

I went out of the house and down to the garage. Vinnie was polishing the already polished hubcaps of the black Cadillac. He clearly took pride in his cars.

I got right to the point. "Vinnie, I get the impression that you get along with your grandmother better than with your grandfather. Am I right?"

He gave me a shocked look, then shook his head. "Nah. What do you mean?"

"I mean you call your grandma Grandma, but you call your grandpa boss, and you frown when he tells you what to do."

Vinnie ran all that through his head. It took a while. "I don't know what you mean," he said, sullenly. "I don't hate Grandpa. I don't hate nobody at all. I don't know what you mean."

"She gives you money, he gives you work. That's what I mean."

Vinnie thought some more. "They got me out of some trouble," he said. "They brought me down here."

"But you'd rather be back in the city."

He shook his head. "Nah. Who told you that?"

I studied him. He stared back. There was not a lot of intellect in his eyes. I changed the subject.

"Vinnie, you've dated Maggie Vanderbeck a few times. Do you remember ever telling her about Luciano's plans to go up to Boston to see that performance of *Carmen*?"

Vinnie rubbed his handsome jaw. He frowned and looked at some spot of empty air. Then he smiled and shrugged. "Maybe. It wasn't no secret or anything. I don't remember telling her, and I don't remember not telling her. I don't know why I would have told her, but maybe I did."

"While you were at UMass Boston, you met some of the other college kids who live here on the island. Aside from Maggie, do you date any of the other UMass girls down here, or hang around with them or the guys? You know, at a party or a dance or the movies? Anything like that?"

Vinnie nodded and ran a hand through his hair, smoothing an errant curl. His smile was white. "Sure. I date some of the girls. And I been to parties, or we go to the Connection there in Oak Bluffs."

"You ever mention that Luciano was going up to the opera?"

"Jeez," said Vinnie. "Like I say, maybe I did, and maybe I didn't. Why you want to know?" Then it came to him. I could almost see the lightbulb brighten in his brain. "Oh, I get it. You think maybe I told somebody about the boss going to that opera, and that's how those hoods in Boston knew he'd be there. Sure, I get it now."

"You're smart, Vinnie." I gave him an approving smile. "I've talked a little with Maggie Vanderbeck, but I'm going to talk with her again. And I want to talk with the other people you might have told about Luciano and the opera. I want you to tell me who your friends are."

Vinnie got wary. "I don't know. My friends ain't killers. They go to college. I don't know if I should tell you who they are. I don't want to get anybody in trouble. Besides, what'll they think of me when they find out you're asking them questions because of me?" He shook his head. "Nah. I don't know whether I want to do this. You know what I mean?"

"I know what you mean," I said. "But I'll tell you what might have happened. You might have told one of them, and that person told somebody else, just talking, you know, and that person told somebody else until, finally, the guy up in Boston heard it. You understand? So I need to talk to the people you might have talked to."

Vinnie fidgeted. "I don't know. You know what I mean?"

"You know I'm working for Luciano," I said as smoothly as I could. "I just finished talking with him, and he told me I could talk with you. You don't want to give me the names, I want you to go up to his office right now, and ask him what you should do."

Vinnie hesitated some more, his handsome face full of indecision.

"There's another thing," I said. "The cops are investigating this case, too. If you don't help me, you may have to talk with them. Would you rather have your friends talk with me or with the cops? I think it's going to be one or the other."

Vinnie gave me names. I recognized two of them.

I assured Vinnie that he'd done the right thing, got into the Land Cruiser, and drove out of the sunshine down into the fog.

18

I found Toni Vanderbeck at her shop on top of the Gay
Head cliffs. By sheer chance, a car full of tourists, no
doubt frustrated by the fog that blocked their view of the
cliffs, of Cuttyhunk, and of points beyond, had backed
out of its slot on the side of the road just as I had arrived,
so I had been able to park immediately. When you can't
do that, you have to drive around in circles watched by
the eagle-eyed Gay Head traffic cops who patrol the
town's miles of no-parking areas, or, worse yet, pay the
outrageous fee required to use the town parking lot,
down by the even more outrageous pay toilets—an
abomination in the eyes of man and God.

The cluster of buildings at the famous clay cliffs is
made up of eating places and souvenir shops, all dedicated
to separating visitors from their travel money. The restaurants offer classic American fare such as hamburgers and
hot dogs, and Vineyard specialties such as fish chowder,
clams, and stuffed quahogs. The souvenirs mostly consist
of quasi-Indian goods from Taiwan or other Eastern civ-
ilizations: Chinese bows and arrows, Korean rubber tom-
ahawks, Japanese feather headdresses. Mixed with these
are genuine Vineyard and Indian crafts. Toni Vanderbeck's shop specialized in the latter.

"I'm looking for your sister," I said.

"You came to the right spot," she said. "She's working
here today."

Maggie Vanderbeck came out of a back room, bringing with her what looked like an Acoma pot. She smiled
her pretty smile.

"Hi," she said. "You want to see me?"

"I have a couple of questions."

"Ask." She put the pot on a shelf.

"When you and Vinnie Cecilio were dating, did he
ever tell you that Luciano Marcus was going up to
Boston to see *Carmen*?"

She looked surprised. "If he did, I don't remember it."

"Another question. Do either of you know these people?" I gave them the names of Wally and his friend.

"I know them," said Toni. "Macho types. They side
with Mom a lot when the arguments start."

"Bullies?"

She frowned. "Maybe. They're a couple of hotheads.
I know that much. Why?"

"I had a talk with them this morning. I just wanted to
know what kind of people they are."

"Did they try to bully you?"

"Maybe."

She nodded. "They found out that you and Mom had
words, didn't they? And they tried to scare you off.
Goons!"

"Nothing came of it," I said. "No blood was shed, no
scalps were taken. One last question. If you don't want
to answer this one, I'll understand. What kind of a guy
is your uncle Bill?"

She and her sister exchanged looks.

"Why do you ask?" said Toni.

"You know I'm trying to figure out who took a shot at
Luciano Marcus. I'm asking all of the questions I can
think of. Your uncle Bill is helping your mother out with

this cranberry bog business. I'd like to know as much about him as I can."

She frowned, and when she did, she looked more like her mother. "Uncle Bill had nothing to do with that shooting. He was at home when that happened."

That was probably what Mrs. James said about her son, when the sheriff claimed Jesse was robbing banks.

"Anything you can tell me will be fine," I said.

"I'll tell you about him," said Maggie Vanderbeck. And for the next half hour, between customers, she did that. After a while, Toni joined in.

He was a strange person to them, not at all like his brother, their late father, who had been plain as dirt and solid as stone. Uncle Bill looked ordinary enough, but somehow he wasn't. One thing was, of course, that even if you were looking for him, you might not see him. He had the ability to be there and not be noticed. Another thing was that even though he never talked about it in particular, you got the idea he'd been a lot of places and seen a lot of things, and that he knew something you didn't know. Maybe that was why some people called him shaman; because he was different and hard to understand, and because he sometimes spoke in riddles.

Like Vanderbeck's Axioms. Both of them, when they were little girls, had listened to Vanderbeck's Axioms. They would go to see Uncle Bill and Aunt Polly for an afternoon, and he would take them out to Squibnocket Point and then west along the beach.

"You know how they call you a shaman?" the girls would say to him. "Well, if you're a shaman, you must know the secrets of life. So what are they?"

And he would say he didn't know much about life at all, but he had worked out some axioms. "Vanderbeck's

Axioms," he called them. When they'd asked him what an axiom was, he'd said it was a self-evident truth. Anyway, he'd say they didn't have to believe his axioms, and it might be fun for them to try to come up with a few of their own. His were pretty odd.

The first axiom was, "It's hard to walk on a railroad track." On the rail, that is. Uncle Bill had said he actually stole that one from a friend of his, a guy named Comstock. It was Comstock's First Axiom. But since an axiom can belong to anybody who wants it, Comstock's First Axiom was now also Vanderbeck's First Axiom. Uncle Bill had said that if you didn't believe the axiom, you should try to walk on a railway rail without falling off. For a person with a terrific sense of balance, it wouldn't be an axiom at all, but for most people it would be recognized as a self-evident truth. Of course, there weren't any railroad tracks on Martha's Vineyard, so there was no way for the sisters to check the axiom out.

Vanderbeck's Second Axiom was, "It's not what you think it is." Toni, who was older than Maggie, had figured that this meant that when you thought you knew what something was, you were wrong because it was something else, and that it required even more thinking; Maggie thought that it meant that thinking about things didn't necessarily help you understand them; that maybe, for instance, you should just see and touch and hear things and have feelings about them instead of just thinking about them. Uncle Bill had said he thought maybe both of them might be right, but he never said for sure.

Vanderbeck's Third Axiom was, "It makes no difference." The girls thought that this meant that even if something wasn't what you thought it was, it didn't matter. Or wasn't supposed to matter, even if it seemed like maybe it should. Or something like that. Uncle Bill had agreed. His agreeableness was one of the things they liked about him. They also liked the fact that he could disappear whenever he wanted to, even when there didn't seem to be anything to hide behind.

Vanderbeck's Fourth Axiom was, "This is it." That was a simple one. It meant that whether something was what you thought it was or not, and whether it meant anything or not, it was what you had to deal with, one way or another.

There might have been more of the axioms, but those were all Toni and Maggie could remember at the moment. When Aunt Polly had died, Uncle Bill had gone away for a long time. Where he had been, they didn't know, but they had the impression that it had been far. Then, just last year, he had come home, and their mother had gotten him involved in the business about the cranberry bog.

"And he was the one that brought up the idea of the trade," said Maggie.

What trade? I wondered. "What trade?" I asked.

"Oh, you don't know about the trade idea?" Toni pursed her lips. "Well, there are maps and the deeds and the records of land sales here in Gay Head, and everybody argues over what they mean. You'd think, hearing them wrangle, that Marcus's lawyers would be glad to meet Mom's lawyer on the green at dawn with either swords or pistols. But Uncle Bill wants to go the let's-settle-this-thing-out-of-court route. And he came up with the trade idea.

"There's a little stub of land up on the hill behind Marcus's place that belongs to the tribe. It sticks down into Marcus's land like a sore thumb. Bill thinks maybe

Marcus would give the tribe the bog in exchange for the thumb. The thumb isn't good for much. It's mostly down in a gully where you can't even see the ocean, so you wouldn't want to build there. And it's so rocky you couldn't grow anything if you tried, so the tribe can't use it for anything."

"Why would Marcus want to trade?"

"Well, it would take a kink out of his property line, and it would make him a friend of the tribe instead of an enemy, and it would keep him out of court. If he goes to court, his name will be in the papers, and some people don't like to have their names in the papers. Maybe he's one of them."

Maggie nodded. "Uncle Bill says it's good to avoid war, if you can. I think he's right."

So did I.

"Mom is talking this trade idea over with her lawyer and the tribal council. And I think that Uncle Bill is going to talk it over with Mr. Marcus."

I wondered how he was going to manage that, since Marcus lived inside a sort of fortress designed to keep visitors out, but I didn't say so. Instead, I thanked them both very much, and told them they'd been a big help, and left.

Martha's Vineyard has little weather systems all its own. Mainland forecasts do not apply to it at all, and, moreover, small as the island is, consisting of only a hundred and thirty or so square miles of land, the weather is often radically different in one part of the island than it is in another. Today, for example, the fog hung heavy in Gay Head, but thinned to a mist in Chilmark, and was gone completely by the time I got to West Tisbury. In Vineyard Haven, the sun was shining brightly, just as it had been on Marcus's hilltop. I drove to John Dings's house, and knocked on the door.

Sandy Dings recognized me at once. She didn't seem too happy about it.

"I'd like to talk with your daughter," I said.

"Jean has to go to work in a little while. I'm trying to get her to get dressed."

"This won't take long." I stood there.

Sandy Dings was not a very good doorkeeper. "Oh well," she sighed. "Come on in. She's out on the deck trying to get a tan. You can't get a tan when you're working almost every day as a waitress. I don't think she should be getting a tan, anyway, what with all this skin cancer business. You wait here. I'll call her."

"If she can talk and tan at the same time, I'll talk to her out there," I said.

She hesitated, then said: "You wait a minute till I see what she's got on."

She went out and came back, shaking her head. "That girl better start getting ready for work or she'll be late again. She says for you to come on out. Don't be shocked. I swear these girls wear less every year."

"I don't know about that," I said. "I think they were wearing bikinis when you were her age."

Sandy Dings's face got red, but she smiled in spite of herself. It took about five years off of her. "You go on out there, now." She waved toward the back porch. "But don't keep her too long. She's got to get ready for work."

I went out there and found Jean Dings, clad in dark glasses and a bit of cloth. She had zinc oxide on her nose. She had that young and juicy look.

"Hi," she said. "Mom says you want to talk to me. What about?"

"Vinnie Cecilio says that you two have dated a couple of times."

She tugged at the bit of cloth, rearranging it in some microscopic way. "That's right. We dated up in Boston, while he was still in school, and we've dated a couple of times down here. Vinnie's not much for long thoughts, but he's fun, and he knows how to dance."

"Have you dated him or been at a party with him, or anything like that in the last few months. Say, since March?"

She put the bit of cloth back where it had been before. "Yeah. We were at a party together in April. And when I got home from school in May, he and I caught a movie down at the Strand. Why?"

"Did he ever tell you, or did you ever hear him tell anybody else, that his boss, a guy named Luciano Marcus, was going to go up to Boston to see a performance of *Carmen*?"

She sat up, grinning. "Now, that's about the last question I expected to hear. But, as a matter of fact, I think he did tell me that. I'd forgotten all about it."

"Did you ever tell anyone else?"

"No. Why would I? I'd forgotten all about it till just now."

"Did you ever hear him give that information to anyone else?"

"No. What's so important about it, anyway?"

"Maybe it isn't important," I said. Beyond her, across Tashmoo Pond, I could see her aunt Lillian's house under the trees. There was a neat shed behind the house, and there were some conch or lobster pots stacked behind the shed. A path and wooden steps led from the shed down to a dock, where a dinghy and a Sunfish were tied.

I looked back at Jean. "Your mom says that you and some of your friends were down for a couple of week-ends last April. Was the party that you attended with Vinnie the one that happened the night your dad's shot-gun was stolen?"

"Yeah," she said. "Now that you mention it. Say, what's this all about?" She picked up a wristwatch from the floor and looked at it.

"Can you tell me who was at that party?"

She took off her dark glasses. Her eyes were very blue. "Gosh, I don't know. Let me see . . . There was Vin-nie and me, and Maggie Vanderbeck, and Peter Jeffers, that cop friend of hers up in Gay Head, and my cousin Freddy, and Benny What's-his-name who came down with him that weekend with his girlfriend. Marsha was her name. First time on the island for those two, and they thought it was great." She put on her thinking face. "A couple more people, maybe. But I forget who."

"If you remember, let me know." I wrote my name, address, and telephone number on a piece of paper and gave it to her. "If you lose this, I'm in the book."

She looked at the watch again, and jumped to her feet. "I've got to get ready for work!"

The late Jean Dings. I stepped aside and she went into the house. I looked again at the house across the water, then followed her.

19

I parked the Land Cruiser in the Vineyard Haven Steamship Authority parking lot, found a pay phone, and looked up the number for Toni Begay's shop, hoping that Maggie Vanderbeck was still there. She was.

"I just talked with Jean Dings," I said. "She told me that several of you were at a party together last April. She told me that you were there, that Peter Jeffers was there, that she and Vinnie were there, and that her cousin Freddy was there with a couple of friends from Boston, Benny Something-or-other and a girl named Marsha. She says that there were a couple of other people there, too. Do you remember who they were?"

"Sure," said Maggie. "Neal Otis and Nancy Parks. Freddy was the odd man out. No girl. No wonder, either, if you ask me; he's so moody lately, not like he used to be. But that night he tried to be fun. He danced with everybody else's girl, and made the beer run while the rest of us went for a walk on South Beach, and I guess he had a good time. I remember it was a really warm night for April, and we had all the windows open."

"Jean Dings says that Vinnie told her that night about Luciano Marcus's plans to go up to Boston to see *Carmen*. Did you hear him talking about that?"

"You asked me about that this morning. No, I didn't hear anything about that until today. But it was a party, with a lot of noise, so I probably wouldn't have heard him talking about it unless I was listening. He never said anything to me about it."

"Do you remember anything in particular about the party. Anything unusual, or different?"

There was a pause. Then she said: "No. It was just a party. We had some discs, and we danced and drank beer. A couple of people overdid it. Nothing unusual. Just a party."

I thanked her very much for her time, and went back to the truck.

There are a lot of roads and driveways that lead down to the east side of Tashmoo Pond, and I have never been very good at keeping them straight, so it didn't surprise me when I made a few wrong explorations before I finally found Jimmy Souza's house. There was a wide spot in the road, where his driveway left it. The FOR SALE sign at the end of the driveway was painted in bright colors, and told me which realtor I could call if I was an interested buyer.

The house, when I got to it, wasn't as grand as that owned by the movie star whose place bordered Jimmy's, but it was a comfortable, neat home, only slightly gone to seed since Jimmy's fortunes had declined. Still, it had a sad look about it, although that impression might have been only a reflection of my own melancholy mood.

I parked in the empty yard, got out, and looked across the water at the house of John Dings. Dings's back deck, where recently I'd stood, was in plain view, as were the wooden steps leading from it down to the small dock below.

I walked down to the shed behind the house, and went around back, where the fishing pots were stacked. Close up, I could see that all of them were in need of repair. I looked down at Jimmy's dock, where the Sunfish and dinghy were tied. Then I walked back to the house and knocked on the door.

Nobody home. I'd been hopeful, but I wasn't surprised, since there were no cars in the yard. Jimmy was probably looking for work, trying to make the best buck he could manage while staying constantly drunk. And his wife and kids were no doubt working somewhere, trying to keep the wolves from the door as long as possible, while Jimmy slid down into the pit. Of course, Fred might be out looking for me. The idea irked me, and I thought that maybe I should go looking for him, to get the matter between us over and done with.

I tried the door. It was unlocked. I went in.

There were three bedrooms. One for Jimmy and Lillian, one for a girl in her early teens, whose stuff was piled everywhere, and one for a college-aged boy, according to the clothes in the closet and the textbooks on a shelf. I looked inside the covers of a couple of the textbooks, and saw that they belonged to Fred Souza. I put the books back, and looked around. There was a UMass Boston pennant on the wall. I went through the house, opening closets, looking for Jimmy's shotgun. I didn't find it.

I went outside again, and back to the shed. Inside it was some fishing gear, including a couple of boat rods and reels. There were some boxes and chests, and there were the lawn and garden tools that people put in sheds. No shotgun.

But I hadn't really expected to find one. There were a lot of hunters on Martha's Vineyard, so there was always a market for a good shotgun. The gun would have been one of the first things Jimmy sold, on his way down. Nip money.

I went back into the house, and found a desk where the bills and correspondence were kept. There, amid the clutter of other papers, were some of those forms that come attached to paychecks. Lillian Souza worked at a clothing store on Circuit Avenue. She didn't make a lot of money there, but at least it was a job. I went out to the truck and drove to Oak Bluffs.

Circuit Avenue is Oak Bluffs' main drag, a busy one-way street with angle parking that keeps cars from moving very fast, since drivers have to be careful about people backing out into the driving lane. Most of the passenger ferries bringing day-trippers from the mainland come into Oak Bluffs, so the town is filled with souvenir shops and fast-food restaurants that cater to that clientele.

Oak Bluffs also sports the Fireside Bar, where the working island young mix at night with the college kids who come down to the island to combine work and play. High-tech fake ID's are the order of the day, as is the Mary joke: How do we know that Jesus' mother never drank at the Fireside? Because there are no virgins there. Bonzo, my gentle, childish friend, swabbed the floor and cleaned tables at the Fireside.

Oak Bluffs offers other entertainments as well: the Vineyard Connection, where you can dance between drinks; a couple of good restaurants, and a couple of very expensive ones; and various businesses and stores. One of the latter was where Lillian Souza worked. I found a parking place and went in.

I recognized her immediately. She looked like her sister, but more tired. She was folding clothing and placing it on a shelf. I went to her.

"Mrs. Souza?"

She put a saleswoman's smile on her face. "Yes?"

"I'm looking for your son. Can you tell me where I can find him?"

The smile faded. "He's not on the island. He went up to Boston a week and a half ago. He got a job there, making more money than he can down here. He says he may come down here some weekends. Are you a friend of his?"

"Not really. I heard that his dad was selling a shotgun, but I can't get a hold of Jimmy, so I thought Fred might know something about it."

"Oh," she said. "I'm afraid you're too late to buy Jimmy's shotgun. He sold it last winter. He decided he didn't want to hunt anymore, so he sold his guns." It was such a practiced lie that I imagined that she'd almost come to believe it herself.

I noticed a woman across the room looking at us. She had that slight frown that some employers wear when they think their help isn't moving fast enough, so I picked up a shirt and pretended to examine it.

"I haven't seen Fred's little sister in quite a while," I said in my friendliest voice. "She must be all grown up by now."

Lillian Souza brightened. "Well, I wouldn't call Allison all grown up yet, but she's very mature for her age. She's working down at the ice cream shop on the docks, you know. She's the youngest one there, but her boss says she's the best of the bunch!"

"You must be proud of her," I said. I looked at the shirt one last time, and put it down. Not my style.

I smiled at Mrs. Souza. "Thanks for your time," I said, and walked away. I shifted course so I would pass the frowning woman. I smiled my smile at her, too, and gestured back at Lillian. "Nice lady," I said, going by.

I walked down Circuit Avenue, figuratively shaking my head. Good grief. Just about the time I'd started hearing

Freddy's footsteps in the dark, Fred had actually left the island. Imagination is wonderful but not always dependable.

Down at the docks, I found the ice cream store and Allison Souza, an efficient girl just in her teens who was dressed in a white uniform and a little white cap that made her look rather like a nurse.

"Allison," I said, "I've lost Fred's Boston address. Can you remember what it is?"

"No," she said. "But I know his telephone number." She gave it to me.

I thanked her, and while I was there, I got a double scoop black raspberry cone. Lunch. Delish.

When the ice cream was gone, I drove home and called Aristotle Socarides again. Elusive Aristotle was still not answering his phone. I called the Edgartown police station and asked for the chief. He was out. Downtown. I had apparently used up all my telephone luck with the call to Maggie Vanderbeck.

I drove downtown and spotted the chief in front of the county courthouse.

One of the curiosities of Martha's Vineyard is that Dukes County, of which the Vineyard is the greater part, is not really Dukes County at all, but is officially the County of Dukes County. That is to say, it is Dukes County County, a county whose name is Dukes County. Thus, the courthouse is the County of Dukes County Courthouse, just as the main island airport is the County of Dukes County Airport. This odd nomenclature is due, I'm told, to an ancient error in official writing that, for reasons unknown to me, became the official form. So things go, sometimes.

Naturally, I couldn't find a parking place anywhere

near the courthouse, but the chief was still there when I got back, talking with Dom Agganis, the state cop.

"What do you want?" asked the chief.

I handed him Fred Souza's telephone number. "I want the address that goes with that."

He looked at the paper. "What is this?"

"It's Fred Souza's telephone number."

"Jimmy's boy? Why don't you just call him and ask him yourself? Why don't you just ask his folks, for that matter?"

"I don't want to worry his folks, and I don't want to scare Freddy away. I want to talk to him before he can run."

Dom Agganis tilted his head, listening. The chief looked at the paper again. "Why should Fred run away?"

"Because it's possible that he stole John Dings's shotgun. I can't prove it, but I think it's possible."

"Is that a fact?" said Agganis. "What makes you think so?"

I told then what people had told me, and what I'd seen when I'd walked around the outside of Jimmy Souza's house. I didn't tell them about my explorations inside the house, since it's not a good policy to confess crimes to policemen standing in front of a courthouse.

When I was done, Agganis said: "And that's why you think Freddy Souza stole his uncle's shotgun?" He allowed his lip to curl slightly.

"I didn't say he did it," I said, irked by the curl, as Dom no doubt knew I'd be. "I only said it's possible that he did it, and I want to talk to him before he has a chance to run away."

Agganis snorted. "I think the only running Fred has to do is to a lawyer, who'll probably sue your socks off for harassment, if you lay this trip on his client."

It annoys me when I let somebody annoy me, so I willed my anger away to some far corner of my psyche. I said: "Even you should be able to figure this, Corporal." I ticked off the points of the argument on my fingers, as though to make sure he would get them. "Jimmy Souza is going down the tubes, and taking his family with him. He's lost his boat, his house is for sale, he's had to sell his shotguns and probably other stuff, and he's nipping vodka all day long. He blames the trawlers for all his troubles. He says the trawlers wrecked his pots and other gear, and did him in. They're the bad guys. And guess who owns the trawlers? Luciano Marcus. They're his latest toy. He's got them coming out of New Bedford, Provincetown, and maybe Gloucester, for all I know.

"Now, while Jimmy goes from bad to worse, and his wife has to take a job selling shirts, their boy Freddy is up at UMass Boston, running out of money for school, along with everything else that's gone bad after Jimmy lost his boat. Maggie Vanderbeck says Freddy's gotten moody, not like he used to be, and even in the old days Freddy had a bit of a short fuse. Anyway, one night last April, he and some friends come down from school and have a party. That same night, his uncle John Dings and his aunt Sandy came over to his folks' place for the evening to play cards. His folks probably told him that, but even if they didn't, he knew it, because the Dingses had offered their place for the party, if the kids wanted to have it there.

"He gets to the party down in Katama and overhears Vinnie Cecilio tell Jean Dings about Luciano Marcus's plan to go up to Boston to go to the opera. Like his daddy, Fred blames the trawlers for all the family's problems, so he decides to do something about it. While he's on his beer run, he goes to the Dings's house—maybe by car, or maybe he parks his car at the end of his folks' driveway, sneaks down and takes the dinghy across the pond, I don't know which. He knows Uncle John has a shotgun because John and Jimmy Souza used to go hunting together. And he probably knows where the gun is kept, because he's been in the Dings's house lots of times, and, besides, it's no secret where John Dings keeps the gun.

"So he takes the gun, and gets the beer. With a fake ID, Dom, in case you didn't guess that. He gets the beer and goes back to the party. Now he's got a gun and he knows that Luciano Marcus will show up at a certain time and place. He takes the gun to Boston, finds a helper who's got a hooded sweatshirt, and *voilà*! You follow all that, Dom?"

"Why did he go to Boston, then have his helper wait all that time?" asked Agganis. "According to you, the kid's mad and he's got the gun, and Marcus is right here on the island. The killings that I know about, the bad guy, if he's really worked up, doesn't hang around four months to make his hit. He does it right now, with whatever weapon he's got. A rock or a gun or whatever. None of this long-range planning, or rare poison found only up the Amazon, or any of that kind of crap."

"Maybe Freddy thought of doing that," I said. "Maybe he went up there to Marcus's place, even. But Marcus lives in a high-security house. He's got guards, and dogs at night. Fred couldn't get in there if he tried. Besides, maybe he has some Italian blood in his veins. Maybe revenge is a dish he prefers to eat cold."

Agganis nodded, suddenly agreeable. "I can understand that," he said. "I got one grandmother was Italian.

She was like that." He turned to the chief. "Maybe we should look into this."

The chief gave me a sour look. "Maybe we should. I'll call Sullivan, up in Boston, and drop this story in his ear. Maybe he can do something with it." He held up the piece of paper I'd given him. "That being the case, you probably don't need the address that goes with this, after all. We'll let Sullivan take care of it." He folded the paper and put it in his pocket.

20

Angela Marcus stood, hands on hips, and looked at her garden.

"There's no doubt about it," she said. "Something is eating the leaves of the cucumbers and lettuce." She looked at her cabbage. "Damage there, too. Maria! I wonder if I should finally give in and buy some chemical pest controls? I hate to do it, because I like to do things organically, if I can. What do you think?"

"Something has to be done," I said. "Personally, I'm not above using a few bug killers."

The garden was partially sunken into the side of the slope above and behind the house. There was a low stone wall around it, to cut the winds that blew so steadily across the Gay Head hills. Between the walls, tons of rich earth had been trucked in and spread in a thick layer to replace the original sandy, rocky soil that had been hauled away when the garden had been built. Now flowers grew beside the walls: bright wild flowers mixed with annuals and perennials. Inside the ring of flowers, Angela grew her herbs and vegetables.

It was Angela's garden, and, she had explained to me in the half-hour I'd been there with her, she grew what she wanted to grow in the way she wanted to grow it. None of the men or women who worked on the estate were allowed to say anything about how things were done there, or to offer a single word of advice unless asked to do so, even though Angela knew very well that several of the groundskeepers were far more knowledgeable about plants than she was. Although she was glad to share its bounty with Jonas, the cook, Angela was mistress of the garden just as she was mistress of the house itself.

Now, as the wind tugged gently at the old straw hat she wore, and the summer sun shown bright in the arching blue sky above us, she sighed. "Insect problems." She got down on her knees and peeked under a holey cabbage leaf to see if she could spot the enemy who was eating it. No such luck. She sat back on her heels.

I had come to talk with her about her perceptions of her husband's possible enemies, but had rapidly learned that he had been right about her: She knew nothing that could help, because she could not conceive of anyone wanting to harm Luciano, even though someone clearly had tried to kill him. The only explanation she could think of was, "It was some kind of a mistake. They thought he was somebody else."

Now, sitting on her heels, she was speaking of things she knew something about. "Sometimes an insect likes one kind of plant, but doesn't like another," she was saying. "Maybe I can take advantage of that."

"That's right," said a voice. "Maybe next year you should plant things in alternating rows to discourage some kinds of bugs. They call it companion planting. There are other options you might try, too, before you start using chemicals."

I was startled, because I'd thought we were alone. Angela and I turned our heads and looked toward the voice. The shaman stood there, looking so comfortable that it was almost as if he belonged there, as if he were a member of the staff or one of Luciano's guests.

Angela, too, seemed to think he belonged. "I know there are things I can probably do, but I just don't know what they are," she said, turning back to the cabbage plant and peering through its leaves. "I have enough books, goodness knows. I guess I'll just have to read them more carefully."

"Reading is always good," agreed the shaman. "And if you were to ask me, I'd also say that chemicals aren't always bad. On the other hand, why use them if you don't have to?"

Angela nodded. "My thoughts exactly." She smiled at him and stood up. Together, they looked around the garden.

"Very nice," said the shaman. He nodded to me. "How are you, J.W.?"

"Fine," I said.

Angela was looking around. "Insect problems, for sure. But the garden doesn't look too bad."

"Almost everything you need is already growing here," said the shaman. "Rosemary, sage, geraniums, garlic . . ."

"Luciano and I use a lot of garlic," said Angela. "I think mine is better than anything we can buy in the local stores. And fresh herbs just make all the difference in the world. Jonas—he's the cook. Have you met him? No? Well, Jonas has free rein to take whatever he wants out of here. He's the only one beside me who can do that. He gets a lot of use from it, and Luciano and I eat well, I can tell you. What do you mean, I have almost everything I need?"

"I have my own garden," said the shaman. "There's nothing better than eating fresh vegetables you've grown with your own hands."

"Oh, I agree."

"Let me show you what I mean," he said, and together they moved slowly about the garden, looking first at this, then at that. I followed, wide-eared. "For example," he said, "here's your garlic. Aphids hate garlic . . ."

"Like vampires?" She laughed, and he joined her.

"Just like Vlad Dracul himself," he agreed. "So if you plant your garlic next to, say, your lettuce, the aphids will stay away. And if you plant your tomatoes next to your asparagus, the asparagus beetles will stay away."

"What about my cabbages?"

"Here's your rosemary and there's your sage and there's your thyme. Cabbage butterflies don't like those herbs, so if you plant them near your cabbage, the butterflies go off and eat somebody else's cabbage."

"Now that you say that, I seem to remember reading it somewhere."

"I'm sure you did. I know I didn't discover it single-handed."

She seemed to reach back into her mind. "And there are flowers, too, aren't there? You mentioned geraniums, and I seem to remember reading about nasturtiums, too, and marigolds." She apparently remembered, and spontaneously grasped his wrist. "Japanese beetles! That was it! Japanese beetles don't like marigolds or geraniums! Now, what was it about nasturtiums . . . ?

"You're absolutely right about the marigolds and geraniums." He gestured with his free hand. "And nasturtiums are good for keeping off bean beetles. You have everything you need right here: your flowers, your herbs. All you have to do next year is rearrange them." He looked down at her, and a small smile flickered across his face. "Of course, in the meantime you might want to pop down to your local greenhouse and get some stuff that will do in this year's bugs. We live in an imperfect world, and sometimes we need help we wish we didn't need. When my organic plans don't work out, I'm not above taking advantage of modern science."

She seemed to become conscious of her grip on his wrist and withdrew her hand. He seemed not to have noticed. She looked happy and comfortable in his presence.

"My goodness," she said. "I'm afraid I haven't even introduced myself. I'm Angela Marcus."

"I'm Bill Vanderbeck."

She took off a glove and put out her hand. He shook it with his larger, browner one.

"I don't think we've met," she said. "Are you working here?"

"No, I'm not. I came by to talk to your husband, and I saw you here in your lovely garden, and I'm afraid I got sidetracked."

"Ah. You know Luciano, then?"

"No, we've never met. It's a business matter."

"I see. Well, Mr. Jackson here wants to see him, too. Mr. Jackson, why don't you take Mr. Vanderbeck down to Luciano's office. And afterward, perhaps you'll have time to join us for a drink on the veranda."

"I would enjoy that, but it may not be possible," said Vanderbeck. "Thank you for showing me your wonderful garden."

"You must certainly come back soon and visit it again."

"It would be my pleasure, Mrs. Marcus."

"Call me Angela. I have the feeling that we're to become friends." She again extended her hand, and again he shook it.

"If you're Angela, then I'm Bill."

"Bill."

"Just plain Bill, like in the old radio show."

She laughed. "I used to listen to that program when I was a child. I haven't thought of it in years!"

I led him into the house and down the hallway that led to Luciano's office. We paused outside the closed door. "This is Luciano's realm," I said, and knocked. A voice said to come in, and we did.

Luciano was seated at his desk. Vanderbeck followed me into the room and the door shut behind him.

Luciano's eyes widened, then narrowed. His face paled. He touched a button on his desk, then dropped his hand from sight and appeared to open a silent desk drawer. I wondered how long it had been since he had fired a gun, and if he had imagined that he would ever have to fire one again, particularly in this innermost of sanctums, deep inside his own house. I imagined that it had been Thomas Decker who had insisted that his boss should have a weapon of last resort, and that Luciano had given in, and now he was glad he had.

He looked right through me, staring at Vanderbeck.

"Who are you?"

"Bill Vanderbeck."

"Vanderbeck! How did you get here?"

"I met your wife. She asked J.W. here to bring me down."

"That's right," I said, wondering if there really was a pistol pointing at Vanderbeck, or maybe at me. "Angela asked me to bring him down. She said that maybe we could stay for a drink afterward."

"A drink? You know my wife, then." Marcus's narrow eyes were fixed on Vanderbeck.

"Yes," said Vanderbeck. "We've been in her garden."

"Are you some gardener she met? No, you're one of

those damned Wampanoag Vanderbecks! How did you get up here? You should have been stopped!"

I wondered what Luciano was seeing as he stared at Vanderbeck. Did he see the man I saw? A medium-sized man of indefinite age, dressed in casual summer clothing—jeans, a short-sleeved shirt, boat shoes, a baseball cap with a Colorado Rockies logo. A face that was so ordinary it was hard to describe, brown skin, dark hair. Deep eyes that seemed to be amused, or maybe not amused, but having some kind of odd, not unpleasant expression in them. Or did he see a devil in poor disguise?

Vanderbeck's eyes were roaming the room, no doubt noting what I had noted on earlier visits: the well-hidden TV camera high on the wall, the button on Luciano's desk, and the door to the right, behind which, perhaps, Thomas Decker and some others might even now be looking at the TV screen that showed them the inside of the office, so that they'd know what was going on in there before they came in.

Luciano glared at me. "Do you know this man?"

"We met earlier this week."

"Did you bring him up here in your car? Did you?" His eyes were hot.

I shook my head. "No. I met him in your wife's garden."

"What do you want?" asked Luciano, watching Vanderbeck casually select a chair with its back to the right-hand door, and sit down, putting his hands on the arms of the chair. I had the distinct impression that Vanderbeck had chosen that chair deliberately, so as to make himself more vulnerable to whoever might soon be coming through the door. It was as though Vanderbeck knew Luciano was frightened and wanted to show that he had no need to be.

"I want to talk to you about the cranberry bog and the bit of land just this side of it," said Vanderbeck, as the door behind him swung silently open and Thomas Decker and Vinnie came in, Decker's right hand behind his back. Decker and Vinnie stepped quietly to either side of the chair where Vanderbeck sat. He glanced at them and nodded, then looked back at Luciano.

"Cranberry bog?" asked Luciano in momentary confusion. "What are you talking about?"

"Your cranberry bog," said Vanderbeck. "The one down at the bottom of the hill in front of your house. And about a half acre of land just this side of it."

"What about it?"

"There are some Wampanoags here in town who think that cranberry bog and that half acre of land actually belong to the tribe. They believe that you probably bought it in good faith, but that since it never really belonged to any of the people who probably thought they owned it before you got it, it's not really yours at all, but belongs to the tribe. I came up here to talk to you about that and see if something can be worked out, so nobody has to go to court. I have a trade in mind."

"A trade? Go to court?"

"Well, there are a couple of Wampanoag lawyers now, here in Gay Head, and you know how lawyers are. They make their living by going to court or threatening to. And there are some people in the tribe who are pretty hot about that bog. They say it always belonged to the tribe, and that they want it back right now, and they're ready to hire the lawyers if they have to. On the other hand, some other people want to avoid the whole court business. They asked me to drop by and talk with you personally, about maybe you trading the bog for a piece of

Wampanoag land that breaks up your north property line,
before we start dragging the lawyers into the situation."

Marcus stared. "Why did they send you? You some sort of
chief or something? A damned lawyer yourself, probably."

Vanderbeck shook his head. "No, I'm nobody official,
nor any lawyer, either. Just a neighbor of yours come by
to see if we can work this thing out together."

Luciano glared. "You even a Wampanoag?"

"So some people say."

Luciano, feeling more comfortable now that Decker
and Vinnie were there, brought his hand out from
behind the desk and leaned back. "I can't figure out why
they sent you. Why you?"

Vanderbeck smiled. "Probably because they thought I
could I could get in here. It isn't always easy to meet with
an important man with a lot of business interests. Usually you have to meet a secretary first and explain what
you want, then the secretary has to talk with the boss,
and the boss may decide not to see you at all. They figured I could probably get to see you."

Luciano's earlier fear seemed to be replaced by confidence and some irritation.

"Look," he said. "As far as my land is concerned, I
bought it fair and square. I want to be a good neighbor to
everybody in town, Indians and all, but that cranberry
bog is mine and I plan to keep it. And if we have to go to
court, well, I have a couple of lawyers of my own that I'll
stack up against your Wampanoag lawyers any day."

Vanderbeck nodded pleasantly. "You talk with your
lawyers, and have them check the records for that bog
and the bit of land I mentioned. You look at a map of
your place, you'll see what piece of land I mean. Afterward, you may change your mind about that bog." He

flowed to his feet. "No need to try to resolve things right now. I'll be back one of these days, and we can talk some more. Maybe we can work something out."

"I don't expect to change my mind," said Marcus, standing up.

"Neither do those Wampanoags who are calling that bog sacred Indian Land," said Vanderbeck. "Personally, I can't imagine calling a cranberry bog sacred land, but people think about things in different ways. Well, see you later." He turned to Thomas Decker and pointed to the right-hand door. "That leads outside, I reckon. Maybe your friend there will walk out with me. I think your boss and you will probably want to have a talk. So long, J.W."

He gave Vinnie a long look, then moved past Decker, opened the door, and walked out. Vinnie, frowning, followed him.

"Take him as far as the main gate, Vinnie," said Decker. When the door closed, he and Luciano looked at each other.

"That man walked right in here," said Luciano. "You find out how that happened and make sure it doesn't happen again."

Decker nodded, his hard face even harder-looking than usual. "I'll take care of it."

When Decker was gone, Luciano sat and thought. It was as though he had forgotten I was there. The fear he'd experienced when Vanderbeck had first appeared flickered back across his face. I could imagine what was going through his mind: What if Decker couldn't stop Vanderbeck from coming to the house? That was a scary thought. He'd built this fine house and surrounded it with trusted people so he'd never be confronted by anyone he didn't want to see. And now this Vanderbeck had just walked in. He must suddenly have felt vulnerable and a little older than an hour before.

He reached into his shirt pocket and got out another one of those pills. He put it into his mouth. After a bit, his breathing was better, and he suddenly seemed to remember me.

"You have something to tell me?"

"Yes."

He held up his hand. "First tell me how you met Vanderbeck earlier this week. Then tell me how you met him up in the garden just now. How did he get there without anyone seeing him?"

So I told him about my talks with Linda Vanderbeck and the various members of her family, including Bill Vanderbeck. Then I told him my theory about Fred Souza, and about meeting the shaman in the garden, and that I hadn't the slightest idea how he'd gotten there.

He listened, frowning at times. I had the impression that Vanderbeck worried him more than Fred Souza did. He could understand someone like Fred. But the shaman was a mystery beyond his ken, and he didn't like that at all.

When I was done with my tale, he said, "So you think this boy Souza is the one?"

"He had motive and opportunity, and that makes him a candidate at least."

"And now the police are investigating?"

"I think so. I also think I owe you some money. If Fred Souza is the guy who hired the shooter, the job didn't take as long as I thought it would."

"I'll tell Thornberry Security about this Souza kid," he said. "As for the money, you keep it. Besides, we can't be sure yet that the Souza boy did it."

True enough. I stood up. "Since I keep the money, I'll stay on the job a little longer, just in case there are some loose ends, or if Freddy didn't do it. If he didn't, somebody else did." He nodded, then frowned. "Yeah. Do that. There is one thing you can do for me. You can keep that damned Indian off my land!"

Fat chance of that, I thought. But I didn't say it.

21

"So that's why you think Fred Souza might be the one," said Zee, looking out over Sengekontacket, and nibbling on a cracker stacked with bluefish pâté.

Out on the horizon I could see the *Shenandoah*, the wind a bit aft of her beam, working her way back to Vineyard Haven, her home port. She seemed like something from another age. "That's why," I said. "I might have figured it out a little faster, if I'd been paying attention. I knew that Jimmy Souza's son was named Fred, and I knew that the boat Jimmy owned before he went belly-up was named the *Lucky Lil*, and I knew that Jimmy blamed the trawlers for his problems. And then Sandy Dings told me that her sister's name was Lillian, and Jean Dings told me her cousin's name was Freddy. But somehow I never put that all together until yesterday. Dumbness."

"Probably you were so bedazzled by being married that you couldn't really think clearly. I imagine that's it, and I think it's sweet." She smiled her shimmering smile.

"Maybe I'll get over it in time."

"Let's hope not." She sipped her Lukusowa. "But tell me, if you've solved the mystery, why do you still have that little wrinkle in your forehead?"

I hadn't known about the little wrinkle, which probably helps to explain why I'm not the world's champion poker player; but I was aware of being less than quite content. "For one thing, the kid with the sweatshirt up in Boston wasn't Fred Souza. I know what Fred looks like. I used to see him when Jimmy still had his boat and Freddy crewed for him, and the kid in Boston wasn't him."

"Somebody he hired? A friend?"

"I thought that for a while. But do you have any friends you could hire to kill somebody? Or do you know how to get in touch with somebody who'd do the job for you? No? Well, neither do I, and I'm having a hard time figuring that a college kid like Freddy knows any hit men, either. Even amateurs, like this guy."

Zee tried another cracker. "Oh, I don't know about that. Remember that schoolteacher in New Hampshire? She got some of her students to knock off her husband."

Touché.

"And another thing," I said. "Whoever the guy was, he knows we can ID him, and he's still out there. Until the cops find him, I want you to be careful." I told her about Wally and his friend. "And these local guys only brought their fists," I said. "The kid in Boston is a gunner."

Zee stopped nibbling. "You mean to tell me that two guys attacked you right here? This morning? While I was asleep?"

"Well, it wasn't much of an attack. The point is that the next one might be."

Zee reached across and put her hand on my arm. "The police will find Freddy, and they'll learn who the shooter was, and they'll bring him in, and we won't have to worry anymore. They may have him already." I didn't think she sounded quite as confident as she had before.

I finished my drink. "How's the target practice going?"

"It's going fine, and it's fun. But I'm not going to start carrying my trusty Beretta around with me, if that's what you're thinking."

That's what I'd been thinking. "I won't ask you to do that," I said.

"The wrinkle is still there, Jefferson."

I ironed it out. "Gone," I said. "Let's go down and eat."

But after the supper dishes were washed and stacked, I found her staring at me.

"It's back again?" I asked.

She nodded.

"Probably a sign of age. Your insatiable carnal demands are wearing me out and turning me into an old man."

She slowly shook her head back and forth, and allowed a little smile to cross her face. "Oh no. Those make us younger, not older. It's something else."

True. I told her about Vanderbeck's Axioms, then said, "One of them says things are not what you think they are. That's what I've been thinking about. Freddy Souza seems too perfect. Motive, opportunity, and all that. The thing is, I can't imagine who else might have stolen that shotgun. Who else knew where it was and that the house would be empty that night?"

"It's true that things are almost never exactly what they seem," said Zee. "They're always at least a little bit different. More complex, usually. It's the way things are. On the other hand, aren't you the one who's always talking about Occam's razor: the simplest explanation that accounts for the facts is probably the proper one?"

I put my hands on her shoulders. "Haste makes waste, but the early bird gets the worm. That's the trouble with truisms: there's always one that contradicts another one."

"You sound tired," said Zee. "Bring your worm, and I'll bring my bird, and the four of us will go to bed."

So we did that.

Later, Zee said, "You should have another talk with Bill Vanderbeck. Maybe he can tell you more about these axioms of his."

She tucked her knees up against the back of mine, and put her arm over me, and gave me a squeeze, then got out of bed, and put on her uniform and went to work. I was awake awhile longer, missing her warmth against me, but feeling blessed.

The next morning I drove again to Gay Head, running things through my mind. I drove past Gubatose's driveway, on to Bill Vanderbeck's house. There was an extra car in his yard. Then the door of the house opened and the shaman came out and waved me in.

I parked the Land Cruiser and went up onto the porch. "I don't want to interrupt anything."

"No problem," he said, putting one brown hand on my shoulder and shaking my hand with the other. "It's only my niece, Toni. Come in. You might be able to help her out, as a matter of fact. She's here to talk about her husband."

I followed him inside. Toni Begay smiled at me and said hello. She had a cup of coffee in her hand. Vanderbeck went to the kitchen and came back with a cup for me. We sat.

"Toni here is wondering if she knows enough about her husband," said Vanderbeck. "Can you tell her anything she doesn't know?"

No one had ever asked me to do anything like that before. "I doubt it," I said. I thought Toni Begay was as surprised by her uncle's request as I was.

"Anything at all," said Vanderbeck.

I could think of little. "You know that I met him in

Vietnam. But I wasn't there long enough to learn much about him. He had a reputation for doing his job and for bringing his people back alive, which wasn't the easiest thing to do. He saved my life, I know that."

"Toni, here, says that Joe doesn't tell her much about himself."

"It's not that, exactly," said Toni. "It's like he really believes that his life isn't worth much discussion. If I ask him something in particular, he'll tell me whatever I want to know, and he seems good-humored about it, if you know what I mean, and goes into as much detail as I want. But if I don't ask, he doesn't tell. Is that normal?"

Actually, it sounded pretty normal to me. I wondered what Zee would say, if she were here.

"For instance," Toni went on. "He's never really told me anything about his business. I mean I know about him growing up out there in Arizona, and I know he was in the army in Vietnam and that he got wounded there, and I know that he worked as a rep for a company, or maybe several companies. That gidget business. You remember? But he never really tells me much. Whenever I ask him, he seems to tell me what he's done, but actually never does. It bothers me, but I don't know if it should."

"So she called me up and I told her to come over for coffee," said the shaman. "I figured she could think about it some more on the drive. Besides, I have some green beans she can take home, and maybe give some to her mother, too. They're growing like crazy, and I have more than I can ever eat by myself. You're welcome to some yourself, J.W."

There was a bowl of fresh green string beans on the table, which reminded me that I had better get to picking mine again. It doesn't take beans long to grow you out of house and home. When they're ready, you have to pick them almost every day. I wasn't an hour past breakfast, but thinking about fresh string beans for supper made me hungry.

"Thanks," I said. "But I have all the beans I need."

"Some men don't want their wives to know what they do," said the shaman to his niece. "Some of those men like to have something to hold over their women's heads."

"Joe's not that way. He's never held anything over my head. It's something else."

"Maybe he's ashamed of what he's had to do, and doesn't want you to know about it."

"I don't know what it is. I just wish he'd tell me. I wish he trusted me."

"Maybe he thinks it's better if you don't know. Maybe he's done something illegal that would affect you if you knew."

"Joe wouldn't ever do anything illegal!" she frowned.

"I do illegal things all the time," said the shaman. "So do most people. I drive over the speed limit, I trespass where there are NO TRESPASSING signs. I do that on purpose, by the way, just because I don't like NO TRESPASSING signs. And another thing. There's a law in Massachusetts that says that anytime you find something worth more than, I think, about three dollars, you're supposed to report it. But when I find a buoy or a fishing plug washed up on the beach, or a five-dollar bill, or any other thing like that, I never report it; I keep it."

"Yes, but what if you found a wallet full of money, or something like that? You'd turn that in. I know you would."

"Maybe," said the shaman. "Maybe not."

"You're just being stubborn. You know you would."

He smiled. "Maybe so. The point is that people in business bend the law all the time. Good people do illegal things. Or sometimes they do legal things, but get into trouble anyway. Or they do legal things that most people think are immoral . . ."

That seemed to make Toni almost angry. "Joe would never do anything immoral!"

The shaman drank some coffee.I thought of the immoral things I had done.

"He probably just doesn't want to bore you," I said.

"He won't tell me some things."

We sat quietly for a time. Then the shaman spoke again: "Do you trust him?"

"I want to trust him. I want to!" She turned toward him. "I do trust him! But tell me this, Uncle Bill. I need to know. Do you trust him?"

He met her gaze. "The important thing is that you trust him."

"But you're a shaman. You're not like other people, not like the rest of us. You know things about people. I want to know if you trust him."

He looked at his coffee cup, and turned it in his hand. "You shouldn't base your faith on what a shaman tells you," he said, almost sadly. "You're a grown-up woman. You have to depend on yourself, on your own understandings."

"I said I trusted him, and I do." She stared out the window at the barn. "This business of being grown-up and married is hard. I don't know that I like having to decide so many things by myself."

"It is your fate," smiled her uncle. "It's the fate of all grown-up people. Children get to have someone else tell them what to think and what to do, but grown-ups have to decide for themselves. And getting married is part of it.

When you get married, the two of you are responsible for the marriage. If you take that responsibility, the marriage may either thrive or break apart; but whatever happens, it will be the right thing. Sometimes, if the two people were wrong about thinking they could live well together, the breaking is the right thing. But if you decide that you can live well together, you are responsible for making sure that happens, even during the worst of times." The shaman nibbled another bean, then went on:

"You ask me if I trust Joe. I do. I think he is a strong, imperfect man who loves you but doesn't think yet that you're quite grown-up enough for him to tell you everything. You're almost twenty years younger than he is, remember, and part of him still thinks of you as some sort of wonderful child who shouldn't yet be introduced to some of the unpleasant aspects of life, of his life. I think that's why he won't tell you certain things."

"But I am grown-up. I'm a woman. I haven't been a little girl for a long time!"

The shaman ate a bean. "They say that there is a bit of woman in every girl and a bit of boy in every man. Maybe it's the boy in him that can't see the woman in you."

"You always did talk in riddles." Still, she smiled.

"Another thing to consider: Sometimes a lover or husband can be afraid of what his woman will think or feel if he tells her the truth. That's not unusual in men."

"What should I do?"

He shrugged. "Trust him until he knows he can trust you. Until he knows he can tell you anything. Until he's either not afraid anymore or is willing to take the risks that go with fear."

She shook her head. "I don't think Joe Begay is afraid of anything."

"He may be afraid of you," said the shaman. He turned to me. "You're a married man. Are you afraid of your wife?"

"No."

"Does she know everything about your life?"

"No."

"Do you know everything about hers?"

"No."

"Do you want to?"

"We have an agreement. What happened to us before we met doesn't count."

The shaman nodded, and looked back at his niece. "Maybe that's something for you to think about."

She looked at me. "What will you do if something comes out of the past into your new life?"

"I won't know until it happens."

"How will you handle it?"

The question made me uneasy. "I don't know."

"I don't know how I will, either. But meanwhile, you don't need to know any more?"

"I know all I need to know about Zee. I'm not her judge. I'm her husband."

"What is it you know?" she asked. "Tell me."

"I'm not Solomon," I said. "You'll get no great wisdom from me."

"Try."

I thought awhile. Then I said, "What I know is that Zee was born to be loved and protected, and that I was born to love and protect her."

Toni looked at me. Then she shook her head and smiled. "You men. You're all hopeless romantics."

I needed to change the subject, so I turned to the shaman. "Maybe you can tell me something."

"Maybe. Ask me. If I can, I will."

"Yesterday up in Luciano's office, you gave Vinnie Cecilio an odd look when you left. What was that all about?"

"Ah," he said. "Vinnie. The young man who escorted me off of the property." He looked thoughtful. "Vinnie has an odd aura. He's not like us. He has no heart."

22

No heart. Not like us.

Vinnie, Luciano's eldest grandchild, the apple of Angela's eye, had no heart.

I stared at Vanderbeck. "What do you mean by that?"

He frowned. "Some people have heart. Others don't. How shall I say this? If you have heart, you face the world. If you have great heart, you face it very well. If you have little heart, you face it badly. If you have no heart . . ." He shrugged.

"And Vinnie has no heart?"

He looked sad. "I saw none."

"He's a shaman," said Toni to me.

Vanderbeck smiled his enigmatic smile and shook his head. "Shamans are like everyone else. There are good ones and bad ones, strong ones and weak ones. If I am a shaman at all, I'm a very imperfect one whose readings of auras should be taken with salt. I am no Passaconnaway."

I didn't know who Passaconnaway was, and I was inclined to take what most people said with salt. But I wasn't sure what I believed about Bill Vanderbeck.

"Who else around here has no heart?" I asked.

"Why, very few people," said Vanderbeck. "Some tourists. No one who lives in this town."

"Not anyone else up at Luciano Marcus's place?"

He shook his head. "No one that I saw. All others I saw there have heart."

I tried another angle. "Are the heartless people the evil ones?"

"Many people you would call evil have strong hearts."

There was something missing in his words, and I wanted to know what it was. "What are you saying? Why do you say they're people I would call evil?"

His eyes revealed nothing. "Sometimes I try to imagine that I am God, and I try to see things as God must see them. When I do that, I seem to understand that much of what men call good and evil is not that at all. I seem to see that good and evil are human notions that mean nothing." Then he laughed, ironic and full of humor. "But as soon as I stop playing God, I see good and evil everywhere once again, as usual."

Actually, I didn't see it everywhere. But I did see it sometimes.

"And you," I said. "Do you have heart?"

"I hope so," he smiled. "But it's probably true that no one really knows himself. We are all good at self-deception."

"Even shamans?"

Again the laugher. "Especially shamans, I would think!"

I drove to the Edgartown library, on North Water Street. It being yet another fine summer day with most people at the beaches, I found a parking place no more than three blocks away, up near the Harborview Hotel, and walked back. On my right, the great white houses that lined the street, making it Edgartown's loveliest, towered over me, and their gardens were bright with flowers. To my left, yachts swung at their moorings, and I could see the buildings and pier of the Chappaquiddick Beach Club, one of many Vineyard places I had never been. For so small an island, there were many such places. In fact, when I thought about it, I hadn't been most places on the island.

I had, however, been in most of its libraries. I am fond of libraries because they're full of information and people who actually like to help you find it. Just as there is no bad beer, there are no bad libraries, although some are better than others. Edgartown's is one of the island's best.

Inside, I looked up Passaconnaway. He, according to the books I found, turned out to have been no Wampanoag at all, but the great sachem of the Pennacooks, who lived up around Lowell. And he had been not only a sachem but a powahee, capable of incantations and visionary ecstasy. The English of the 1600s had called him a prophet and magic maker, and his reputation had made the Pennacooks the only people feared by the Tarentines of Maine, who, in 1618, had attacked and decimated the Agawams and other Massachusetts tribes before going back north for a while.

Passaconnaway could make fire in the snow, could cuddle poisonous snakes, and could predict the future. A comet he saw led him to predict the plague of 1616, which wiped out two thirds of the Massachusetts coastal tribes, before the Tarentines pretty much finished the job two years later. When a group of Boston riflemen came to arrest him for troublemaking in 1642, he stopped them with a storm, and escaped.

Passaconnaway's magic had been considerable, but not strong enough, finally, to hold back the English.

"They fought me with fire and thunder," he was quoted as saying. "I tried sorcery against them, but still they increased and prevailed. I am powerless and must bend before the storm."

Passaconnaway had lived to be a hundred and twenty years old. He had died in 1666 after converting to Christianity and warning his people not to quarrel with the English lest they be "destroyed and rooted off of the earth." Old Passaconnaway, a prophet to the last, had seen the future clearly, I thought. His people had been, in the end, pretty much rooted off of the earth.

And now Linda Vanderbeck was set on getting at least some of that earth back.

While I was there, I read more of New England history. About the European explorers and settlers, and the people they found waiting for them when they landed. About Champlain and Block, John Smith and Cotton Mather, Gosnold, Standish, and Bradford, and their adventures and misadventures with the native folk. And about Winepoykin of the Nahumkeikes, who had his nose cut off while fighting the Tarentines and who was afterward known to the English as "No-nose George"; and about Samoset, and Squanto, and Coneconum; and about Massasoit of the Pokanokets, who were also known as the Wampanoags, and who, after the Terentines had devastated the Massachusetts tribes in 1618, became the most powerful people in southern New England.

I read about the conflicts between the Wampanoags and the Narragansetts, the wars between the Algonquins and the Iroquois, especially those between the Mohawks and the Mohegans, and about the torture and mutilations that seem to go with all wars, particularly those between relatives. I read about Massasoit's sons, Wamsutta and Metacomet, called Alexander and Philip by the English, and of "King Philip's War" between the native peoples and the Europeans that ended only with the death of Metacomet, King Philip, in 1676.

It was a bloody history of betrayals, killings, and bru-
tality, and its ending all but guaranteed that Passaconnaway's last, dark prophecy of doom for his people
would come true.

I thought about Linda Vanderbeck. In the seven-
teenth century, there had been women leaders of some
of the native peoples in New England, squaw-sachems,
who were tribal commanders. A phrase appeared in my
mind: Queen Linda's War. I put aside my books, and
thought awhile, then got up and left the library, wondering what I had learned, if anything, that might be
useful to me or make me wise. Outside, the sun was
bright and the wind was sweet, and King Philip was a
long time dead.

It was past noon, and I was suddenly conscious of
being hungry and in need of a beer, so I walked down to
the Navigator Room for a sandwich and something to
wash it down. When I came outside afterward, I looked
up the street and saw the chief standing at the four corners, where Main Street crosses Water Street. He was
talking to a summer cop. I walked up, arriving just as
the summer cop left.

In spite of the fine beach weather, there were, as
usual, a lot of people in town. A mixture of tanned July
people and pale August people.

"What brings you downtown?" asked the chief.
"You're usually hanging out in the woods, or off fishing
someplace this time of day."

"Scholarship," I said. "My never-ending quest for wisdom has brought me to the library."

"I didn't know they had a library in the Navigator
Room," said the chief.

"Ha, ha. That was my after-library lunch."

"It must be nice to have a job that lets you drink beer all day." His eyes were roving here and there, as usual.

"What do you hear from Boston?" I asked.

"You mean about your notion that Fred Souza stole that shotgun and is behind that attack on your boss, Luciano Marcus? Well, as a matter of fact, I talked with Gordon Sullivan, up in Boston, an hour or so ago. He's talked with Fred Souza and some people who know him, and so far, at least, it looks like your theory will fly about as well as a lead kite. Freddy is working for the summer at UMass Boston, he's going to summer school, and he's got another job flipping burgers at night in a diner. In his spare time, he studies and sleeps, and that's about all. He doesn't hang around with any hard cases, and he doesn't seem to have the time or money or energy to date girls or to party. He's broke, and he's unhappy about his father, but Sullivan thinks he's too busy and tired to be involved with anything but his work and his classes."

"Sullivan could be wrong, of course."

"Sure, he could."

"But if Freddy didn't steal that shotgun, who did?"

"There are two hundred million other people living in the United States," said the chief. "If it wasn't him, I'd guess that it was one of them. See you later." He walked up Main Street.

I looked at my watch, then walked up Water Street, thinking. At home, still running things through my mind, I found Zee washing her long black hair. I wondered if she'd like to go fishing.

"No. I don't need to get my hair all salted up before it's even dry."

I repeated my theory that the reason women don't

rule the world is because they don't have time to do that and wash their hair, too.

"Get out of here," said Zee.

I put both regular and light rods on the roof rack, my tackle box and a five-gallon bucket in the back of the Land Cruiser, some beer in a cooler, and headed for the Jetties. Fishing is good for the soul, and mine felt like it needed some TLC right at the moment.

FWD's lined the Norton's Point Beach, and there were kites flying above them. Swimmers, sunbathers, and picnickers were enjoying the bright blue afternoon. At Wasque, there were more Jeeps and four-by-fours and more sunbathers, mixed with fishermen who were not catching any fish, but who didn't seem unhappy about it. I saw someone in an inner tube floating west in the falling tide, right in front of the surf casters. Had fish been there, that person would have been the subject of furious abuse and maybe even more, but today the warm and lazy fishermen simply held their casts until he sailed by.

I drove up East Beach, then cut inside to the Dike Bridge and went on north past the narrows to Cape Pogue Pond. I drove along the pond's east side until I could cut back outside to Arruda's Point, where, perhaps, a Spanish mackerel or maybe a bonito might be waiting for my Swedish Pimple.

There were a couple of trucks there already, but there was still room for me, so I got down my light rod and went to work.

While I fished, and felt the soul release that I get from casting for the fruits of the sea, I thought some more about the stolen shotgun.

After a while, I got back into the truck and drove on to the Jetties, over the soft sands that lie between there and

Arruda's. There were more trucks at the Jetties, but room for me again, so I tried my luck there for a while. Nobody was catching anything, but that was all right. If bringing home a fish is the only reason you go fishing, you should get one at the A & P instead of trying to catch one.

When I had been casting for about a half hour, I got my first hit. And lost it. The hit encouraged everybody, however, and pretty soon a guy on the other side of the rocks actually landed a mackerel. Everyone was happy for him. A little later I landed one of my own. I cut its throat and stood it, head down, in my five-gallon pail full of salt water. Before I left, I had another one standing on its head beside the first one. Not bad, for a short trip to the beach. I opened a celebratory beer, and drove home, looking at the birds, feeling better than when I'd left the house.

I cleaned the fish and got one ready for supper. When that was done, I phoned Thornberry Security. Thornberry was out. His secretary was willing to take my message: Had Thornberry checked out Fred Souza?

Then I called Aristotle Socarides. No answer. Where did that guy spend his time? Wasn't he ever home? And why didn't he have an answering machine? Everybody had an answering machine these days.

Except me, of course.

Zee's hair was dry. Our martini glasses were in the freezer, chilled and waiting, but she'd gotten her bag of shooting gear out of the gun cabinet. Apparently shooting didn't get your hair salty. I wasn't surprised when she said she'd take the martini later, after she and Manny finished their evening shoot. She invited me to come along, and I did that, not forgetting to take my own earplugs.

She and Manny worked hard, and the targets disintegrated before their pistols.

"Jessica James," I said, when she pulled the plugs out of her ears and packed her gear away.

"The lady can shoot," said Manny, approvingly.

At home, while Zee cleaned her Beretta, I got the drinks and appetizers ready, and took them up to the balcony. Zee came up and we sat and looked out over the evening waters. Life seemed strange and beautiful. I thought back to what Vanderbeck had said, and tried to imagine what God saw when examining the world. But I was not God, and could not guess.

23

The next morning, I called Detective Gordon R. Sullivan. He didn't seem too happy to hear from me.

"What is it this time? Another hot lead?"

"A few years back, a kid named Vinny Cecilio stole a car . . ."

"Every other kid in Boston has stolen a car," said Sullivan. "You want to talk to somebody about a stolen car, I'll connect you."

"This kid was Luciano Marcus's grandson. He still is. Nowadays, he's the old man's chauffeur. He was driving Gramp's car when the guy went at Luciano with the shotgun."

"So?" Sullivan was a little more interested, but not a lot.

"There were a couple of other kids with Vinny when they hooked the car. One of them was named Benny White, and the other one was called Roger the Dodger. I'd like to know what they're doing these days."

"I have things to do, Mr. Jackson. I don't have a lot of time to run around looking up juvenile records. If I tried to keep track of every kid who stole a car in Boston, I wouldn't have time to do anything else."

"You sound jaded," I said, putting a note of obviously false sympathy in my voice. "Okay, forget it. I'll call Thornberry Security. And I know a reporter over at the *Globe*. I'll see if he can help me out. Sorry to have bothered you."

Cops often have good relations with reporters, and

sometimes they actually get along with private cops. But they don't like it when those reporters and PI's have information and they don't.

"All right, all right," said Sullivan. "But what's the deal here? Why do you want to know who those kids were?"

"Because somebody took a shot at Luciano Marcus, and if it wasn't Fred Souza, it was somebody else. The only name I have that ties the Vineyard to Boston is Vinny Cecilio's, and aside from the island kids who knew him at UMass, those two names are the only ones I have that are tied to him."

"You telling me that Vinny tried to pop his own grandfather?"

"No. But if he did, it wouldn't be the first time some kid did it."

"There aren't any first times anymore," said Sullivan. "I got a lot of people to talk to. I'll add those to the list. It's the best I can do."

"One more thing. Those other two guys who were shotgunned. When did the shootings happen? Was it since the shotgun was stolen down on the island?"

"Yeah. One in May, and one in June. And now this latest one in July. Sounds like Joe Lewis."

I didn't get that one, and said so. "You're too young," said Sullivan. "Joe Lewis knocked them down so fast that they said he had a bum-of-the-month club. This shootist may have his own bum-of-the-month hit list. May, June, and a whack at Luciano in July."

Great. And now it was August.

I rang off and called Thornberry Security, I got Jason himself this time, and gave him the two names.

"So far," said Thornberry, "your tips have not gotten us very far."

"They've gotten you as far as yours have gotten me," I said, and told him what I'd been up to since last we'd talked. He told me nothing, of course. Jason the silent.

I thought about the people I'd talked to and the people I hadn't. I thought about people I hadn't even seen. I thought about Vinnie Cecilio. I decided to talk with Angela Marcus. Grandma.

How many times had I driven to Gay Head in the past few days? I was spending more time there than down island, where I belonged.

I drove up the Marcus's long driveway and parked. No one came to meet me. Nobody was watching the television screen. Security was lax. I knocked on the door, and Priscilla opened it. I told her I wanted to talk with Mrs. Marcus.

"She's in her garden," said Priscilla. I followed her along a hall and up some stairs. We passed Luciano's office en route. Priscilla opened a door and I went past her, out into the light of the August day. I walked along a path and came to Angela's garden. She was alone, on her knees, peering at her basil. She glanced up and smiled as I approached.

"Bugs," she said. "I've put some beer traps here. Did you ever use beer traps?"

I thought of the cans and bottles I'd emptied over the years. I was probably in a beer trap myself.

"Yes," I said. "I use them sometimes. And sometimes they even work." I knelt beside her, as she sat back on her heels and wiped her brow with the back of a gardening glove. "I've talked to everyone, and I'd like to talk to you some more. About the shooting."

She lifted a leaf and looked under it. "I'm afraid I won't be able to help you, but I'll try, if you like."

I liked Angela. She didn't seem to have any bad bones.
"You're probably right," I said, "but I'll ask you a few
questions anyway."

"All right."

"Do you know anyone who might want to harm your
husband?"

"No, I don't."

I wanted to protect her as much as I wanted to question her. "I understand that when he was younger, his,
ah, business activities may have created enemies."

"That was a long time ago," she said. "Luciano has not
been involved in such things for years."

"Ah. You knew about them, then?"

She looked at me. "I'm not one of those wives who
shuts her eyes to her family, who sees nothing but good
in her husband and children. I love them, but I know
who they are. Luciano did things that he felt he had to
do. And he did them knowing that I did not approve.
But he loved me and I loved him, and in time he stopped
doing those things. All that was a long time ago."

"Tell me about your grandson Vinnie."

Her gaze was steady. "Vincent is a naive young man
who has neither great intellect nor ambition. In part I
blame our daughter and her husband for that, though
perhaps I shouldn't, since neither of them values
thought or hard work, either. Perhaps it's genetic. My
sons are intelligent and industrious, like their father, but
my daughter is like my mother, good-natured and
clever, but lazy. Worse yet, she married a man much like
herself, and Vincent is the product of that union. So
what he is, is probably not his fault. It's probably mine,
for not having brought him down here earlier, before his
weaknesses got him into trouble."

"But you give him money. Isn't that catering to those very weaknesses?"

She shrugged. "I have it to give. Perhaps I spoil him a little. But a boy needs a little money." She smiled. "It's like that good cop, bad cop business I see on the TV programs. Luciano is the bad cop, and I'm the good cop. Together, we get the work done. We get Vincent to become a man, instead of a child."

"You love him."

"Of course. He's my grandson."

"And does he love you and his grandfather?"

"What a question! Of course he does!"

"One of the motives behind crimes is money. Who will benefit from Luciano's will?"

Her back stiffened. She put her hands on her knees and looked down at them. When she spoke, her voice was tight.

"A good deal of the money will be in trusts. If I survive Luciano, most of the rest of it will come to me, but some will go to the children and grandchildren. I don't think you should be thinking along these lines, Mr. Jackson."

"I gather that the estate will be considerable. Who'll control the businesses? What you've said about your daughter suggests that she's not the one to leave in charge."

Some of the anger seemed to go out of her. She sighed. "Cynthia and her husband would very much like to get control of the family businesses, but Luciano has put those businesses in our sons' hands. Our daughter and her family receive the income from a trust, and from the businesses as well. It will keep them comfortable, though probably not as comfortable as they might wish. But what is it they say about wishes? If they were horses, beggars would ride? We love our daughter very much and are fond of our son-in-law, but we no longer hope that someday they'll become responsible enough to trust with the large amounts of money. When Luciano dies, they will, of course, receive a very nice cash legacy, as will the other members of the family, but their principal inheritance will be another trust."

"And the boys will get the businesses."

"No. Our sons will control the businesses, but they will continue to be owned, in part, by their sister."

"But she'll have no hand in running things."

"That's right. Cynthia is like her son. When she has money, she spends it and wants more. She's a wonderfully pleasant person, but she never looks beyond her present desires. We're working hard to see that Vincent won't turn out the same way. Vincent . . ." Her voice fell away.

It was interesting to have it affirmed that rich people had almost as many money problems as I did. They were just of a different kind. Mine came from having almost too little cash; theirs came from having almost too much. I wondered what it was about Vinnie that made her voice fade away like that.

A shadow fell across the basil, and we both turned and saw Bill Vanderbeck peering down. I glanced down at Angela. Her face, which had been troubled, seemed immediately very happy.

"It's doing very well," he said, nodding.

"We love pesto," she said. "I think we might eat it every day if our cook would let us."

He smiled at me. "Hello, J.W."

How had he gotten there? As usual, I'd heard and seen nothing of his coming. I shook his hand, and stepped back. He knelt beside Angela, and together they worked their way down the row of basil plants, pulling the occa-

sional weeds that had emerged since Angela had last
worked along this row, and discussing Angela's herbs
and vegetables. When they were done with the basil,
they started on the beans.

"Wonderful beans," said Bill. "You could live on
pesto, I could live on fresh-picked green beans."

"Me, too," agreed Angela. She paused and sat back on
her heels and looked around. "In fact, there's nothing
here that I wouldn't be able to live on." She smiled at
him, and her teeth flashed in the summer sun.

"You take care of your garden, and your garden will
take care of you."

She pushed a strand of hair from her forehead. "I
imagine you've come to talk with Luciano again about
the cranberry bog."

"So he told you about the bog, eh? That's good. Some
men never tell their wives much."

"Well, I'm not saying he tells me everything, but I do
know about your people wanting the cranberry bog."

"They're not necessarily my people," said the
shaman, plucking a single stem of grass from beside a
hearty bean plant. "To tell you the truth, I'm not very
happy about people identifying themselves as members
of groups. If they have to belong to some group or other,
I think they'd be better off if they just thought of themselves as members of the human being group. But
you're right about some of the local Wampanoags wanting that bog. And the thing is, I believe they've got a
case. I've seen the old maps and papers they talk about,
and even though I'm not a lawyer . . ."

"That reminds me," she interrupted. "I meant to ask
you before. What do you do for a living?" She laughed.
"I know now that you're not a lawyer, but what are you?"

"I'm retired."

"What did you retire from?" she asked, her hands busy amid the beans.

He worked steadily beside her. "I guess you might say that I never really had a regular job, a steady job, like being a doctor, or digging ditches, or driving a truck. I've done a lot of things during my life."

"One of them must have been gardening."

"That, too. Gardening's been one of the jobs I've gone back to many times."

"I should warn you that Luciano seems very firm about keeping the cranberry bog."

"I'm sure he is, but I still hope to get him to change his mind. There's a piece of land that the Wampanoags are willing to exchange for the bog and the half acre that goes with it. It sticks down inside the northern boundary of your property and it's actually bigger than the bog land, so you'd be getting more land for less and straightening out your northern boundary line at the same time, if your husband could see fit to make the trade. It would be a good deal for everybody."

She climbed to her feet. "I suppose I'd better let the two of you get at your negotiations, then. I tell you, Bill, it would please me if you and Luciano could work this thing out. I don't like to think about my neighbors being mad at us. I'd rather be friends. I should tell you, though, that Luciano is very unhappy about the way you come up here without any of his men seeing you. It's very disturbing to him."

"I'll try not to anger him."

She swept the garden with her eyes, seeing more work that needed doing. Then she looked at him. "I know you won't," she said.

"Don't bother showing me in," he said. "I know the way." He turned to me. "Maybe you'd like to come along, J.W. That way, Luciano won't be all alone."

Angela nodded. "Yes, J.W., I think that's a good idea."

When Luciano opened his office door in response to what I guessed he thought was Angela's knock, he seemed stunned to find himself looking at Bill Vanderbeck.

"How the hell did you get in here?"

In answer to his question, Vanderbeck made a vague gesture that took in the house beyond the office door, the grounds outside the house, and the greater part of Gay Head. "I was helping your wife with her weeding," he said.

"Well, you can damn well stop seeing my wife in her garden! And you can get yourself out of here before I have you thrown out! And the next time you try to get in here, I'll have you arrested!" He glared at me. "And what the hell are you doing here with this man?"

"We met up in the garden again," I said. "I was talking with your wife."

Vanderbeck floated across the room and took the same chair he had taken before. He pointed a bony forefinger at Luciano's desk. "If you push that button there, you can have some men in here pretty quickly. I won't be too long, in any case. I just came by to see if you've had a chance to talk with your lawyers about the Wampanoag claim to the cranberry bog."

Luciano stalked behind his desk and fell into his chair. "I've talked with them. They think they can beat you in court."

I was suddenly very conscious of Vanderbeck's gentle yet piercing eyes, eyes that seemed to peer into Luciano's psyche and to root out the truth that

Luciano's lawyers were, in fact, none too sure that they would prevail against a determined Wampanoag legal suit. Luciano, who normally was unreadable, save for his anger, seemed almost transparent.

Vanderbeck produced a folded paper and laid it on Luciano's desk. "You may not have seen this map. It shows the boundaries of your estate. You'll notice a piece of land sort of sticking down into the northwest corner of your place. Some Wampanoags own that. They're willing to trade that piece for the cranberry bog and that half acre that goes with it."

"The sacred Indian Land," said Luciano, his lip curling. Still, he took the map and looked at it.

"Show that to your lawyers and ask them what they think of a trade. That piece of land on the north has a title solid as a state biologist's head. There'll be no question in anybody's mind about your owning it, if you decide to make the trade."

"I'm not interested in making any goddamned trade!"

Vanderbeck got up. "You talk to your lawyers before you decide. I'll see you again in a few days, and you can let me know what you think."

"You're not, by God, coming back! I don't know how you got back in this time, but it won't happen again!"

Vanderbeck pointed at the desk. "It's not necessary, but you'll want somebody to escort me off your place. So just punch that button, and I'll be on my way."

Luciano jabbed at the button, and soon Vinnie and two other men were in the room, staring at Vanderbeck, then looking nervously at their boss.

"Hello, Vinnie," said the shaman.

Vinnie, who had no heart.

"How the hell did this bozo get in here?" shouted

Luciano, slamming his fist on the desk. "And where's Thomas? He was supposed to make sure this guy never came back! Damn! Vinnie, you take this guy to the gate and make sure he never gets back in again!"

"Yes, boss," said Vinnie. He hesitated. "You want I should, ah, give him a lesson, like. You know, so he'll know to stay away?"

Vanderbeck gave Vinnie a smile, then smiled in turn at Luciano.

"No!" said Luciano. "Just get the guy off my land and keep him off!"

"We'll get together later, Mr. Marcus," said the shaman. "Come along, Vinnie." He turned and led Vinnie and the other two men out of the room.

Luciano put his hands on his desk and saw that they were trembling. He was pale. He looked at me. "The doctor tells me not to get too stressed out about things, to take it easy. Now this damned Indian, or whatever he is, is coming into my office whenever he damned pleases!" He took a pill from his pocket and put it under his tongue.

I had a bad feeling. "Take it easy," I said.

But Luciano wasn't listening. "And now he says he's going to come again, and I know damned well he'll do just that, in spite of Vinny and Thomas and all the rest of them who are supposed to be guarding the place! He's like a goddamned ghost or something!"

Luciano sat and looked at his trembling hands, as if trying to will the chill of fear out of his soul. After a while, his hands stopped their shaking. He picked up the map and looked at it. Then he lifted a phone and glared at me. "I'm calling my lawyers! Goddamn that Vanderbeck!"

It seemed a good time for me to leave. So I did.

24

Since I was already in Gay Head, I drove on up to the cliffs where, by a miracle, I found a parking place. Maybe Gay Head was beginning to think I was a native and had decided to treat me like a human being instead of just another money-producing tourist. I walked up to the lookout to see if I could spot Block Island, way out to the west. I have a theory that if conditions are just right, if it's a perfectly clear, dry day, I should be able to see it, even though I never have. Today was no different. I could see Cuttyhunk, and the mainland of America beyond it, and the Texas Tower lighthouse out in the middle of the mouth of Buzzards Bay, and, way off there in the distance, what might be Point Judith, Rhode Island; but all I could see where Block Island should be was a little white cloud hanging over a thin haze on the horizon.

On my right the bright clay cliffs fell down to the sea. Along the beach, far below, the water was colored by the hues of the clay, and the beach walkers were tiny ants. Fishing boats moved over the waters, and the wind was warm.

I went down to the stores and bought myself a cola and a Wampanoag hamburger. When I was finished with them, I went into Toni Begay's shop.

"How's married life?" I asked.

She laughed. "Well, it's not what I expected when I was a little girl."

"Little boys don't even think about marriage," I said. "I imagine it's one of those gender things I hear about."

She idly arranged items on the shelves, moving here and there. "I had a talk with Joe," she said.

"Ah."

"He told me some more about what he does."

I said nothing.

"He says he was sort of an aide-de-camp, a simplifier, an untangler. He says there are people like that in a lot of organizations. Their bosses trust them and when there's some kind of a problem—in communications, for instance, or some sort of a mix-up in the organization—guys like Joe, who can speak for the boss, straighten out the problem. He says that nine times out of ten, it's some personality thing. One manager doesn't like another one, so he won't cooperate with him. That sort of stuff. He says that his company and some other one might be trying to do a deal, and there are some little problems that have to be worked out. So he and the other company's guy, who did the same work he did, work them out, and have a drink or two afterward, and maybe see each other a couple of times later. He says that's some of what he used to do. Did you know there are people who do that sort of thing?"

"I don't know anything about business," I said. "But it sounds logical. I know that every time something's done, somebody does it. It doesn't get done by itself."

"He put his hands on my shoulders and pushed me back so he could look down into my face, and he said he was out of that business, and that now he's going to be a fisherman. He asked me to be patient with him a little longer."

I remembered the movement of his hand across his

chest when Bill Vanderbeck had startled us. "You don't need to tell me this," I said.

"You're his friend. He said there's a lot about me that he doesn't know, but that he'll tell me everything I want to know about him. He says we're going to be married a long time, and the time will come that I'll know so much about his boring life that I'll be sorry I asked."

I thought back over my own life. It certainly didn't seem to be worth much discussion. "Maybe he's right," I said.

"No, he isn't! I know he's lived an exciting life."

"What is it that sailors say? That cruising consists of days of boredom interspersed with moments of stark terror? That's probably a pretty good description of most men's lives. Lots of dull stuff and a few high points."

"Anyway, he says he'll tell me everything."

"Good."

"And that then I can judge for myself what kind of life he's led."

"Probably he's like me," I said. "Probably he figures his past life was nothing compared to the one he'll be living with his new wife."

She flashed me a smile. "You and Zee will have to come to our place for dinner."

"Fine. I'll have Zee give you a call, so we can find a good time. Meanwhile, I'd like to talk to your husband. Do you know where I can find him?"

He was down at the boat, in Menemsha. I drove there, parked in the lot by the beach, and walked along the dock until I saw Joe Begay and another man working together on the deck of a boat called *Matilda*.

Menemsha is a genuine fishing village, but looks so perfect that you suspect it was designed by Walt Disney. Its post office is sufficiently quaint to have once been painted by Norman Rockwell as a *Saturday Evening Post* cover. There is a Coast Guard station there, a restaurant where the lobster is good, an antique shop, a boutique, a couple of fish markets, some snack shops, and not much else. Like the citizens of many of the island's communities, Menemsha residents believe their spot is the island's finest, and wouldn't think of living anywhere else. They only wish that not so many people knew about it.

Joe Begay and the other man were working on lines for conch pots. Coils of line lay in the cockpit of the boat under their feet, as they spliced.

Joe Begay made introductions. "Buddy, this is J. W. Jackson. J.W., this is Buddy Malone."

I shook Buddy Malone's hand. "You're the guy who sold this boat to Joe."

"That's right. Now he gets to try his hand at it. I'm going into another line of work."

"I do some scalloping down in Edgartown, but I've never done this sort of fishing."

"I been at it long enough. It's like any other job. There's good parts to it and there's bad parts. If you like it, and if you work hard enough at it, and if you're lucky, you can do all right."

Begay tugged at the bill of his cap and picked up a line. "Buddy's showing me the ropes. He hasn't painted any rosy pictures for me, either."

"I wouldn't do that," said Buddy, taking up a line and working at a new splice. His scarred fingers were still nimble, and he was at least twice as fast as Begay, who worked slowly and methodically, making sure that his work was strong. In time, he would need to work faster, if he was to keep his gear in shape.

"You have trouble with trawlers wrecking your gear?" I asked.

Buddy snorted. "Does a bear shit in the woods? We lose gear all the time. If it isn't the trawlers, it's the storms. We can't afford insurance, fuel costs more every day, the market is down, taxes are up. You name the problem, the fishermen have got it."

"He's a terrific salesman," said Begay, with a grin. "Makes me wish I'd gone into the business ten years ago."

"Buddy, did you ever hear of a guy named Luciano Marcus?"

Buddy's fingers flew. Then he shook his head. "Nope. Never heard the name."

"You guys have a fishermen's association of some kind, don't you? You never heard anybody talk about Luciano Marcus?"

He thought some more, then shook his head again. "Nope. Who's Luciano Marcus?"

"He's a guy who owns several of those trawlers that tear up your gear. Somebody took a shot at him the other day, and I was wondering if any of the pot fishermen on the island might have had something to do with it. Jimmy Souza says he lost his boat and has his house on the market, because the trawlers put him out of business. That might be motive enough for somebody to take a shot at somebody."

Buddy Malone's hands moved to the next splice. "I know Jimmy. It wasn't the trawlers that cost him his boat. It was the booze. The booze is a problem for a lot of fishermen. It keeps them warm when they're cold, it makes them happy when they're sad, it lets them forget things they want to forget. It can get so the booze is the most important thing. You start off drinking so you can keep on fishing, and you end up fishing so you can keep on drinking. And then you get to be the next Jimmy Souza." He looked up from his work. "That's one reason I'm getting out of the game. I'm beginning to like the juice too much. But as for this Marcus guy, if somebody is mad enough to shoot him, I never heard about it."

I looked around the boat. It was about thirty feet long, with a forward steering station and a wide, open deck, where you could stack pots and other gear. It was beamy and had a fairly high bow, but had low freeboard amidships. There was a rig to haul pots, and a spare outboard motor mounted on the stern, in case the inboard ever failed. It was sturdy and without frills, a classic New England fishing boat, the kind you see going out for lobsters off Maine, or dropping fish traps off the southern coasts.

The lines Joe Begay and Buddy Malone were working on would string pots together on the ocean floor. There would be a float at either end of the line, topped by a radar reflector, so the fisherman could find them even in fog or darkness. He'd start at one end of the line, and pull up the pots one by one. When a pot came up, he'd keep what catch he could sell, dump out the garbage, rebait the pot, and drop it overboard again. Then he'd go on to the next pot. It was not romantic work, but fishing and farming are only romantic pastimes to those who have never practiced them.

Trawlers would cross his lines and wreck his pots, storms would set the floats ashore, lines would part, pots would break up, and his catch would not wait for fair weather to be gathered. The fisherman would be out there in all but the very worst weather, often in an old boat without insurance, harvesting the sea.

And the fisherman himself was often his own worst enemy, overharvesting depleting stocks of game, taking no thought for the future other than tomorrow and the next boat payment. He fished out grounds, and bitterly complained when he could no longer bring back the catches he'd gotten in the old days. He sank boats to collect insurance money, if he was lucky enough to have insurance. He glutted the market when the fishing was good, and complained about the low prices he got.

It was a job I was glad I didn't have, although I had admiration for those who stuck at the trade, in spite of their shortsightedness and self-destructive inclinations.

They that go down to the sea in ships.

"You hear anything about Jimmy Souza going to an AA meeting?" asked Buddy.

"No. Is he doing that?"

Buddy shrugged. "I don't know. Somebody mentioned it. I guess I hope he is."

I'd read that AA didn't help unless you were ready for it. I didn't know if Jimmy was ready.

"I guess I do, too," I said.

I sat in the afternoon sun and for a while watched Buddy Malone's flying fingers and Joe Begay's slower, careful ones. Then I went home.

While I picked beans, watered the flowers in the boxes along the fence and in the hanging pots, and refilled the bird feeders, I ran things through my head. A few pieces were missing from the jigsaw puzzle, but if I was lucky, I might have them soon. It all depended on whether Sullivan or Thornberry checked out the names I'd given them, on what they found when they did so, and on whether they'd tell me what they learned, which they might well not do.

I was in one of those They Also Serve situations that irk me. I don't like to depend on other people to solve my problems, but short of going up to Boston myself, I'd have to, in this case.

I went inside and called Aristotle Socarides. Naturally, he wasn't answering his phone. What else was new?

I went out and looked at my hydrangea. Still not blue.

I went in and started supper. At least I could accomplish that.

25

When the information finally came, two days later, it came like catsup from the catsup bottle. Two catsup bottles, in fact, one shaken by Gordon Sullivan and one by Jason Thornberry. Blobs of data about Benny White.

Sullivan was friendlier than he had been the last time we talked. "I checked Mr. Benny White out, and the kid they call Roger the Dodger. Roger's brain wouldn't light a twenty-amp lightbulb, but he hangs around with Benny, like a dog. You know the type. Benny's something else. A real hard-ass. Beginning to make a name for himself in the street. A bad boy, getting worse. Likes to muscle people. You know he went to college? Yeah, UMass Boston. For a semester. Ran a little numbers game there with—guess who?—your boy Vinnie Cecilio. They both dropped out about the same time."

"And stole cars together."

"One, at least, that we know of. Probably more that we don't. But that was just the start, for Benny. Since then, he's been brought in for questioning about aggravated assault, assault, battery, and rape, but nothing's stuck. People won't testify, or they drop charges. You know how it is."

"Yeah. They know he'll be back on the street about five minutes after he gets probation, and they're afraid he'll come after them."

"He runs some girls, and probably is into gambling

and dope, too, but mostly he seems to want to be muscle for hire. I get the idea he just likes to beat people up. He likes people to be afraid of him."

"You think he's a killer?"

"There are rumors about that, too. Maybe you can help us out there. We don't have a mug shot of Mr. White, but we've got a couple of what you might call informal snapshots, and I'm going to fax one down to the Edgartown police. Maybe you and your wife can take a look at it and let us know if he's the guy who tried for Luciano Marcus. If you can ID this slimeball, I can get a warrant to search his place. He lives with Mom, down in Dorchester, and she'll probably swear that he's home every night by seven and leads the church choir on Sundays. But we might find something that will help us nail him."

I'd barely hung up the phone when it rang again. *Quelle surprise!* Jason Thornberry was on the line.

"J.W., Jason Thornberry here. I have some information I think might interest you."

Surprise again. Jason Thornberry was actually going to give me information instead of just accepting it? "Shoot," I said.

"Following up on those names you gave me, one of our operatives managed to get inside the home of Mrs. James White, the mother of Mr. Benjamin White. It was done quite legally, I assure you."

"I'm sure." I was, too. There's no law in Massachusetts against lying about who you are, unless you lie about being a policeman and try to act like one. You can pass yourself off as anyone, real or imaginary, and nobody can charge you with anything, although some aggrieved party can no doubt find a lawyer who'll give it a try. Probably a Thornberry operative wearing gas company coveralls, or some such outfit, carrying a clipboard, and armed with one of those neat ID's that look so official, knocked on Mrs. White's door, said something about a meter or the smell of gas in the neighborhood, and was invited in.

If it was me, I'd have used the smell-of-gas story, and would have asked the old lady to step across the street, just to be on the safe side, while I checked things out. Then, while she was gone, I'd have done some fast snooping before telling her all was well, and bringing her back inside.

Thornberry didn't give the details about the entrance, but got right to the point about what was found.

"In the boy's room, our operative found a box of double-aught buckshot shotgun shells, about half full. Found a box of latex gloves. Found a good deal of money in a drawer. Found some white powder in a cellophane bag. Found a pistol. A .38 or a 9-millimeter. Found an address book with Vincent Cecilio's address and telephone number in it." He paused. "Seemed to our operative that, considering all the stuff he kept in his room, Benjamin had a lot of confidence that nobody would ever come to his place. Our operative had a casual little chat with Mrs. White. Her husband is dead. The boy is an only child. Mom does everything for him, except clean his room. You can guess why he doesn't want her in there. Something else, too." Another pause. Even when I'd first known him in Boston years before, Thornberry was a man who knew the value of drama. Even then he wore one of those little Errol Flynn mustaches, and worked hard at looking like Henry Fonda in *Fort Apache*.

I played along. "What?"

"It seems that her son had an accident a while back. Slammed his hand in a car door and broke his little finger."

Ah.

"You going to tell all this to the cops?" I asked.

"My first obligation is to my client. We want to contact the other person, Roger the Dodger, before we make any reports to anyone. This call to you is simply to keep you up to date, since you gave us the lead."

"I appreciate it."

And I did. As soon as Thornberry rang off, I drove into Edgartown and went into the police station. Naturally, the chief wasn't there, but I asked the officer at the desk to get in touch with him and tell him about the fax coming down from Boston. She got on the horn, and I found a chair and sat down.

The Edgartown police station is the finest on Martha's Vineyard, with several offices, a gym, showers, storage areas for recovered stolen goods, labs, and everything else a small-town cop could ask for. It is the envy of the other five towns on the island, and rightly so. The chief's office has a private entry, so he doesn't have to come through the front door if he doesn't want to. He can also use his private door as a way to sneak outside to smoke his pipe.

He came in through that door just as the fax arrived, and the two of us took a look at the mug shot Sullivan had sent us.

Bingo.

Benny White wasn't a big guy, but a gun would make him as big as anyone, and bigger than most. A shotgun, loaded with double-aught buckshot, would, at close quarters, make him a giant.

"Is that him?" asked the chief.

"It looks like him to me."

"Let's run up to the hospital and let Zee have a look."

"Can we use the siren and the blue lights and break the speed limit with impunity?"

"Now I know the real reason they kicked you out of the Boston PD," said the chief. "Come on."

We drove up to the blinkers on the Vineyard Haven Road, took a right on County Road, drove past Bill Clinton's favorite island golf course, and went on to the hospital, where we parked in the emergency room parking lot.

"I'll pretend to be bleeding," I said. "That way they may let us talk to Zee without having to fill out forms first. If you're bleeding, sometimes they take you right away, but if you're not, you always have to fill out the forms before anything else happens."

"I'll tell them that you're unconscious. They'll believe that."

We went in and there was Zee, looking splendid in her white uniform, talking to a young doctor who was informally garbed in shorts and a tee-shirt. She was taller than he was, I noticed when she looked over his head, saw us, and smiled.

We crossed over to her and showed her the picture. She nodded her head. "That's him."

"You're sure this is the guy?" asked the chief.

"It looks like him to me," said Zee.

The chief nodded. "We'll give Sullivan a call, then."

"You look great," I said to Zee. "See you later." I gave her a kiss and followed the chief out to the car.

"The scenic route, Jeeves," I said.

We drove through Oak Bluffs and back to Edgartown along the shore road, which was lined with the cars of

August people enjoying the sun and water of the long beach between the towns. There were umbrellas rising from the sand, and kites in the air. Bicycles moved along the bike path. When we got to the big bridge, I could see my house across Sengekontacket pond. Beneath that same bridge, many years before, the giant *Jaws* shark had chewed off some poor guy's leg in the movie that kept a lot of people out of the water the summer it was released.

I felt simultaneously light and happy and depressed, because I knew who had done the shooting and why. The knowing felt good, but what was known felt bad.

In the chief's office, we called Sullivan. The chief told him that Zee and I had ID'd Benny, and I told him what Thornberry had told me.

Sullivan gave a contented grunt. "This should be enough to get me warrants to search his place and to bring him in. I'll get right at it."

"You might try to round up Roger the Dodger while you're at it," I said. "If he's as dumb as you say, he might tell you a lot about Benny."

"It may surprise you to learn that I already thought of that," said Sullivan, with a sigh. "Lemme talk to the chief."

I listened while the chief yessed, uh-huhed, and mmmmmed. When he hung up, he looked at me. "With a little bit of luck, this case might actually work out. It's the Boston PD's baby now, so you can go back to loafing in the woods. Sullivan's going to give me a call when they bring White in. When I get the call, I'll let you know."

I went out and sat in the Land Cruiser for a while. I had problems the chief didn't know about. The biggest one was figuring out how to tell Luciano and Angela Marcus that their grandson was behind the assassination attempt on Luciano. Another one was making sure that Vinnie didn't walk away from all this without a scratch. If he was willing to arrange for the killing of his own grandfather, he would probably be willing to kill somebody else, if he thought he could get away with it.

"One thing that's irksome," I said to Zee, as we sat on the balcony that evening with drinks and hors d'oeuvres, "is that if I'd been paying attention, I'd have known sooner that it was probably Vinnie. But I couldn't figure out how he could have gotten the shotgun, so I scratched him off the list. Dumbness once again."

Zee nodded. "Don't fret about it. When Sullivan gets into Benny's house, and brings Benny in, and grills Roger the Dodger, there should be enough evidence to make a case against Benny. And if there's a case against Benny, he might cop a plea and testify against Vinnie. What made you decide, finally, that it was Vinnie?"

"I was pretty slow. I thought it was probably Fred Souza. He seemed to have motive and opportunity. His dad blamed the trawlers for destroying his career and wrecking the family finances. He knew where the shotgun was kept, and he left the party alone the night it was stolen. I figured that Fred had a grudge and had given the shotgun to some friend or hired thug in Boston to do the job."

"What made you change your mind?"

"Buddy Malone had a hand in it. Buddy's been pot fishing for a long time, and he's probably as mad at the trawlers as anybody else, but he never heard of Luciano Marcus and had no idea he owned a lot of those boats. If Buddy didn't know, would Freddy somehow know? It didn't seem likely.

"Then there was Vanderbeck's Second Axiom. It's not

what you think it is. I don't know what Bill Vanderbeck thinks that means, but I began thinking that maybe what seemed to be true really wasn't. So I started all over again, and remembered things people told me, and I suddenly realized that Vinnie was probably the guy.

"He's lazy, he hung around with some young Boston hoods and stole at least one car; he likes his grandma, probably because she gives him money, but he calls Luciano boss. He's greedy and immature, and when Luciano dies, Vinnie stands to get his hands on some real money. That's motive enough.

"Then Bill Vanderbeck said Vinnie had no heart. That's another one of those things Bill says but doesn't really explain, but it rang right to me. A lot of killers aren't much different than you and me, but the ones I know about are mostly stunted somehow. They're children in grown-up bodies. They're not too bright, and their moral development is way back down there where it was when they were two years old. They want what they want when they want it and they don't see any reason why they shouldn't have it.

"Angela says Vinnie's mom is just as childish in some ways, so maybe Vinnie got it from her. Anyway, people like Vinnie only value people who do good things for them or whom they fear. Nobody else counts. They have no heart. They're what some shrinks call sociopaths."

"But Vinnie is a charmer," said Zee. "Lots of people like him. Look at his girlfriends. He treats them well."

"Yeah. He's sweet on the outside, all right. But he's got the motive, the right character, and he had the opportunity: He knew when Luciano would be going to the opera."

"But how did he get the shotgun?"

"He stole it. John Dings had taken him duck hunting once, but it was too cold and miserable for Vinnie to ever do it again. Vinnie doesn't like to do anything that gets him dirty or uncomfortable. He doesn't like clamming or fishing or freezing in a duck blind or anything like that. I think that's why he hired his pal Benny to bump off the old man: Vinnie didn't want to get his own hands dirty. Too gross for Vinnie. Anyway, John Dings kept his shotgun in the hall closet, and probably either took it out of there when Vinnie came to go shooting that morning, or put it back when they came home. It wasn't any secret where he kept the gun.

"The night it was stolen, John and Sandy Dings were already gone, across the pond at her sister's place, playing cards. Vinnie came by to pick up Jean Dings, but Jean is always late, and everybody who knows her knows it. So Vinnie knocks on the door and goes in, and Jean says she'll just be a minute, which probably means five or ten, at least. Vinnie sees his chance, gets the shotgun out of the closet, and takes it out to his Cherokee—borrowed from Luciano, of course—puts it under a blanket in the back, or something like that, and is back in the house reading a magazine when Jean shows up."

"He was taking quite a chance, wasn't he? What if she really had just been a minute?"

"She'd have found him outside, instead of inside. Unless she saw him with the gun, he'd just have had to say he was out looking at the stars, or some such thing. No problem."

"And now he had the gun."

"And his friend Benny was at the party."

"And Benny takes the gun back to Boston and saws it off so it will fit under that long sweatshirt . . ."

"And maybe shoots a couple of other people before he takes a crack at Luciano."

"A bad apple," said Zee, with a little shiver. "I'm glad there aren't many like him."

"It doesn't take many to ruin the barrel."

"I'll be glad when the chief calls and tells us that they've got him."

"Me, too."

But when the chief's call came a little later, it was with other news: "Sullivan missed him. Seems that when Benny came home today, his mom told him about the man who'd come to the house earlier. By the time Sullivan's people got there with his warrant, Benny was gone, and so was a lot of the stuff that Thornberry's man saw in the room, including the pistol."

"Terrific."

"It gets worse. The guys Sullivan sent to pick up Roger the Dodger didn't find him, either."

"Great."

"But some other cops already had. They'd responded to a report of gunshots and found Roger in an alley, very dead. Three shots at close range, right in the pump. They won't know for sure for a while, but Sullivan says it looks like a .38 or a Nine."

"And Benny is gone."

"Nobody knows where. But if Benny did Roger, he may want to do other people who know what he's been up to. So be careful."

I thought that was excellent advice.

26

When the chief hung up, I told Zee what he'd told me. Her great dark eyes widened, then narrowed. "There are only three people I know about who can ID Benny. You, me, and Vinnie. And we're all here on the island."

"The cops will be watching the boats," I said.

Zee did not look relieved, and no wonder. In the wintertime, Martha's Vineyard has a population of about ten thousand people, but in the summer there are ten times that many, and the visitors are constantly coming and going on the ferries and planes. Hundreds of new faces arrive every day, and hundreds of others leave. Thus, if Benny White could bring himself to shed his city garb of baggy clothes and oversize sweatshirts, and don the collegiate summer-on-the-Vineyard costume of shorts, sandals, and tee-shirt and tote a gym bag—no problem for an old UMass man like himself—he could probably walk off a ferry past a dozen cops flicking their eyes back and forth between their copies of his picture and the faces of the people unloading onto the island. It would be the hide-in-plain-sight theory of anonymity, and it often worked.

"You'd better call Vinnie," said Zee. "He may not know about this."

"Vinnie is the mastermind," I said. "What do you care about Vinnie?"

"He's a human being," said Zee. "So far he hasn't

actually killed anybody. He should be told that Benny's on the loose!"

I thought about that. Yeah. Maybe if Vinnie thought that Benny White was coming down to shoot him and shut him up, he might decide to help us find Benny before Benny found him.

"You're right," I said.

Priscilla answered when I called the Marcus's number. Vinnie had his own phone. An unlisted number. She hesitated.

"Tell Luciano that I need to talk to Vinnie," I said.

She went away and came back and gave me Vinnie's number. "But I don't think he's in," she said. "I think he went out."

"Why? He have a date?"

"I don't know."

"Where'd he go?"

"I don't know that, either. I'm not his secretary."

"When did he leave?"

"Not too long ago. A half-hour, maybe. I think it was him in the Cherokee."

I dialed Vinnie's number and let the phone ring. Vinnie, unlike Aristotle Socarides, had an answering machine. I left a message: Benny White is on the prowl, with the police after him; Roger the Dodger has been shot dead, maybe by Benny; call me right away.

I got out the ferry schedule. Several more boats would be coming in before they stopped running for the night. Benny might be on any one of them. Or none of them. Or he might be here already.

If Benny had called Vinnie, maybe Vinnie was planning to meet him, which meant, maybe, that Vinnie didn't know about Roger the Dodger, and was soon to become

Benny's next victim. Or maybe it meant that Vinnie did know about Roger, and planned to help Benny find me and Zee, and make us the next victims, so he and Benny could both live happily ever after. Or maybe Benny never called him at all, and Vinnie was just out on a date, or was going to a movie, or to a bar.

Or maybe Vinnie still had Luciano on his mind. I felt stupid for not having thought of that earlier, and called the Marcus number again. This time Thomas Decker answered. Good. He could decide what to tell Luciano and Angela, and how to do it. I told him about the ties between Benny White, Roger the Dodger, and Vinnie, and about what had happened in Boston this afternoon. Decker listened without a word, until I was through. Then he said: "Are you telling me that Vinnie is the guy who tried to get Luciano killed?"

"It could be."

There was a silence. Then he said. "That's pretty strong stuff. Are you sure you're right?"

"I've been wrong lots of times. But if I'm right, it could be dangerous for Luciano. Luciano's got himself a sort of fortress up there on the hill, but Vinnie can drive in and out whenever he wants to and nobody even gives him a glance. It occurred to me that he could bring Benny White in with him."

There was another pause. Then: "Luciano and Angela aren't going to like hearing this."

I was sure that was true. "Maybe you can just tell them the Benny White part for the moment, and leave out the Vinnie part. Tell them that Benny looks like the shooter, and that he may be on the island to finish the job. Tell them it'll be safer if they leave for a few days."

"Luciano won't want to go."

"Tell him that Benny may have found a way into the house. Bill Vanderbeck knows how to do it, so maybe Luciano will believe that Benny does, too. Tell Angela that Luciano is in danger, and tell Luciano that Angela is. Play one against the other. The three of you should get on Luciano's boat and go to Block Island, or some place until the dust settles. I think you should go right now, because Benny may already be here."

"It will kill Angela if Vinnie really is in on this."

"Benny may kill her and Luciano both if they don't get off the island."

Decker made up his mind. "I'll get them off. Later, I'll phone you from the boat to find out what's happening. I won't be able to keep them out there very long."

"You may not have to."

I hung up, and looked at Zee, who had been listening. "Where's your pistol?" I asked.

She frowned. "It's in its paper bag, where it always is."

"Of course it's not loaded."

"Of course not. Loaded guns are dangerous. You know that."

"I don't suppose that under the circumstances I can prevail upon you to load it and keep it close to you."

"You don't suppose correctly. There are plenty of police on this island, and all of them have guns. They don't need me or my gun to deal with Benny White."

She was right about the number of police and police forces on the island. Aside from the six town police forces, there were state cops, environmental cops, registry cops, the sheriff's department cops, and maybe even some other cops I didn't know about. The fact that the six island towns don't combine forces into one is yet another example of the rivalries that exist on the Vineyard. Every town is sure it will get worse service for more money, if an island force is created. Besides, who will be chief? Some guy in Oak Bluffs, or Chilmark? What will he know about how things are in Vineyard Haven or West Tisbury? So we have an island with ten thousand permanent residents and ten police forces to look after them.

"You're probably a better shot than most of them," I said.

"I shoot at targets, not at people. Now, let's not talk about this anymore. Let's have supper, and let the police do their job."

So we had supper, and I said nothing more about her pistol. But after supper I had coffee instead of cognac, and when Zee went to bed, I stayed up. I turned the yard light on, and stuffed some shells into my 12-gauge. I leaned the gun beside the door, turned the inside lights off, and sat on the dark porch as the night deepened.

After a while, Zee came out. "Are you coming to bed?"

"Not right now."

"Are you mad at me? Because I won't carry the gun?"

I was surprised. It hadn't occurred to me that she'd think that. I got up and took her in my arms. "No. I'm just going to sit up for a while. Sit with me, if you will."

So she sat beside me in the lounge, and we looked out through the screens at the bright stars and the Milky Way arching over us. A summer wind moved through the trees. Finally she said, "You're standing guard, aren't you?"

"It's just that Vinnie's not at home, and he knows where we live."

"He won't come here."

"Probably not."

A while later, she said: "You're not coming to bed tonight, are you?"

"I may come in later. I'm not really sleepy. Too much coffee. You go in. No need for both of us to be out here."

The stars turned in the sky. Finally, she kissed me and went in.

I stayed up.

No one came through our woods or down our driveway.

When the sun climbed out of Nantucket Sound, I went inside, rinsed my face in cold water, took a couple of aspirin, and peeked into the bedroom. Zee was looking at me with tired, red eyes.

I put a smile on my face. "You were supposed to get some sleep."

"I got some." She held up her arms and I went to her. She pulled me down on top of her. "We'll have breakfast, then you come to bed, and I'll stay up."

"But you have to go to work."

She rolled me onto the bed beside her, and feigned disgust. "It must be really nice to live a life where you don't have to keep track of the days of the week. This is Saturday! I have the weekend off!"

I'd forgotten. I was overcome with weariness and felt like lead, as if I were sinking into the mattress. "Forget breakfast," I said. "Wake me up for lunch." The world went away.

I slept for six hours, then swam awake on the scent of coffee, ham, eggs, and something more. I followed my nose out into the kitchen and found Zee, clad in Tevas, shorts, and a loose hanging shirt with rolled-up sleeves. Her hair was put up in the blue babushka she favored when we went fishing. She met me with a kiss, and waved at the table.

"Sit down. Here's coffee and juice. The eggs Benedict are on their way."

She served, and we ate. Delish! I felt the last of my fatigue fade away. Cholesterol is wonderful.

"I thought of something this morning," she said. "We don't have to find Benny. All we have to do is find Vinnie. If we find Vinnie, we'll probably find Benny, and we should be able to find Vinnie, if he's still on the island, because we know what he looks like, where he lives, who his island friends are, and what kind of a car he's driving."

"You are smarter than the average bear," I said. "I think you should pass that on to the local fuzz."

"I'm several hours ahead of you," she said. "I talked to the chief this morning. He's going to take care of it. I thought we should give him a chance to do that, so while you've been snoozing, I've been loading up the Land Cruiser for a run down the beach. We'll get out of every-body's way, while the wheels of justice grind exceeding fine. By the time we get back, all may be well. What do you think?"

"A good plan," I said.

I brushed my teeth, climbed first into my daring bikini bathing suit, and then into my shorts and tee-shirt, and we went off to East Beach. There, beneath the warm August sun, we fished in vain for the wily bonito at the Jetties, then drove back to Pocha Pond, where Zee lay on the old bedspread that we use for a beach blanket while I waded out and raked a basket of chowder quahogs before coming in and lying down beside her. The sun burned the tension out of me, and I napped. Tans replenished, we pulled clothes on over our bathing suits and left the beach in the late afternoon. We drove to the police station, to see if, as we hoped, all was, indeed, well.

All was not well. Neither Vinnie nor his Cherokee had been found. They had both been gone since last night.

"You know how many Jeeps there are on this island." said the chief. "He could be parked on a street someplace, or on some dirt road, or even in a parking lot, and we'd never know unless we happened to see him. Everybody's looking, and we'll find him sooner or later, but so far no dice. You go home and sit tight. We'll get him."

A lot of life is a psychological proposition. The reality that seems so objective to us often in fact exists only in our minds. The world we see as full of terrors is the same as the world we might as easily see as full of joy. The troubles that keep us tossing late at night are often gone in the morning, although nothing has changed but ourselves. Wealth, fame, and political power, which seem so real, in fact exist only because we and others agree that they do. If they didn't exist in our minds, they wouldn't exist at all.

I thought again about Vanderbeck's Axioms, and considered the possibility that the Benny White in my mind lived there and there alone. Maybe he wasn't the gunman, maybe he hadn't shot Roger the Dodger, maybe he'd never even thought about coming to the island.

Maybe the moon was made of green cheese.

I was suddenly tired of being pushed and pulled around by fear of some hood who might not even be there.

"Let's drive around awhile," I said to Zee when we left the station. "Maybe we can see something nobody else has seen."

So we drove through the streets and parking lots of Edgartown, looking for a green Cherokee with darkened window glass. There aren't a lot of streets in

Edgartown, but there are enough to keep you busy for a while, even if you have nothing else to do, and the cops all had other things to do at the same time they were looking for Vinnie, which meant they didn't have time to look everywhere. We saw a lot of Cherokees, but not the right one. We drove up and down street after street, but saw nothing.

We were about to give it up when I remembered Maggie Vanderbeck saying that some friends of Vinnie's had once taken him clamming in the Eel Pond. Vinnie hadn't liked the experience, as I recalled, but he knew where the pond was. There were two dead-end roads where people parked when they went to the Eel Pond: the road to the boat landing, off the Pease Point Way extension, and Gaines Way, off Fuller Street. Unless you drove down to the end of either of those streets, you wouldn't know if anybody was there.

We drove to the landing. Two pickups were there, but no Cherokee.

We drove back to Cottage Street and took a left, then took another left onto Fuller and yet another onto Gaines Way. There, where the pavement ended, parked where the shellfishermen park under the trees, was a green Cherokee with dark-tinted windows.

I parked the Land Cruiser crosswise in the street, blocking it off, and set the emergency brake. Then I got out and dug under the seat for the pistol. I wished I could see into the Cherokee. If there was anyone inside, he could certainly see me. I put the pistol in my waistband, under my tee-shirt, and walked to the Cherokee. The driver's door wasn't locked. I took a breath and opened it.

27

No one was in the car. I exhaled. There's a little path that leads through the trees and undergrowth out onto the marsh that lies along the southwest shore of the Eel Pond. You take that path when you want to go clamming, stepping over drainage ditches and sending the little crabs that live there scuttling into their holes. If you turn to the east once you get out onto the marshlands, you can cross to Little Beach.

I walked along the path until I was clear of the undergrowth, and looked both ways. Where would a couple of city kids go while they waited to make their next moves? To the beach, of course. I walked back to the Land Cruiser.

"We need some help," I said. "If they didn't just abandon the car, I think they're out there on the beach. But there's too much of it for us to cover alone. They could be out on the point, or they could be clear down to the lighthouse. Or any place in between. Time to call the cops."

Zee ran a map through her head. "If they're on the beach, they can only get off it in three places. Here, down at the lighthouse, and at the end of Fuller Street. I'll find a phone. You stay here and make sure they don't get away in the Cherokee."

She went to the nearest house and knocked on the door. It opened and she spoke to the woman there, then went in. I went back to the Cherokee, opened the driver's door, popped the hood, and pulled a few wires loose. Zee came out of the house as I moved the Land Cruiser to the side of the street.

"They're on their way," she said. "A couple of the guys will start working their way up from the lighthouse, and some others will be here right away. They said for us to wait."

"You wait," I said. "I'm going to cut around to the end of Fuller Street to make sure they don't slip out that way while we're waiting here." I pulled the .38 out of my waistband. "Here. I know you won't shoot anybody, but if they happen to come out this way, shoot into the air or something. That should stop them."

"And what will you do to stop them, if they come out at Fuller Street? You keep that old revolver of yours." She made a sort of strange face, reached into her purse, and brought out her Beretta .380. "If I have to shoot into the air, I have a better chance at hitting it with this. Go on, now."

I wondered what my own face looked like when I saw her pistol. I put the .38 back under my shirt, turned, and trotted to Fuller Street.

Where Fuller Street ends, there is a path that leads over a short bridge to Little Beach. I've gotten scallops in the shallows beyond the beach, although it's not my favorite scalloping ground. Sometimes, though, after a wicked nor'easter, the scallops are piled two feet high along the beach and the fish wardens abandon all regulations about limits, so that Edgartownians can salvage as many of the shellfish as possible before they die and become food for only the gulls.

In August, though, we were still two months away

from scallop season, and were in the sunning season instead. I crossed the bridge and went out on the beach. Looking to my right I could see Edgartown Light, around which were crowded the brown-skinned all-summer people, and the pale August people who were working to become brown themselves in spite of medical warnings that it was bad for their health. Between me and the light was a scattering of towels, blankets, and umbrellas.

I saw neither Vinnie nor Benny. I turned and looked the other way, toward the Eel Pond, and saw fewer sun-bathers, including two pale young men in shorts, seated on beach towels. There was a gym bag sitting on the sand beside them.

Vinnie. And a friend. Benny White, without a doubt.

They were looking the other direction, at a water-skier leaving the beach behind a noisy motorboat filled with laughing young people. The boat pulled away, and the skier rose from the water.

As I looked at Vinnie and Benny, their heads turned and they looked at me. I turned casually and looked back toward the lighthouse. When I turned back, they were still looking at me. I sat down on the sand and pre-tended to look out to sea. When I glanced at them again, they were walking away from me to the north, toward the towels belonging to the water-skiers.

It seemed certain that Vinnie had recognized me, but in case he hadn't, I pulled off my tee-shirt and hid the pistol inside it, then pulled off my shorts. Wearing my manly bikini, and carrying my bundle of pistol and clothes, I strolled along the beach behind them. Maybe when they next checked behind them, my change of cos-tume would deceive them. Probably it wouldn't.

In not too long a time, they turned off the beach toward the spot where they'd left their car. I felt a little rush of adrenaline, as I thought of Zee waiting there. I slid my hand into my bundle of clothes and got hold of the .38. I began to trot. But at that moment Vinnie and Benny saw something in front of them, and turned back to the beach.

I looked, too, and saw a policeman come down the path by the Cherokee, and out onto the marsh. I looked back at Vinnie and Benny, and saw them looking at me. Then they turned and trotted along the beach to the north, passing the spot where the water-skiers had left their gear. I heard a rush of footsteps behind me, and whirled to find Zee at my back.

"They've got themselves into a trap," said Zee. "Once they get out there on the point, they're stuck."

It was true. Little Beach hooks around the outside of the Eel pond, where I do some of my clamming and most of my musseling, and then ends, leaving a wide opening for boats to enter the pond and moor.

"They're stuck unless they want to swim," I said. "If they don't want to swim, they have to come back this way again. What are you doing here? You were supposed to stay on Gaines Way."

"The police are there." Zee didn't break stride. "You didn't think I was just going to stand there while you were out here, did you? You know, I'll bet these guys don't know where they've gotten themselves. I'll bet they think that they can get out of town along this beach, all the way to Oak Bluffs, if necessary. I'll bet they've never looked at a map of this town."

That made sense to me. Nobody on the run would deliberately get himself trapped on a spit of sand that led nowhere, but neither Vinnie nor Benny knew where they were. I wondered if Vinnie had a gun, too. I had to presume that he did. I wondered how good he was with it, and whether Zee and I would need the pistols we were carrying.

"Look," I said. "We don't both need to trail along after him like this. Why don't you stop here and make sure the chief and the others are coming along. I'll go ahead and keep an eye on them."

"You're not a really champion patronizer like some men I know," said Zee, "but you do have your moments."

"If a woman patronized a guy, is that matronizing?"

Far ahead, Vinnie and Benny walked on. When they paused and glanced back, Zee and I stopped and pretended to be watching seagulls, just in case they really didn't know yet who we were. When they went on, we followed. The more they looked back, the longer they looked. Every other look or so, Zee and I kept walking, so they wouldn't wonder why we stopped every time they stopped.

"I don't think we're fooling them," I said. "I really think you should go back."

"They haven't got much farther to go," said Zee. "They're about out of sand."

It was true. Vinnie and Benny had come nearly to the end of Little Beach and could now see that it ended with a last bit of sand covered with gulls, terns, and cormorants. Across the pond several small boats, both sail and power, were moored. But they were a long swim, almost as far as the other shore.

We stopped and looked at Vinnie and Benny. What would they do? They were looking across the pond at the houses there, and looking at the boats. There were several catboats on moorings, ready to go, if you knew how to sail. Did either of them know how to sail? It would be ironic if they escaped in a slow-moving catboat.

Then at the top of the launching ramp across the way, where I park the Land Cruiser when I'm shell fishing, a police car appeared. Then another one pulled alongside of the first. People got out and looked across the pond toward Vinnie and Benny. The sun glinted on a badge or two and what looked like some long guns.

So much for swimming across to the land or to a boat. Vinnie and Benny turned back and saw us standing there, watching them. Benny made his decision and started toward us, his free hand slipping into the gym bag. Vinnie hesitated. I looked behind us and saw that the motorboat had come ashore, its crew clowning and laughing on the beach. There were police officers coming toward us along the sand, but they were quite far back, well beyond the boat. Benny was much closer.

I read part of his mind. He'd take the motorboat, if he could get to it. But at what cost? What else, in this tight place, would he do? Would he be willing to shoot us, if we stood between him and the boat?

Or would he, thinking that he could not escape, decide to shoot us anyway, before surrendering? Just for laughs? Massachusetts has no death penalty, so he wouldn't be risking his life if he decided to take ours. Or would he decide to go out in a blaze of gunfire and glory, shooting until the cops shot him? Or, since nobody had yet proved he'd ever actually killed anyone, would he just surrender peaceably, knowing that he stood a good chance of walking away pretty untouched by the judicial system?

Unless Vinnie Cecilio talked, in which case Benny was

looking at long jail time. I thought of Roger the Dodger, who might also have talked.

Vinnie lacked Benny's toughness. I heard his voice say, "They got us, Benny. We gotta give up."

Benny's face registered contempt. His hand appeared, holding a pistol. He turned and shot Vinnie in the chest. Vinnie went over backward. Benny let his gun hand swing by his side, turned, and came running toward us.

"I think it's retreat time," said Zee, touching my sleeve.

That seemed like a good plan, but since I didn't fancy turning my back to Benny, I turned half away and shuffled sideways, like a pair of ragged claws scuttling across the floors of silent seas, trying to watch Benny and the beach under my feet at the same time, a hopeless effort that only resulted in my tripping and banging a knee on a rock. The pain was like a knife.

Zee, faster than I was, looked back. "Get up! Come on, come on!"

I looked beyond her and was surprised to note that the water-skiers apparently hadn't even heard the shot. Rather, they were looking the other way, watching the policemen coming toward them.

Zee's eyes widened, and I looked back toward Benny and saw him racing over the sand, closing the distance between us with breathtaking speed. I was filled with a terrible fear for Zee. I got up.

I cried, "Run!" and started toward her. But I already knew that the pain in my knee would not let me move fast enough. As she turned and fled down the beach, I stopped and turned and got the .38 in my hand. I sat on the sand, resting my elbows on my knees. I cocked the pistol and pointed it at Benny, as he came fast along the beach.

When he was twenty yards away, I shouted, "Stop!"

To my amazement, he did.

"Toss away the gun," I said.

Instead, he lifted his pistol and fired.

But he was panting from his run and his aim was off. The bullet kicked up sand to my right. I took cold and careful aim as he started walking toward me, firing again, and again missing.

Then, as my finger tightened on the trigger, but before I could shoot, he spun around, staggered, and collapsed, the pistol dropping from his hand.

From across the pond came the sound of the rifle shot that had felled him.

I stood up and looked across the pond and waved my hand. In reply, someone over there lifted a long gun overhead. I thought the man looked like the chief, and the long gun looked like the new 30.06 he'd gotten for deer hunting in Maine.

I limped to where Benny lay, his blood seeping into the sand. His pale face was peculiarly peaceful, the splinted little finger of his right hand looked oddly innocent in spite of the pistol that lay near it. I put a finger to his throat, but could feel no pulse.

Then Zee was by my side, tucking away her little .380. Her hands were on Benny's chest, working in vain to get him breathing again, as the police came running toward us.

28

In September, Zee and I signed up for the Bass and Bluefish Derby, and headed for the beaches. As usual for that time of year, the blues were out where the boats could get them, but were scarce for surf casters. After the weigh-in the first night, we weren't even close to the leaders. I compensated for this by retelling Zee about the twenty-one-pounder I'd once caught when I was the only one on the beach.

"Yeah," said Zee. "I remember you waving it under my nose. But as I recall, you didn't catch it until the derby was over."

"Details, details."

We walked out of the weigh station into a soft fall night. The Edgartown parking lot at the foot of Main was thick with fishermen and onlookers, and on the float behind the weigh station the filleters were busy with their knives, filleting fish for elderly and other people who could no longer go out and catch their own. No fish went to waste.

Between the yacht club and the Reading Room, the *Shirley J.* swung at her stake, and beyond her, out in the harbor the last yachts of the season lay at their moorings. There was a police car in the parking lot, and the chief was leaning against it, smoking his pipe and looking pretty well recovered from having killed Benny White. In his decades as a police officer, it had been the first shot he'd ever fired in the line of duty, and it had taken him a while to get over it.

Zee and I walked across.

"Quite a mob," said Zee, leaning on the car beside him, and looking at the crowd.

"A mere nothing," said the chief. "After Labor Day, the real crowds are gone. You can even find a parking place on the street, sometimes."

"I still see a lot of tourists around," I said.

"Only a few, by comparison. And none with kids over five. School has carried those folks off to America, and peace has once again arrived in Edgartown, more or less."

"Well," said Zee, "you still have the local slimeballs around, so you won't be bored completely to death."

"Yes," he agreed, "we still have the hometown drunks and thieves and wife beaters and vandals and the rest, but we know who they are, mostly, even though we may not be able to prove it in court, so it's not the same as when we have eighty or ninety thousand extra people on the island. Did you hear about Luciano Marcus?"

The last time I'd talked with Luciano was on the phone, just after the shootings on the beach. He'd called from Hyannis, where they'd anchored for the night, to find out what was going on. I'd decided that telling the truth about Vinnie would be no benefit to him or Angela, so I'd told him that Vinnie had gotten shot trying to stop Benny from shooting me.

The news of Vinnie's death had stopped Luciano from thinking too clearly, but he'd listened while I told him something about bad Benny leading good but not-too-bright Vinnie astray, and about Benny stealing the shotgun that weekend he'd come down from Boston and exploiting poor naive Vinnie's knowledge of Luciano and his fat wallet being at the opera that day in Boston, and then about my guess that once the cops were on his trail, Benny had decided to come down and shoot Zee and me so nobody could ID him, and about heroic Vinnie trying to stop him and getting himself killed in the process.

Luciano had hung up the phone, breathing hard. I had imagined him popping another pill under his tongue.

Now I said to the chief, "No. What about Luciano?"

The chief removed his pipe from his mouth and looked at it.

"They brought Luciano to the hospital this afternoon, then they flew him up to Boston. Heart attack. He's in bad shape."

I felt a surge of sympathy for Angela, who had loved him all the years of their marriage, in spite of who he was or what he had done.

"Poor Angela," said Zee, echoing my thoughts. "I'll call the house when we get home."

I thought of the fisher king in the Arthurian tales. The man who, because of spiritual sin, had brought ruin to his kingdom, and to those he loved.

"You two win anything tonight?" asked the chief.

"No triumph of justice for us," said Zee. "We were skunked good and proper. My hubby here thinks it may mean there is no God."

The chief raised his eyes to the night sky. "As Sister Luke used to say, after we're dead, all of this will be explained to us. Well, this crowd looks pretty peaceful, so I guess I can leave." He got into the cruiser and drove away.

"If we go home right now," said Zee, "we can mess around awhile and still have time to get some rest before we hit Wasque early tomorrow morning."

"An excellent idea."

For the rest of the derby, we fished the Chappy beaches from Metcalf's Hole to the Cape Pogue Gut, and when the blues came back close to shore we did our best to nail them. As the derby wore on, the truly dedicated fisherpeople became haggard from lack of sleep, and were occasionally testy.

October 1 dawned clear and chilly, and presented us with a moral dilemma: whether to hit the beaches again, or take a scalloping break on the first day of that season.

"Why not both?" asked Zee, checking out the tide tables. "We can go to Wasque early, then get home in time for low tide in Katama Bay. We can get our bushel of scallops and be home again by noon. We can have the scallops shucked by two, and be back on the beach by three."

"Done. But does that leave us time for sex?"

"Let's see. Maybe we can delay getting back to the beach until three-oh-five."

"I'm fast," I said, "but I don't know if I'm that fast."

"Actually," said Zee, smiling up at me, "you're slow. Very slow. It's one of your charms."

"Would you like to list some of the others?"

"Not right now."

That afternoon, on Wasque Point, just before sundown, some pretty big blues came in. The beach was shoulder to shoulder with fisherpeople, but they were regulars, so few lines were crossed and few tempers lost. Zee and I brought in big fish, as did everyone else, and about nine, the trucks began to peel away and head for

Edgartown so their drivers could get to the weigh-in station before it closed at ten.

"On the board at last," grinned Zee, pointing. She was best of the day for shore blues, and I was third by a whisker. Happiness.

"Hello, kid," said a voice behind me. I turned and looked into Joe Begay's eyes. He dropped his to Zee's. "And hello to you, too, Mrs. Jackson." His eyes came back to mine. "How were you lucky enough to win this woman?"

"I didn't get her by luck," I said. "It was a combination of skill and lies."

"Ah," said Begay. "The same time-honored technique I used to court Toni. I see you both made the board. Let me buy you two a drink to celebrate your fleeting fame as fisherfolk."

We went into the Wharf Pub and found a booth and beer.

"Cheers," said Begay. "This is my first derby. I figured that since I'm going to be an islander, I should join up and learn how to catch bass and bluefish. Turns out that I'm a very fashionable fellow. I can fly-fish."

"It's all the craze," I said.

"When I was a kid, growing up out near Oraibi, my folks used to take a trip up to Emerald Lake in Colorado every year, for a week of trout fishing and camping. My dad taught me how to fish with dry flies, and now, all these years later, I'm using those ancient skills. I've been fishing up at the other end of the island."

"How are things up that way?" I asked. "It seemed like I lived up there last month, but I haven't been back since."

"Interesting," said Begay. "I'm getting some callouses

from hauling pots, and I'm getting a lot more respect for the guys who go down to the sea in ships. Someday, I may even begin to make some money at it." He paused and glanced at Zee then back at me, and arched a brow.

"She knows everything I know," I said.

"Good grief," said Zee, putting down her beer and looking at Begay. "Don't tell me you're one of those dare-I-speak-of-manly-things-in-the-presence-of-the-little-woman guys. If you are, it's time you wised up!"

"Jesus," said Begay, laughing. "You sound just like Toni!" He sipped his beer and thought. "You're right. It's a bad habit. If it makes you feel any better, it isn't a man/woman thing in my case, it's just the result of the kind of work I used to do. In that work, you never told anybody any more than you had to."

"And what kind of work was that?"

He shook his head. "Sorry, Mrs. Jackson. I've begun telling Toni about it, but so far it's just between her and me."

"Very mysterious," said Zee, intrigued. "I'm glad to hear that you've at least started to tell her things, but she must be going crazy, wanting to know everything."

"Does your husband know everything about you, Mrs. Jackson?"

To my surprise, Zee blushed. A rather weak smile appeared on her face. "Well, almost," she said.

"And does your wife know all about you, J.W.?"

"My life is an open book," I lied.

"There you have it," said Begay, making a small gesture with a large brown hand. "Well, now, about things up in Gay Head. For one thing, you might be interested to hear that I've got myself a crewman. Jimmy Souza. Sober, and trying to stay that way. Guy knows a hell of a lot about pot fishing. If I make any money on the boat this year, it'll be because of him."

I was pleased. Maybe the chief had been right; maybe Jimmy was again going to be a good man. I hoped so.

"And another thing," said Begay. "It seems that my mother-in-law, Linda Vanderbeck, got proposed to by Bill Vanderbeck."

Zee's ears opened. "No kidding!"

Begay smiled at her sudden interest. "Yeah."

"And?" Zee had both hands on her stein.

"And she said no, she'd already been married to enough Vanderbecks for one life, and besides she didn't want to get married again anyhow because she has enough to do trying to make sure the tribe—that's the Gay Head Wampanoags, of course—get what's coming to them from you European invaders. The job will take all her time, she figures, and she doesn't have room for a husband in her plans."

"Shucks." Zee sipped her beer. Then she brightened."You and Toni will have to come down for supper. Jeff is a great cook, and the two of you can catch up on old times while Linda and I get to know each other better. You men can serve us drinks and goodies while we sit in front of the fire and talk about womanly things."

Begay faked a frown. "I thought it was politically incorrect for men to talk about manly things and women to talk about womanly things."

"Not quite," said Zee. "It's only incorrect for men to talk about manly things when their women want them to talk about something interesting instead. The woman-to-woman part is entirely okay, if that's what the women want to do. If they don't want to do that, they don't have to."

Begay looked at me. "With this wife, I think you're going to have your hands full, buddy."

I leered at Zee. "I certainly hope so."

"One other thing you might want to know," said Begay. "Linda found out about Wally Madison and his pal trying to work you over. I hear she tracked them down and gave them such hell that they both went to the mainland just to get away from her." He laughed.

In Friday's *Gazette* we found our names in the weekly summary of the derby results, and read that Luciano Marcus, of Gay Head and New York, had died in Boston. I thought of stupid, amoral Vinnie. If he hadn't gotten greedy and had just waited a few weeks, he'd have had his inheritance and been alive to spend it. Life is quirky some times.

Then, for some reason, I thought of Aristotle Socarides, the PI over on the cape who never answered his phone. Did Aristotle read the *Gazette*? Did he know his onetime boss was dead? A lot of lives had been changed because of silly, venal Vinnie Cecilio: Roger the Dodger and Benny White and Vinnie himself had been touched hardest, but Zee and I had been affected, too, as Jason Thornberry had been, and the Marcus family, and Gordon R. Sullivan, and the Edgartown cops, particularly the chief, and the Dings, and the Vanderbecks, and God only knew who else. The tree of evil throws a long shadow.

December. The wind was cold, Main Street in Edgartown was decorated with Christmas lights, and Zee and I, bundled in our down coats, were window-shopping along the almost empty street, when the chief pulled over beside us, stopped the cruiser, and rolled down his window.

"Merry Christmas," he said.

"And to you."

"Are you two trying for the red nose championship of the island? All of the sensible people are inside by their fires."

"We're fearless in the face of howling winds and driving snow," I said.

The chief shook his head, and put an envelope into Zee's hand. "Here," he said. "A Christmas present." He rolled up his window, and drove on.

Zee opened the envelope. It was her license to carry.

"Oh, good," she said. "And Manny will be very happy, because now I can't be arrested for carrying weapons. Did I tell you that he wants me to go with him to some competitions?"

"No."

"Well, he does."

"When you win the gold medal, you'll be able to protect me better than ever from scary things. Not that I'm ever scared, of course. I'm as brave as a barrel full of bears."

"Me, too," said Zee. "I chase lions down the stairs."

"I'm like a tiger in a rage."

"I'm even braver than that."

"No, you're not."

"Yes, I am."

"Want to bet?"

"Anything. A million dollars."

"You don't have a million dollars."

"I don't need it. I'm going to win."

"No, you're not. What else do you want to bet?"

Zee thought about that. "We can't bet money, because it wouldn't mean anything since all our money goes into the same account."

"How about the grab of your choice? The winner gets to grab the loser wherever he or she chooses. How about that?"

"You're on!"

"All right. You win, I lose. I admit defeat. I was lying about being brave. You're the bravest. Grab away."

Zee looked up and down the street. "Right here?"

"Hey, you're the winner."

"I'm not sure this is fair. You're wearing an awful lot of clothes . . ."

"I'll wait till we get home and I take some of them off," I said. "And I guess I should warn you that I might grab back."

"I think I've window-shopped enough for today," said Zee, flexing her hands.

We headed for the Land Cruiser.

Early in January, Toni and Joe Begay arrived for supper. I was serving chowder, which I figured was just right for a cold winter's night.

While the women talked in the living room over mugs of mulled cider, Joe came into the kitchen, carrying a mug of his own.

"You know all that business about trading some Wampanoag land up on the Lobsterville side of Marcus's place for a cranberry bog and another little hunk of land Marcus owned down on the Squibnocket side?"

"Yeah. Luciano wouldn't have anything to do with it."

"Well, it seems that Angela Marcus, who's gotten to be good friends with Bill, and maybe more, some say, what with Linda turning him down and all, has decided that she'll make the trade after all."

I looked at Joe, and raised a brow. "No kidding. Well,

that ought to make Linda Vanderbeck happy. Does this mean that someday you might not only have a shaman for a brother-in-law, but a mafioso widow for a sister-in-law?"

"These are exciting times," said Begay. "Anything is possible." He sipped his cider.

We could hear the women's voices in the living room. Suddenly Begay put up a hand.

"I do believe I just heard some mention of babies," he said. "Do you think we should go in and get involved in the conversation?"

My heart made a little jump. "I think we should," I said.

I took a quick taste of the chowder. Delish! Then Joe and I walked into the living room.